Yet, Home

Irene Noor

First Printing: 2016

ISBN: 978-1-365-52241-3

irenenoor2016@gmail.com

Ordering Information:

Special discounts are available on quantity purchases by corporations, associations, educators, and others. For details, contact the author at the above listed email address.

U.S. trade bookstores and wholesalers: Please email irenenoor2016@gmail.com.

To my parents,

whose choices shaped our lives,

and whose love gave them grace.

Acknowledgements

Writing a book is pretty fun. Writing a book that is good enough for others to read is an odyssey. I was fortunate to have a number of people who were willing to spend their precious time reading through the roughest of drafts and who encouraged me through the manuscript's development. More importantly, they were honest — brutally honest when necessary — and this book is all the better for it. Still, it is my first book, and so the thing I needed most was encouragement during the many difficult moments, and that they gave generously.

For reading at least one full draft and for their invaluable feedback, I am deeply grateful to Anne Morgan Chopra, Mona El-Shamaa, Nancy Kaddis, Mary Morgan, Dell Hagan Rhodes, and Nicole Strange. For her enthusiastic support and feedback, I am also grateful for Kylee Easton. From the Bundaberg Writers' Workshop, I am grateful to Liz Filleul for her confidence that there was something worthwhile in this book; for his critical eye that pushed me to up my game, I am grateful to John Galassi at the Brisbane Writers Festival. I am grateful to my mother for input about the scenes in Egypt; this book is that much more authentic for it. My most affectionate gratitude is for my husband, whose faith in me and support of me were true and strong always, and whose feedback as a reader was much more valuable than he realizes. The writing of this book was, among other things, an opportunity to appreciate the treasure that my family and friends are in my life, and for that I am truly blessed.

PART ONE

TAYIB

1

Cairo
1987

The smells of expensive perfumes and roasting meat mingled with the sound of laughter. Cocktail-party laughter, I called it. Gleeful and carefree, and inconsequential. I moved towards a window, and through the wooden shutters, I heard a rooster crowing, but as it was late evening, the misinformed rooster was either far too late or hours too early. Still, its call and the warm breeze against my collar recalled to my mind another sound: the rumble of the fuul vendor's cart.

I would be sitting on our balcony, the early morning heat already having set in, and listening to that irritable rooster, when I would hear and then see the wooden cart being dragged along by the vendor, one of hundreds who have rolled their carts along Cairo's streets for as long as I can remember. His long tunic would be perhaps a little stained, and he would be broadcasting his goods in a sing-song voice. "Fuul," he would call, "fuul for just a piastre!" The fava beans, slow cooked in enormous crockery pots, would be emanating the smell of cumin and lemon. It was one of my favourite childhood memories, hearing that fuul vendor on Friday mornings. In my family, we rarely actually bought fuul from him, my mother insisting she could make it herself just as well—and she could and did—and for even less money. And the sachet that back then cost a piaster now cost a pound. The price had increased, literally, a hundred-fold in my lifetime. Still, the only times that my mother would allow us children to call down to the vendor and buy our breakfast from him were on the occasional Sundays when we had returned from early mass and she was too tired, and too placid, to go into the kitchen. But those days were rare. My father had died when I was 9 years old, and there was rarely enough money for more than the necessities.

I was startled out of my reverie by a gale of sharp laughter. My best friend Aziz, whose enthusiastic relationship with his whiskey was often at the center of these parties, was telling a story about his last visit to his mother. My God, I was ready to get out of here. All the excited greetings and enthusiastic questions, just to fill up space. I always felt like people expected me to be funnier than I was, more interesting than I was, tell better stories than I actually told. I would prefer a quiet evening with Aziz and a good bottle of whiskey any night over this charade. Yet I too often found myself in just this kind of situation.

Sometimes, I wonder how my life must look to a stranger. No different, I suppose, than any other well-dressed, well-to-do, middle-aged professional walking from his air-conditioned office to his air-conditioned Cairene apartment every day, socializing with his equally affluent friends in immaculately furnished living rooms every weekend. It is true that I have long since lost interest in the nation's politics, but it is not, as a stranger might suppose, because I only care to the degree that those affairs affect my own wallet. Rather, it is because caring about the government's decisions and yet not being able to do anything about them only leads me to bitterness and frustration, and I am not inclined to allow my circumstances to change my disposition. But they have changed me, haven't they?

I glanced past Aziz and caught the gaze of my young daughter. She had that smile on her face. She knew her father did not want to be here. Why was I? Out of some duty not to deprive my family of what they might enjoy, I suppose. But I suspected that, given the choice, she probably wouldn't be here either. She had always been a kindred spirit, that one. She preferred the quiet of the early morning, and would sit in silence with me while I sipped tea on our apartment balcony and watched the city come to life. She had done this since she was maybe four or five years old. She was eleven now, and not quite yet on the edge of young womanhood.

I myself am forty. How is it that the years have passed so fast? Passed so fast — what a cliché. They have not passed fast, if I really think about it. Every day has been a long marathon, and yet looking back, they all blur together into a few seconds. But those long days at work, and the evenings of trying to be as present and lively as I could be for my girl, and for her mother, despite the fatigue, those days do not seem to pass quickly at the time.

Even now, I sometimes find myself wishing for the bustling, hopeful life of my youth, and the city Cairo was then: a city steeped in history and yet struggling mightily to modernize itself. This was the Cairo I would call to mind every time I would ask myself, after a particularly tough day at work, why I had become an architect. I could have done anything else; I had the grades for anything. But architecture would allow me to combine my capacity, if not love, for maths with the love I had for my city. I had started my career thinking I would spend the next forty years building the perfect compromise: buildings that were modern and built to provide comfort to the new Egyptian society, but whose style and structure paid homage to the illustrious millennia of history that my country boasted. Little did I know then that my colleagues would all turn out to be nothing more than imitators, all wanting to build a city that looked like the European cities they had visited on their expensive vacations—and a shoddy imitation at that.

"Tayib," my wife's voice called now, pulling me back out of my thoughts. "Are you ready to go?" I smiled in return and got up, following her and our daughter outside. The air was cooler out here, after the confinement of the party inside, but still warm enough, I noticed, that neither of them put on the cardigans they had brought with them as a precaution. The scent of tuberose filled the air, and the light from the half moon and the street lights further down the street cast a soft light on my family's beautiful faces. The noise of traffic had died down, and all I could hear above the sound of car motors in the distance now was the laughing voices of my friends inside.

Alexandria
1988

I looked at my daughter and my wife, walking ahead along Alexandria's boardwalk. We have tried to make this trip to Alexandria every year to take in the Mediterranean Sea breezes. I hope it will be like this for many more years. But it would not be long before our daughter would consider the ghazl el-banat that she was now happily pulling apart to be too childish, or too sugary. Between sticky bites, she would say something to her mother as we continued to walk along the Corniche. It's such an ordinary treat, cotton candy, yet its colloquial name quaintly suggests that the fine threads can only be spun by good little girls. Our girl, if she spun, would more likely spin steel than easily melted sugar crystals, I should think, yet she is the very definition of a good girl.

It was a warm evening, kept from being too warm by the breeze blowing off the sea. I glanced at the other walkers and bicyclists passing by the well-loved Alexandrian boardwalk, each, no doubt, listening to the waves pound their leisurely rhythm against the sandy shores. I was reminded suddenly of the trips to Alexandria my mother, walking alongside me now, would arrange for us, if not every year, then perhaps every other year. Like us, there were so many families who struggled back then—as there are now, I suppose. But people still exuded happiness in those days. The neighbours and friends we had, and the amount of time we spent with loved ones, had given me a charmed childhood. That community had wrapped my childhood in joy and knowledge that my sister and mother and I were loved and valued, despite—or perhaps especially because of—my father's death.

I want to give my daughter the same kind of childhood, but it seems more difficult, despite our improved living standards. I sometimes wonder what has changed. The society of that age seems to have disappeared. Everyone I know now talks mostly about politics, or what real estate to invest in. The kids I see are always being rushed off in their parents' late model cars to tutoring sessions whose purpose is to get them into the best universities. Rarely do the children have nothing to do, unlike in my day, when boredom would lead my friends and I to gather in one of our apartments. There, invented games and lazy conversations would fill the hours, our parents happy to have us safely occupied.

This shift to industriousness, I suppose, is what everyone perceives to be westernization, and therefore something to aspire to. Families are building wealth for future generations, giving their children opportunities, often in the west, that they never had. But I have been abroad enough times now to know that families in western countries suffer from their own poverties: there never seemed to be enough time for a leisurely meal or an unscheduled conversation with an old friend, at least not in my experience. Family sometimes meant only blood ties, and friendships meant only scheduled monthly gatherings. I fear that my own beloved country has made a fatal decision, leaping to achieve material abundance at the expense of its abundance of spirit.

The Egypt I was born into had no shortage of heroes: Saad Zaghlool, Mustafa Kamel, Makram Abeed. These men had led the country to independence from the British. When I was young, it was so easy to believe Egypt was capable of tremendous greatness, as it had been in ages past. But I have become disillusioned over time; the current generation has swallowed wholesale the myth that wealth brings happiness. I now believe that greatness will not come to my country until these so called leaders have been replaced. Perhaps the hope lies with the younger generation. It saddens me to think that the dreams with which I'd begun my adult life are not going to be realized in my lifetime. I have often wondered if I chose correctly. Maybe if I had chosen a different field, or taken a different life path, I could have carved out a life I would have taken greater pride in. There were a thousand decisions that had brought our lives to the present, weren't there? Which ones would have meant any real difference? Which ones would prove to be significant in the future?

"Do you think we've made the right decisions for her? For us?" I asked my mother, who had remained quiet as we walked.

She was quiet a minute longer, and then responded, "We wanted what was best for you and Amira, just as you want what's best for her, and it will be important one day that she knows that. But maybe it is not for you to set up the circumstances that will give her the best life. What do we mean by the best life anyway, Tayib? The easiest life? Look at your life; look at mine.

"Would we be happier or better if our lives had been any easier? On the contrary, you are everything you are precisely because of what you — we — went through. I don't give you parenting advice often, Tayib, but if there is one thing I would tell you, it is this: don't deny her the same chance to grow into who she can become. Don't choose for her."

DALIA

2

South Pacific Ocean
2008

The water shimmered as far as the eye could see, daring the passengers of the behemoth of a ship to carry on worrying about their little lives in the face of its even greater vastness. Dalia thought, not for the first time, that this perspective was what she had been craving. Life had been so intense these last few months. Her cases had kept her up at night; she would end each night by checking email and start every morning with another anxious check before even getting out of bed. Why had separating work and life got harder lately? She knew why: her responsibilities had increased. She was the youngest solicitor at the firm to be promoted to Senior Associate, and would likely be asked to be a partner before she turned forty — that is, if she didn't choose to become a barrister instead. Not for the first time, she thought how much she was turning into her father with his increased responsibilities and late nights at work.

She enjoyed the challenge of her work. She enjoyed knowing that the reason she was on the harder cases was precisely because she was a good solicitor — exceptional, even, and the senior partners at the firm knew it. The stress of handling these cases came with the satisfaction of knowing she had found the best possible solution to the problems their clients brought. It was rewarding in its own right. And of course, even more than the money, the respect of her colleagues was very satisfying.

Then she remembered that Liam was upset with her for not going to his family's annual reunion last weekend. She had tried to explain how much she needed that weekend to finish up her case. She wished Liam understood how valuable her work was to her. He tried to be supportive; she knew that. But she needed a break, the truly luxurious kind, with the sun rising over water every morning and no obligation to be social or even interested in others. Also, she did not want to endure another weekend of hints about when they might take their relationship to the "next level," or the praise, its sincerity unclear, by his aunts about her clothes or hair. "Dalia," one of them would say, "you are so lucky to have the curls that you have. My hair is so straight and limp; I would kill to have hair like yours." As for Liam's parents, even though she was sure they approved of her, she did not feel she could fully relax around them yet. And what she needed most at that moment was just that: a chance to relax, completely, into utter stillness.

So, despite Liam's icy silence, she had finished her work and then gone straight home. It has been weeks since her apartment had been tidied up or cleaned, which only added to her stress. And so, after turning on the vacation response of her work email, she had thrown on an old t-shirt and yoga pants, turned some of her favourite music from her university years on loud and begun sweeping, wiping, and scrubbing every surface and corner of the place back to its pristine state. There were, she lectured to her freshly made bed, few pleasures greater than coming home from vacation to a clean home. Liam would get over his annoyance with her.

He'd go back to being the supportive guy she could rely on: buying take-away and dropping it by the office when he knew she had a long night of work ahead, and taking her out for lavish meals when a big case was over. He did all the cliché things that a good boyfriend was supposed to do. "Boyfriend." That's a word she really didn't like. Saying it brought to mind two teenagers, play-acting at an adult relationship and all the responsibilities that came with it, when really all they were experiencing was the heady joy of having found someone they connected to on that unique level that people called love. Maybe she'd start calling him her partner. No, too business-like, despite the fact that everyone else seemed to use it. Her lover, maybe? Too scandalous. Her significant other? Too long. The English language just was not expressive enough to describe the kind of relationship that she and Liam had.

Of course, Arabic may not be any better. If she and Liam had this relationship in Egypt…well, they just wouldn't. Dating for three years, as they had done, would have been two years too long. They would have been engaged or married by now. So it really wasn't fair to accuse Liam's family of being impatient; her extended family would be far more so.

She thought now that perhaps her own parents were just as impatient, but they didn't show it—or if they did, she chose to ignore the signs. Keeping secrets from her parents was not something she liked to do, with perhaps a few exceptions during her wildest period in high school. Keeping more things to herself would have been much easier, but it had never been in her. She remembered now that she and Liam had only been together for a few months when she suggested that Liam meet her parents. They would have dinner at her parents' house; Liam had been nervous beforehand. "What should I call them?" he'd asked. "Dr. and Mrs. Salib? Or just Tayib and Aida? Am I pronouncing their names right?"

It was the first time she had seen him ever be nervous, and had, of course, found it endearing. But, as she knew he would, he behaved beautifully once they arrived at the house. Liam and her father had taken an immediate liking to each other. Her mother, however, would not be moved by Liam's charm, no matter how high he turned it.

After Liam had left that night, Dalia had confronted her mother as they cleared the table. "Mama, why did you have to be so rude to him?"

"Rude? I wasn't being rude."

"Well, you weren't being very friendly, either."

"Do I need to be friendly with him? Are you serious about him?"

"I really like him, and I think we're really good together, if—"

"Yes, but do you like him enough to marry him, Dalia? Can you see him being a father to your children?"

"Mama," Dalia began, "are you—"

Just then, her father had walked in and looked at her mother. "What's wrong, Aida? Dalia, what are you talking about?"

"Just whether Mama liked Liam or not. You liked him, didn't you, Baba?"

"Yes, I did. Charming young man. And very smart too. We had a really nice conversation. But it's too early to say yet whether I think he deserves my Dalia." He said this with a twinkle in his eye, but Dalia knew that undergirding it was a serious sentiment. Her expectations for men, just as they were for her education and career, were to be high.

The next time mother and daughter saw each other, it was the following Saturday. Dalia had invited her to spend the afternoon doing something they never did: window-shop along Sydney's George Street, with its mixture of designer and quotidian shops. Its stream of tourists coming to and from the Circular Quay provided a great opportunity for people-watching, something both Aida and Dalia enjoyed. Sitting at a café a couple hours later, Dalia approached the topic she'd been waiting all afternoon to find the opening to revisit. "Mama, I've been thinking about our conversation after dinner that night when Liam came over. I think you're assuming something about me— about what I want—that isn't quite right. I think you are assuming that I'm not happy with my life as it is. That I have to want what everyone supposedly wants: a husband, kids, a family. But having a family was your dream," Dalia said. "And you have one. We have a great family. I can't imagine wanting a different family."

Aida smiled at this, and reached out to squeeze Dalia's hand.

Dalia smiled back but continued, "I love being you and Baba's daughter. And it's enough for me. I don't feel the need to become someone's wife, or someone's mother. It's enough for me to be your daughter. My work and you guys—and maybe Liam—are enough. Can you understand that?"

"Is it enough for him?" she asked. "Will it be enough for him, or for you, five years from now? Ten?"

The smell of freshly sprayed sunscreen lotion brought her abruptly back to the present, where passengers were strolling around the ship's deck, some hand-in-hand. Others were sitting in small groups, looking out at the water and sipping their drinks, or engrossed in conversation. The frequent sound of laughter would peel out, usually from young women in small bikinis chattering in Italian or Spanish. Other sun-worshipers, of course, were resolutely ignoring their surroundings, eyes hidden behind sunglasses, and earphones in their ears, or a magazine in hand. But their bikinis were just as small. Dalia looked at her own bikini: not as small as most, but a bikini nonetheless. She mused again at how the young women around her were obviously brought up with a relationship to their bodies that was so different from hers. They seemed perfectly comfortable exposing almost their entire bodies. Bikinis were so common, in fact, that the one-pieces she and her peers with immigrant parents had been made to wear seemed downright provincial. She, and some of her friends had, as teenagers, eventually rebelled and worn what they liked, but not without the straining of relationships. Her thoughts were interrupted suddenly by the clang of metal against metal. She turned to see one of the masts being struck, repeatedly, by a metal hook at the end of a swinging rope. Distractedly, she wondered if it shouldn't be secured somehow, and then, seeing someone who looked like a crewmember walking towards it, decided to get another Mai Tai from the bar.

Her mind wandered back to her relationship with Liam. It wasn't just her mother whose perspective she'd heard or seen implied. Acquaintances worried she was getting older. She did not think 32 was 'older,' but reckoned she might have a generation ago; then, she would have been surrounded by peers who were all married and maybe even had children by the time they were thirty. Everyone assumed that she wanted marriage and children, because didn't everyone? Someone to grow old with, and someone to take care of you when you could no longer care for yourself. But Dalia liked her own company, and she was a careful saver; she would have the resources to take care of herself after retirement.

Besides, Dalia's friend Amy now had two little ones at home. During her evenings visiting there, Dalia had gotten a preview of what life would look like were she to take a similar path. And she did not want that life. She could not imagine trading late nights of writing and creative problem-solving with late nights of listening to babies cry and being woken up from precious sleep at the whim of a toddler. She could not imagine spending her evenings pretending to marvel at a piece of scribbled "artwork" when she could spend her evenings, as she did now — when she wasn't working, that is—attending real gallery exhibitions and theatre performances.

Maybe that is why she liked cruises so much. Yes, there were children here, but only in certain areas. The parts of the ship she tended to frequent were serenely absent of children: the adult-only section of the pool, the library, the art gallery, the gym, the nautical-themed pub, and the formal dining rooms. It was the pub that she found herself sitting in now, flipping through a magazine, her pre-dinner drink in hand. On the armchairs a few feet away, a small group of grey-haired women were chatting. "I found a new dentist closer to home," one was saying. "You won't believe it. He's actually an Australian dentist. Do you know how hard it is to find an Australian dentist these days? Especially in Sydney? They're all Chinese or Indian or something. Or Arab!" Dalia glanced over to see the other earnest heads nodding in agreement. "It's all I can do just to remember their names, let alone pronounce them. I just called my old dentist, 'Dr.' It's alright, of course, they all speak English alright. But it's nice to be able to remember my dentist's name. Except I can't because I'm getting too old!" At that, there was a round of appreciative cackles from the other ladies. Quietly, Dalia stood up. Maybe this pub swung a little too far in the adult direction. Maybe she would head to dinner a little early; the other passengers assigned to her table had regaled each other with travel stories last night; with any luck, they'd have a similar conversation tonight.

The ringing was urgent, its persistence cutting through the blanket of sleep she'd sunk into—what—

hours ago? She propped up onto her elbow and followed the sound to the unfamiliar nightstand with its chorded phone blinking. That's right; she was in her cabin on the ship, but what time was it?

"Hi, love," Liam's familiar voice said. He sounded relaxed and lively, so clearly it wasn't an emergency.

"Hi," she answered. "What time is it?"

"I think it's 10:30 your time. Were you asleep?" Liam sounded surprised. "You never sleep this early. You alright?"

"Yeah, I'm fine. I must have been more tuckered out than I realized. None of the shows tonight seemed any good, and bed sounded much better. So how are you going? What are you up to?"

"Not much," he replied. He had just had dinner with some friends; they were about to go out for some drinks. He gave a summary of his day at work. Then, haltingly, "I miss you. I kind of wish I'd come with you, Dalia."

The truth is, she hadn't actually invited him to come along. If he had asked to come, she wouldn't have refused. When she had pictured a break, she had pictured looking at the water, eating nice meals, listening to some jazz, silently soaking in the sun. But she hadn't thought of bringing Liam. What did that say about their relationship? What did it say about her, she wondered?

"Maybe we can plan a trip together soon," she said. "A trip together would be nice. And being here reminds me how much I need these getaways."

Liam gave a grunt of acknowledgment. Dalia thought she could hear a note of doubt in it. It reminded her of a conversation they'd had several months ago, when she had cancelled plans at the last minute in order to work. "Why do you keep doing this, Dalia?" he'd asked, as if she'd done this before—or at least often before. "It's like you're careening very fast in some direction, with a goal I can't name—and neither, I reckon, could you."

"Will you say hi to everyone tonight for me?" she asked now.

"Of course I will," he responded. "Alright, we'll chat more later. I'll try calling tomorrow, a little earlier?"

"Sounds good. Love you, Liam." She waited for him to hang up before falling back on her pillow. She enjoyed Liam's friends, and for a moment wished she was with them. She looked around the room, small and compact, everything neatly in its place. This was a nine night cruise, long enough that, upon having her bags delivered to the room that first day, she had unpacked her things into drawers and onto hangers, and arranged all her toiletries neatly on the bathroom counter. It felt cozy, and for a minute she pictured the ocean outside, waves gently rippling by. Then she thought about the complex life going on under the water, all the coral life, and algae, and fish and sharks and whatnot. Were there sharks in these parts? She didn't really know all that much about marine life. She had not been one of those children who loved learning about the different types of whales and fish. Unlike many of her primary school classmates, she had never dreamed of becoming a marine biologist when she grew up.

What she had loved—and loved still—was the beach. Some of her favourite childhood memories were of Mediterranean Sea summers spent with relatives, and Pacific Ocean summers spent on the Gold Coast. She remembered early morning walks along the shoreline of the Mediterranean with her aunt Amira, after which they would go into the kitchen of the house Dalia's parents had let, the rest of the house still asleep. Tunt Amira would make a cup of warm milk for her, and tea for herself. I felt like the world belonged just to them on those mornings. There was nothing to disturb the sun, its rays already warming their skin and casting long shadows, and the sound of the waves, which could be heard even three blocks in from the shore. Dalia had her aunt's attention all to herself, and as they walked, they would talk of everything. Sometimes Tunt Amira would tell her stories about her own childhood, or about what Dalia's father had been like when he was a boy. Sometimes Dalia would tell Tunt Amira about her school and her friends, or her parents. Other times, they would just point out what each saw: the sun appearing over a particularly cloudy morning, or the bread baker in front of his wood-burning clay oven, swapping out the baked bread from the oven with the newly kneaded loaves. He made it look easy, but of course, it wasn't. Dalia remembered the one time she had tried to make pita bread during university; she hadn't even been able to get the dough to stay in one piece long enough to go in the oven.

She often times wondered about the lives of people like the bread baker. He learned the trade most likely from a member of his family, and at a young age. His education level probably was not past primary or secondary school, and he had no other prospects in life. Selling bread gave him enough to buy some vegetables or beans, maybe occasionally some meat. He had enough to replace clothing that had gotten too threadbare, but not enough for much else. And yet that baker in the seaside town of her childhood, and others she'd encountered like him, had never seemed unhappy. That baker always had greetings for his customers, a joke or laugh to share with the people he saw every day, and contentment—even pride—in his day's work. Dalia wondered if that was in fact true, or only appeared so. Surely he must hope for better lives for his children, or at least the chance to choose a life.

She thought about her own life. Was it the life she had chosen? Chosen, yes, unlike that bread baker. She had known from the time she was fifteen or sixteen that she wanted to study law in university. And when she had received that acceptance letter, she had felt so completely in possession of her destiny. She was going to make sure that justice won out in every case that she was involved in. But what no one told her then was that acquiring the skills to successfully handle cases was a long and grueling journey. The moments of triumph and satisfaction were dwarfed by all those research and briefing hours, both during and after university, that had eventually necessitated her getting glasses. What no one said back then was that succeeding at the practice of law, and making the world a more just place, were not the same thing.

So was this the life she wanted? Did it mean anything that she was succeeding in it? All those hours in the library had soon put her at the top of her class. Later, the firm's senior partners granted her her first promotion after only three years. But there was no arriving, she'd quickly realized. Each milestone she reached, each accomplishment meant that she was offered a higher profile case or bigger client that required more hours, and challenged her in new ways. She wouldn't really rest until retirement, which was alright. She had the focus and the energy; she didn't have the competing interests of partners and children that so many of her colleagues had. This was the bargain she had known she would have to strike, and had long ago reconciled to it. And she would make the same choice again.

LAYLA

3

London
2008

Layla sighed, leaning her slender torso against the rim of the counter. How much of the past three days, she wondered, had she stood here at the sink, washing the dishes? She spent her days, it seemed, endlessly moving from one household task to the next. Her friend Faiza, on a recent visit, had remarked that Layla never stopped moving. Did she even remember how to sit still, Faiza had asked? Everyone said, Layla had responded gamely, that this was how life was with small children, and that it would get better. Layla believed this; she had to. But there remained years before that change would come.

"Mama!" Layla looked down to see her four-year-old, Maggie, holding her finger up to her. "Tado got orange play-doh on my finger. I told him not to touch it but he did, and now it's on my finger." Her voice started to rise in indignation. Maggie's features were delicate and feminine, like her mother's, which made her anguished expression now all the more dramatic.

"Remember, sweetie, that Tado is a baby," Layla responded. "Don't be upset. You're the big sister; you can get the play-doh off your finger." "Tado" was Maggie's name for her two-year-old brother Matthew. Layla helped Maggie peel off the offending play-doh and then led her back to where she had been playing. Without really looking at him, Layla scooped Matthew up and put him at a further distance from his sister, placing some new toys around him.

Seeing them both occupied for a moment, Layla ran her fingers through her hair, noticing as she did that it needed to be blow-dried straight again; its natural curl had started to assert itself again. But not now; now, Layla stepped outside to get the post. Flipping through the solicitations and occasional bill, she came across a hand-written address. 'No one ever writes actual letters anymore,' she thought. The return address was Lisbon, Portugal. She didn't know anyone in Portugal, and as far as she knew, neither did Peter. She sat down at the kitchen table and opened the envelope carefully. She was surprised to see that it was in Arabic, despite the English address on the envelope.

Dear Madame Layla,

Please allow me to introduce myself. My name is Hany Abdelmallek, and I grew up in the same neighbourhood as your father, Mr. Tayib. I hope this letter finds you and your family in good health, and I write with the warmest regards.

As it has happened, once your father and I grew up, I moved overseas, and am now in Portugal, where I have lived for over twenty years. Your father and I have lost touch, but I hope he would remember me. I have something, from our

24

childhood, I want to speak to you about, but I'd like to speak to you in person.

    I am sorry to contact you like this, out of the blue, but I hope you will consider writing back.

Sincerely yours,

Dr. Hany Abdelmallek

At the end was a street address in Lisbon. Layla stared at the letter, wondering if someone among their acquaintances might be playing this prank on her. Would any of them have been so malicious? She and her parents had not spoken for a year, and this purported connection to her father was a painful reminder. She tried to remember if she had ever heard her father speak of a friend from childhood called Hany. She didn't think so.

"Mama!"

Layla looked up to see Tado sitting in the middle of a cloud of flour, having somehow managed to get into the kitchen and pull the flour canister out of the cabinet. She sighed and got up, silently cursing the fact that she'd never gotten locks on the cabinet doors. The letter, and what to do about it, would have to wait until Peter got home that night.

Layla was picking toys off the floor when Peter came downstairs, having put the kids to bed. "You'll never guess what came in the mail today," she said, jutting her chin towards the corner of the kitchen counter, where the mysterious letter lay hastily tucked under the phone.

She could hear the sigh that Peter tried to keep inaudible. He always came home tired from work these days, but always insisted that he put the kids to bed. It was, he maintained, his best chance to spend time with them each day. And spending time with one's children every day is what good parents did these days. She didn't remember her parents spending such deliberate time with her at bedtime, Layla thought, and she'd turned out alright. Of course, she and her parents had other rituals in her childhood, but as she remembered it, the foundation of their relationship was built upon countless moments of laughter, and talking with them about any number of things.

The problem with Peter's insistence on a bedtime routine, Layla thought now, is that it left little time for the two of them to spend any time in adult conversation. As soon as the kids were in bed, Peter would retreat to his office, open up his laptop, and finish the work he had left undone earlier so that he could have these couple of hours with the family.

"So do you know anyone in Portugal?"

He glanced up at her as he picked up the letter, one eyebrow raised. "No, of course not," he responded. He was silent as he read the letter, and Layla had to remind herself that he read Arabic a little slower than she did. "What is this?" he asked.

Layla shook her head. "I have no idea. I don't know what to make of it. For a moment I thought it might be a joke that someone decided to play on me. But to bring my dad into it? No one we know would do that." She paused for a moment, knowing what he was suspecting. "I suppose I could respond and see...just see what he says. If he mentions anything about expecting payment for this information, or whatever it is he says he has for me, we'll know it's a hoax and can drop the whole thing. No harm done."

Peter was re-reading the letter, and she watched his eyelashes—ridiculously long eyelashes that no man should have and which had so charmed her when she'd first met him. "You don't remember knowing the Abdelmallek family when you were little?"

"Not when I was little," she responded. "When my dad was. And no, I don't remember him mentioning a Hany Abdelmallek. Then again, I don't remember much about what he said about his childhood friends, so it's very possible this was really a friend."

Peter looked at Layla for a minute. She knew that it bothered him that she and her parents weren't speaking. For his own kids' sakes, of course, it bothered him. They should know their grandparents. But it also bothered him for Layla's sake. He knew how much she loved her father especially, and that they had always been so close. This letter, whatever it was, seemed like yet another reminder of how painful this rift was, and as Peter had hinted before, how unnecessary.

"There's no harm in responding," he replied. "It's like you said. You can find out a little more and see where it leads. Although it does worry me a bit that this man, whoever he is, has our address. Where would he have gotten it?"

"I still go by my maiden name officially," Layla responded, "and we never bothered to get our directory information unlisted, remember? Something about paying an annual fee. It seemed pointless." She paused. "I looked up my last name on Google today, just to see what would come up, and when I included an address request, I found our address. On the second page, but still. Maybe we should have gotten our address unlisted after all."

27

"Well, we've gone this long without needing it unlisted," Peter replied, hesitatingly. "And it's done now…but maybe we can start looking into installing a security system if this character seems at all shady." Layla murmured a half-hearted consent. She saw no need to overreact. Anyway, she did want to find out more from this man, whoever he was.

She realized with a pang of shame that she'd been expecting Peter to tell her to respond—or to forbid her from responding and then handling it himself. But of course, Peter never forbade her from doing anything. Sometimes, she realized with surprise, she wished he would. Sometimes making all the decisions was so exhausting, even when, like here, they were decisions about her. She would never say this out loud of course; it sounded so childish. But on the flip side, wasn't that what married people did? Decide things together? Peter would talk through the decision with her if she pressed him to, she knew, but she could see he wanted to get into the office and finish his work. If she was going to find out more about this Abdelmallek fellow, it seemed she would have to take the lead. 'Done,' she thought, 'I'll write back tomorrow.'

PART TWO

4

Cairo
16th of January, 1967

The dawn call to prayer began at precisely the same time it had for as long as I could remember. It was the sound I woke up to, the loudspeakers blaring from that mosque at the end of the street. I did not, of course, participate in the prayers, but, secretly, I'd always found the tune quite beautiful, even when the imam calling out the prayer would change on occasion. I'd heard the call in our old apartment, then even when our family moved to this apartment after my father's death. Our apartment wasn't far from the old one, but it was smaller and a little shabbier, but most importantly, the rent was affordable on our reduced income. My mother always used to joke that it was the best of both worlds: we still had our neighbours and friends and every place we ever went was still close by, but we paid less for it — and we were the only ones of our friends who sported a turn-of-the-century kitchen. She was sure, my mother would intone with a big smile, that it would come back into style any day now.

I was in university, a second year architect student. Life was rich. My classmates and I studied hard, but it was a carefree existence, and we made many good memories during this time. My friends and I would spend weekends on trips to the seaside, or going camping, or catching a concert in Cairo, a city which at that time was growing rapidly but also prospering.

That is why, in fact, I had decided to become an architect. A couple of my primary school friends and I had stayed together until now, studying architecture together. We took the bus to classes together and studied together. We would meet at the library if there wasn't some event or protest or construction preventing us, or we would meet at one of our homes, where the tea and biscuits were plentiful, but the interruptions from family frequent, if not unwelcome. My friends never said so, but I knew they preferred coming to my house, where my mother would only engage in a little small talk before sending us off with a pot of tea and her renowned biscuits.

The biscuits were something that my father always used to compliment my mother about; she'd perfected the recipe early in their marriage and he had always, without fail, praised them. "Iriny," I remember him saying, "there are no better biscuits in the whole neighbourhood—no, in all of Cairo!" These days, the biscuits reminded her of my father, just as they did me. I knew that is why my mother always had a batch around, and that she missed him, still, every day. It was a kindness to me and to my sister that she didn't let the grief show on her face and in her motions, which she kept as energetic as ever. Amira and I were both teenagers now—me not for much longer though— and the apartment was always filled with friends and activities. I was happy to take part in this life, knowing my mother wanted to see us normal and carefree, but knowing too that there were many days when she— and I too if I were being honest—would have preferred the quiet that would allow my father's absence to be felt, and in that way honoured.

I had tried talking to my mother about all of it a few years ago. I wasn't sure why. Perhaps I wanted her to know I was old enough and strong enough to carry her grief with her, though of course I didn't really know that I could. My mother was my anchor. It was to her that I took all of my thoughts and plans, and so even though I remembered my father and missed certain things about him — the music he liked to play, the way he laughed — I no longer felt like I needed him there every day. I needed my mother every day, and so maybe that is why I worried over her. And I was old enough now to wonder what she did when she needed refuge or the counsel of that one person. And so, in the way that so many of my age did — but which, in retrospect, I recognize as rather naive — I tried to at least open the door for her to be sad with me.

It was only much later, when I myself became the parent of someone that age that I realised what an impossible expectation I had been placing on my mother, and on myself. The shape of that grief was, well, unutterable. How does one express the loss, sudden and absolute, of one's spouse and life's mate? But even if my mother had managed to express it, the weight of such sadness would have been too difficult for someone my age, for whom life offered nothing but possibilities and promises yet to be made good on.

Maybe I was thinking about all this on that particular morning, or maybe I was thinking about something else. In any case, upon hearing that call to prayer, I had reached for my watch, looked at it even though I knew exactly what time it was, and gotten up. It was still early, and I usually allowed myself to go back to sleep for at least an hour or two before getting up, but today was different. It was the first day of classes following the Ramadan holiday, and my friends and I had arranged to meet at the coffee shop across the street from the university entrance at 6:00am. The only other people who would be up then would be the workers and labourers whose days started early to avoid the midday heat. They would either ignore my friends and I, or greet us with a tired 'good morning' as they prepared for their own day.

I wasn't entirely sure, actually, why we were meeting there. We had hatched this plan one night as we were joking and letting off steam about the events of the past couple of weeks. We were all in a design class in which the professor was lecturing on the concept of axial force. He had decided to make an example out of my friends and I when it became clear that we — and the majority of the class along with us, to be sure — were struggling to grasp this concept. We had gone home and tried to read through it again, but still it remained hazy.

When we had been walking out of yet another humiliating class session the last week before the holidays, a young woman had approached us, a classmate of ours. There were very few women in architecture, and very few women in general who initiated conversation with anyone other than their few close girl friends. This student introduced herself as Yasmine. She was beautiful and, by the very fact that she was there, clearly very smart and very tough. She went straight to the point. "Listen," she said, "I don't think everything in our classes is easy, but this concept of axial force is something I actually understand, and I'm happy to explain it to you if you'd like."

My friends and I stared at her. The last thing we were expecting was for a beautiful young woman to come up to us and offer us a chance to pass this class and end the humiliation of the past few weeks. Before I had a chance to say anything, my friend Aziz spoke up. "Why would you want to help us?" he asked. "If you keep your understanding to yourself, you earn a higher grade."

"True," she said. "But I don't think it's fair how he is treating you. All professors know that we all struggle with something at some point. They probably struggled at some point when they were students! Their jobs are to help us understand, not take pleasure in our struggles. That's what I think he's doing." She stopped, as if wondering if she had been too familiar with us.

"Anyway," she said. "I'm happy to help. You can let me know later." With that, she started to walk away. Aziz went after her, and in a minute, he came back.

"Her family is going to Alexandria for the holidays," he said, "but she said she can meet us the morning classes start again. I told her we would be happy to meet with her."

We nodded, relieved he had decided, then spoken, for us. That night, though, as the giddiness of the break was upon us, we started playing with the idea of meeting together before we met with her and figuring it out ourselves. Whether it was out of a desire to impress a pretty girl, or to not have to be schooled by someone who no one expected to be as good at maths as we were, we probably did not examine, even each within himself, back then. We just decided that we would give our brains a break from this class for the duration of the break, in the hopes that when we came back to it with fresh eyes, the answers would be apparent to us.

Sitting here now, despite our eyes becoming less groggy as each cup of Turkish coffee had its effect, it was clear this was not going to happen. We were stumbling just to remember the theories that led up to the concept of axial force; theories that we had mastered at the beginning of the semester we were now having to reacquaint themselves with.

"Come on, gentlemen," Aziz said. "Don't despair. Our minds just need the chance to wake up a bit. It's early still. But we can do this! Tayib, yala, you had gotten this part down pretty well. Explain it to us, please."

And so it had gone on like this for an hour and a half. It was now almost 8am, and we would be meeting with Yasmine in an hour. There would not be enough time to cover everything. A half hour later, we had gotten caught up but again hit a wall when it came to this concept of axial force.

We decided to spend the remaining time catching up on each others' news instead. As we meandered towards the library, where we would be meeting Yasmine, we talked about the usual things. We had been friends for so long, it occurred to me, that we didn't bother even with the niceties that we employed with our other friends.

At the door of the library, we saw Yasmine sitting at a table on the far end of the room. With her were a couple of her friends — the only other women architecture students. This made us all feel better; this would be more like a regular study session between classmates now. We sat down. As my friends and I began pulling out our notebooks and pencils, Aziz asked the girls how their holidays had gone and made jokes, as only he knew how to, until everyone at the table was smiling, any discomfort or unfamiliarity dissipated. Yasmine asked where we wanted to start, and before long, the group was deep in conversation, taking notes and passing around diagrams. At one point, I looked up and caught Yasmine's gaze, but she quickly looked away. I found myself wishing I could talk to her privately, but I wouldn't know what to say, and besides, I didn't know if I felt this way because I had never met a girl as smart as she was, or because she was so gorgeous: not a reason, in my book, to like someone.

5

Cairo
16th of January, 1967

I was in university, a second year architecture
student. It was the first day of classes following the
Ramadan holiday, and my friends and I had arranged
to meet at the coffee shop across the street from the
entrance to the university at 6:00am. I wasn't entirely
sure, actually, why we were going. We had been
struggling with the concept of axial force that was
being taught in one of our classes. The professor, it
seemed, had decided to make an example of us
somehow and took every opportunity to pick on us
during lectures. One of the few girls in our class had
unexpectedly offered to help. I thought her name was
Yasmine. My friends and I—or rather, Aziz on all our
behalfs—had decided to accept her offer, but we were
still going to try to study together first, presumably so
we wouldn't look too stupid when it came time to
study with our classmate. I suspect the fact that she
was beautiful was a motivating factor for my friends.

To be honest, I was starting to doubt if I should even
be in architecture school. I loved looking at buildings,
but the maths and engineering that went into creating
them was about as appealing as rubbing my skin with
sandpaper. I could have chosen to go down another
professional track, of course, like pharmacy, or
medicine. I remembered biology as being very

interesting when I was in secondary school. Over the break, I had decided, I would use this design class as an omen. If I was understanding and enjoying it by the end of the term, I would stick with architecture. If not, I would switch to medicine.

I knew this would upset my mother, and Amira to a lesser degree, and I had already decided what I would tell them. My grades out of secondary school had been high enough to admit me into one of the professional tracks—a fact my mother took great pride in—and I would remain on one of those tracks: medicine, pharmacy, dentistry, law, or engineering. I would still be following a respectable career path, something I knew mattered to my mother. But I could not bear the thought of spending most of my adult life constantly questioning whether I should have chosen a different path. If I switched now, I would have to get special permission to apply for medicine, and I would have to begin again, essentially losing the last two years. I knew my friends would tease me, and the older relatives would be shocked that I would waste so much time. But as far as I was concerned, the last two years had not been a waste. I had learned a lot, even if I never used it again. And besides, what was two years in the face of 35 or 40 years in the wrong field that would otherwise be waiting for me?

These were my thoughts as I sat with my friends in the coffee shop at 6am on that first day of classes. At one point, Aziz looked at me and joked that my mind must still be asleep from the holidays that had just ended. Or that I was nervous about meeting Yasmine, the girl we were going to study with. She was pretty, granted, but I had never been one to let that kind of thing divert my focus.

Just as we were heading onto the university grounds a couple of hours later, I spotted our doorman's son running towards me. "Ostaz Tayib!" the boy yelled, calling me. This was highly unusual. I walked quickly towards him, calling to my friends that I would catch up to them when I could. The boy was breathing hard, as if he had run all the way from our apartment building almost two kilometres away.

"What's wrong, Ibrahim?" I asked.

"Did you see Amira today?" the boy asked. "Is she with you?"

I had not, of course, seen my sister. I had dressed and left the house quietly, before the sun had yet risen. I had assumed that Amira and my mother were both asleep in their beds. Amira was almost fifteen years old by then; certainly old enough to go out on her own, but our mother — and me, if I had to be honest — did not allow her to. The girl would get so lost in her thoughts that she could easily wander beyond the streets of our neighbourhood and not know how to get back. Cairo was not the kind of place where a pretty, young girl's safety could be assured in the hands of strangers; neither my mother or I would take that risk.

I quickly hailed a taxi, and Ibrahim and I jumped in and headed back to the apartment. Upstairs, my mother was frantic. "Her bed was made, just like she always makes it, so I don't think she left in a rush. Where would she have gone? She hasn't been here since I woke up an hour and a half ago. Where would she have gone, Tayib?"

I looked at my watch. Her school day would be starting soon. She wouldn't have gone there early, would she? Not by choice, she wouldn't, unless her small group of friends were too. And if she had something to do there, she would have told us last night.

"Alright, Mama, how about this: I am going to go get Hany and Magdy," I said, referring to my friends who I knew would be home at this hour. "One of us will go to the school to make sure she didn't go there early without telling us, and the other two will split up and start looking for her in all the places she knows. Can you start calling her friends' families? Or maybe asking the neighbours if they have seen her?"

My mother nodded, trying, clearly, to control the panic she was feeling. "It will be fine," I said, not convinced of it myself. "She probably had planned to be somewhere and forgot to tell us." Of course, Amira never varied from her routine; I would have scoffed at this suggestion, coming from someone else.

I gave my mother a quick kiss on the cheek and headed down the stairs. Walking out the door, I turned towards Hany's house, starting a mental list of the places we would make sure to cover. Half a block later, I saw my friend's tall head, bent in conversation with someone, walking towards me. It was only when the distance between us cleared of other pedestrians that I saw it was Amira that Hany was talking to. At first, I felt a surge of gratitude that Hany had found her. And then I noticed that they did not have an air about them of distress, of someone who had been lost or someone who had been looking. They were talking amicably, even excitedly. I felt an unfamiliar tightening in my chest.

"Hany!" I called, but my eyes were on Amira.

The two of them saw me and quickened their gait, as if excited to tell me something. This did nothing to quell my rising anger. Were they not even aware of the panic they had caused?

"Tayib," Amira said. "You'll never guess where we were. It was wonderful; I wish you'd been there."

"Do you know what time it is?" I asked, cutting her off. Amira stopped almost mid-stride and looked at her watch. "Oh my," she said, the surprise clear in her voice. She looked at Hany. "I'm supposed to be on my way to school. How did it get so late? Excuse me." She brushed past me and started walking quickly towards the apartment. Before turning around to follow her there, I looked back to find Hany looking at me with a quizzical look.

"I'm sorry she's going to be late to school," he said. "Why were you worried? Didn't she tell you where we were going?"

I didn't know how to answer. "We'll talk about this later," I said, not trusting myself to say more. I turned around and half ran home.

I arrived in the apartment to find Amira already putting her things in her school bag and pulling on her school sweater. Our mother was adding her lunch to the bag, scolding as she did so. "Didn't you think to tell us you were going out? And since when is it ok to go out alone with Hany? Do you know how many people I've already worried about you this morning?"

Amira was muttering a string of sorries. As soon as her bag was ready, she disappeared out the door. My mother and I stood looking at the slammed door for a minute before either of us spoke.

"What was she doing with Hany?" she finally asked.

"I don't know. I didn't give them a chance to tell me. They started to say something about having seen something wonderful. I don't know what could be so wonderful she would have disappeared so early. Hany seemed to think she had told us about it. He seemed surprised that we were worried."

"Since when do Hany and Amira even talk?"

"I don't know, Mama. Hany's been coming here for years. I guess Amira assumes if he's my friend, he's hers too."

"And is he?"

"Is he what?"

"Her friend? Your friend? What kind of a person takes a young girl out alone like this? And without talking to her parents?"

"Mama, Hany probably sees her like a little sister. Of course he should know better than to have taken her wherever they went without checking with me or you, but honestly I doubt that anything bad happened."

"You doubt? And what about the neighbours who saw them together at this hour? What are they going to think?"

How I detested this. I detested that, ever since my father had died, our reputation as an upstanding family had become even more important, to my mother in particular. Everyone, my mother insisted, would see the slightest sign of imperfection and assume the family, without a father and husband, had fallen; that she had been unable to uphold our reputation, whatever that meant. She would not have her children's future prospects threatened by any shadow of wrongdoing, she had said on more than one occasion. We would be good and decent people, both in fact and in the eyes of those around us. Of this, my mother had always and would always make sure.

"I'll talk to Hany," I said.

"I don't want you to talk to Hany. What can you say to him that would matter at all right now? My concern is Amira. That is who we need to talk to. I need to find out where they were, and I need to make sure this never happens again. Honestly, what am I going to tell everyone who I had already called this morning?"

"Just tell them we found her walking just outside, and that she hadn't realized what time it was. Don't most people have more important things to worry about?" I asked, irritated now with this line of thinking. "In any case, my classes start in less than a half hour. I should go. We'll talk more about this tonight?"

My mother nodded, "Of course. Do you want to take some food with you?"

"I'm fine, Mama," I said. "Bye."

At the lecture hall, I slid into my customary seat just a minute before my friends arrived from their study session. "Everything alright?" they asked.

"Fine," I answered. "Everything's fine. How was the study session? Do you understand axial force now?"

"Actually, yes," said Aziz. "Well, I think so. We'll explain it to you after class."

I sat through the class half concentrating on what was being said, half thinking about Hany and Amira. Honestly, I didn't know what to make of them. Is it possible that there was, in fact, something going on between them? Or were they, as I had assured my mother, just like brother and sister?

I needed to concentrate. I listened as the professor droned on about geometric centres and compression forces, struggling to write down the main concepts. I would make sense of them later, I decided. But as my friends sat with me after class and tried, each talking over the other, to convey his understanding of axial force and whatever other concepts, I knew that something in me had shifted since we were last in class. I did not care about these things, and I didn't really care if I never became an architect. Though I knew it with certainty, I could explain the reason as poorly as I could explain axial force.

―――――――――――

I arrived home later that same day to find Amira and Mama sitting at the table. Whatever they had been saying before I arrived, they had clearly reached an impasse. I started some water boiling for tea and sat down with them. My mother looked up at me and said, "They went to St. Mina's church. There was a special liturgy early this morning for Saint Abraam. It was his feast day, and so they had a special prayer with his relics."

"And I don't know why," Amira added bitterly, "going to church has now become something that requires a family council meeting." She was, after all, almost fifteen, I reminded myself, and every bit the sass that a girl that age would be.

"Amira," I said, trying to bridge the gap between them. "I didn't know you and Hany liked St. Abraam so much. And I know both of you pretty well."

"Well maybe not as well as you thought," she replied. "Your head's been too busy with architecture stuff."

Not anymore, I thought, but this was not the time for that conversation.

"When did you guys come up with the idea to go?"

"A few days ago, while he was helping us with biology," she replied.

"He helps you with your homework?"

"Well, not just me. His cousin Samia is also in my class, so he's been tutoring us two and a couple other students from my class."

This was news to both my mother and me. We knew she studied biology with some friends; we didn't know Hany was there.

"And did all of you go to church this morning?" Mama asked pointedly.

"One of the other girls met us there," Amira responded. "But she lives in the other direction, so that's why you didn't see her walking home with us."

"And was she also late to school?" our mother pressed.

"Well, no. Hany and I stayed talking after church and after she'd already gone home, and I guess I didn't realize how long we had talked."

"Well, he should have realized," Mama said, looking at me as if it were my fault.

"Mama, I already said I'm sorry I was late to school, and I'm so sorry I worried you. Really. I lost track of time: that's the only thing I did wrong. What else can I say?"

I heard, for the first time, a maturity in Amira's voice. She wasn't scared of our mother's wrath, nor was she being petulant. She really was sorry, and she was also ready to move on.

But Mama wasn't. "And what did you and Hany have to talk about that was so engrossing it made you forget about school?"

"I don't know, Mama. We talked about university, and what classes there are like, and what I might want to study. We talked about what it's like to live in our neighbourhood. Whatever friends talk about." As if realizing there may have been a trap in their mother's question, Amira added, "It's no different than what I talk about with my girl friends."

"Except that he's a university student, and a young man who is significantly older than you."

"Like Tayib is significantly older than me?" Amira asked.

'Ah, the sassiness is back,' I thought. This can only get worse from here. Maybe it was time to switch subjects after all.

"Mama, I'll talk to Hany about this," I interjected. "In the meantime, I have some news for you two."

Mama and Amira looked at me warily.

"I've decided not to continue in architecture. Tomorrow, I'm going to go speak with Professor Ibrahim about switching to medicine."

"What?" Mama asked. "Why? Where did you get such an idea? What about all the work you have put in these two years? What has happened? Are you failing your classes? Because if you are, you should know that medicine will not be any easier."

"I'm not failing," I said. "I'd just rather spend the next forty years of my life working with human beings and their health than on buildings."

"But it will be years before you can properly work," she said. "You'll graduate late, and even then you'll have to spend your postgraduate training years in who knows what outpost of a town. You'll be almost 30 before you even start working. What kind of nonsense is this? What has gotten into my children today? What have I done wrong?"

This made Amira and I look up at her with surprise. Our mother worried, but she was never this dramatic. Perhaps I could have timed my announcement a little more thoughtfully, after all. I looked over at Amira, who looked back at me expectantly.

"I'm sorry to upset you, Mama," I said. "Why don't Amira and I finish getting dinner prepared and call you when it's ready? You should go lie down for a little bit. It has been a busy day." She had gotten up then and gone silently down the hall, not to lie down, the angle of her shoulders and chin said, but to decide how to handle the rebels that had suddenly replaced her children.

"You're sure you're not failing your classes?" Amira said, once we were alone in the kitchen.

"No. I really just don't want to do it anymore."

"What if you decide the same thing about medicine in a few years? Nothing's easy, after all."

I thought how much she sounded like me at her age, when I would coach her through maths. "Then I'll just come live with you and you can take care of me until I'm old," I joked.

She elbowed me with feigned exasperation, and we worked in silence for a moment, she boiling the rice and me cutting up the spinach and beef that would go in the tomato sauce base our mother had started.

"So what *are* you going to study when you go to university?" I finally asked her.

"Not sure. Maybe medicine too. Or pharmacy. At least with pharmacy I can start working right away."

"You'll have to keep your grades really high."

"I will."

Another pause.

"So seriously, you can tell me. There's nothing happening between you and Hany other than studying? You can tell me the truth."

47

Amira hesitated before answering. "Well, I'm sure he would tell you nothing's going on. As far as he's concerned, I think he sees me as just your little sister, just another high school girl. But I don't know. I like spending time with him. He's always really nice to me. Most guys in university — your other friends, even — just ignore me. Which is fine. What do I want to talk to them about? But Hany's nice. Let's just say I wouldn't mind if he liked me," she paused, then added with a false breeziness, "but I'm pretty sure he doesn't."

I didn't know what to say. I had been so wrapped up with my own worries about my courses that I hadn't even known about this budding friendship — or whatever it was — between my sister and my friend. Now I would have to talk to Hany. The thought made my stomach clench. Hany and I had been friends forever, and I considered him like a brother, but this was about Amira now. Innocent, fragile Amira. If she fell for Hany, and Hany allowed her to, I would never forgive him if he broke her heart.

I found I was clenching the bottle of oil I had pulled from the cabinet too tightly. I crouched down to put it back in before Amira could notice my white knuckles or ask for my opinion. "I'm going to go study a little before dinner," I said, and started down the hall.

6

Cairo
February 1967

Studying had become much more pleasurable since that early morning session when Yasmine had managed to explain to my friends and me the theory of axial force. We were back on track, we again felt indomitable. But something else changed that morning too. As if by some unspoken agreement, Yasmine and I had begun to find excuses to organise study dates with our respective groups of friends, but it quickly became clear that the amount of time that the two of us wanted to spend together far exceeded any study needs either group had. So I took her home to meet my mother and Amira, and shortly thereafter, she arranged for my mother and I to have tea with her parents. With their blessing, we got engaged and began openly spending time together, although it was, as custom dictated, always in public places.

We were approaching graduation, and of course our impending marriage. We began having serious conversations about what we would do after. Once we were no longer university students and were husband and wife, what would our life look like? Yasmine wanted to work at one of the architecture firms in Cairo, but not at the same one as me. She predicted, probably correctly, that if we worked at the same place, any work she did would be attributed to me, and that others would expect her to seek my approval of her work. I scoffed at this, pointing out that Egypt was changing, even though I wasn't entirely sure that it was changing enough.

Still, I argued the point, giving as an example the way our classmates treated her and the other women in their class. It was as equals.

"Yes," Yasmine conceded, "but they are classmates. This is still school. Out in the working world, it will be different. You are expected to earn your salary and make the firm successful, not just earn a grade for yourself. And these old guys running the firms? They don't think we women can actually do the work. They just don't, no matter what evidence you show them."

"Well, with that kind of attitude, how do you expect anyone to hire you?" I asked her. I myself had offers from two firms. I had risen, from the days of that almost doomed design class, to the top of the class, along with Aziz and, of course, Yasmine. One of the offers was from a firm of mostly young architects who had a lot of energy and vision for what Cairo could look like; the other had a more established, well respected group of architects who had already built and renovated some of Cairo's most iconic buildings. I was trying to decide which group of architects I could see myself belonging with in the long term. Eventually, I chose the more established firm, deciding that it was the Cairo they had built that I loved, and that by the time I knew enough to have my own ideas, I would be a senior partner and could have a say in the direction the firm took.

As for Yasmine, she soon got a position at a small but respected architecture firm whose partners had connections with her father's business. "It's a start," she'd say. "I will show everyone what I am capable of here, and then the larger firms will be begging to have me work for them."

It was true, I knew, that she was among the best architects, if not the best, in our class. She understood the engineering side of building so easily (I still envied her that), but she brought to her designs a beauty that was breathtaking. 'Perhaps it is best after all,' I remember thinking, 'that we don't work at the same firm. I wouldn't want to have to lose against my wife.'

7

Cairo
January 1967

It had been two days since Amira's morning
excursion with Hany. In that short time, my own life
was coming unraveled. I had made up my mind: I was
not going to continue with architecture, though I was
still having nightly conversations with relatives who
came calling at my mother's behest trying to urge me
to reconsider. Mama, in addition to taking my news so
badly, was still preoccupied with Amira, always
stealing looks at her as if hoping to discover a covert
explanation for her uncharacteristic behaviour.

I still hadn't brought myself to talk to Hany about it,
but that had not been hard to manage. He and I rarely
crossed paths unless we tried to. I did not try. What
would I say to him? What should I say? Moments like
this I wished my father was alive, because if anything it
would be him talking to Hany, or telling me exactly
what I should say to him. And it would probably be
something along the lines of how Amira was too young
to be thinking about boys.

Amira was indeed too young to be thinking about
boys — no, she wasn't too young to be thinking about
boys, but she was too young for men, and talk of
marriage. And if I, at age 20, was a man — and I liked to
think that I was, then so was Hany. Even if he wasn't, it
would not be appropriate for Amira to be involved

with anyone at her age. This is what I'd have to find a way to say to Hany. I'd do it today.

On my way home from class, I stopped at the apartment where Hany lived. I went up the stairs slowly, and paused when I came to his door. This door, which I had knocked on dozens if not hundreds of times in my life, seemed forbidding now, with its lacquered wood and iron-works covered, frosted glass window. I rapped a few short knocks. Hany came to the door a minute later, book in hand. He looked like he was in the middle of studying. The friendly smile froze on his face, and was replaced by a solicitous, questioning tug at the corner of his mouth.

"I hope I'm not disturbing you," I said.

"No, not at all, not at all," Hany replied, his face relaxing. "Listen, my cousins are over with their kids. Let me get my shoes and we can go somewhere quieter — maybe go down to the corner café?"

I nodded and gave him a small smile. As he turned away, I heard him call out to his mother that he was leaving for a little bit with me. It was not unlike the hundreds of times he's called the exact same thing to his mother; it was hard for us not to be completely at ease with each other. I waited until Hany had come back out and closed the door behind him.

We trotted down the stairs and strode out the building. Once we were on the sidewalk, the silence between us became too long. We both started at the same time.

"About the other day," I began.

"Listen, I'm sorry about — " said Hany. Then, as if acknowledging that his account was the one needed, went on. "I didn't think to double check that Amira had told you or your mother where she was going.

And in retrospect, of course it looks bad that she was out so early, and she and I were walking in the street together. I'm so sorry. I wasn't thinking. I forget sometimes that she's not one of my sisters or cousins, you know?" Without waiting for a response, he went on.

"I understand if your mother is upset with me, and I hope she will let me come apologize to her personally if she is…"

"I think she might like that."

"OK, I will then. Our families have been friends for ages, Tayib, and I would hate for my thoughtlessness to ruin that."

This was good, I thought. We don't need to discuss this further; we can just go back to the way things were.

But then Hany continued, "And you know your sister. She is so sensitive. If she thought she had done anything really wrong, she would be devastated. And I would hate to be the cause of that. She's a very sp—" He cut himself off. "Well, she just doesn't deserve that kind of guilt. And besides, how could I cause harm to my dear friend's sister?"

I hadn't missed the affection in my friend's voice. Should I say anything about it? I didn't want to hurt my relationship with Hany, but neither was I one to leave elephants in the room, or on the sidewalk as the case may be.

"Hany, my sister is a very special girl."

Hany nodded as if to say, 'of course.'

"And you've known her since we were kids."

Hany nodded again.

"So you know she's still very young. And impressionable. And right now, she needs to be concentrating on her studies."

"Of course, Tayib. Of course. What are you saying?"

"I'm saying she should not be distracted by anything. And you know young girls, and their thoughts of romance and boys. I just don't want her to get any ideas that you might be interested in her."

"You're saying I might be interested in her? Just because I am spending time with my cousin and her friends?"

"Well, aren't you?"

Hany paused before answering, and in that pause was a resignation that only someone who knew Hany as well as I did would hear. "No, of course not. She's still in secondary school. You know very well we are surrounded by plenty of beautiful women at the university, and they are the right age." Hany was trying to make a joke now, but joking about women didn't suit him.

"I'm sorry, Hany. It's just that my mother is really protective of Amira — we both are — and my mother is concerned about her reputation." Realizing how that could be misinterpreted, I quickly added, "Not that you would damage it, of course, ever. But you know how people are. They see any small thing and they draw conclusions and spread gossip."

"Of course, Tayib. Of course. I'll apologise to your mother. You don't have to worry about this any more."

I knew Hany would keep his word, no matter how he felt about the whole thing. "Thank you, Hany. You are indeed a precious and true friend."

By this time we had reached the café, so we sat down and ordered Turkish coffees.

"So I won't be going to the architecture building for much longer," I said, wanting both to change the topic and to share my news with my old friend.

"Why? What happened?" Hany was instantly concerned.

"I don't want to be an architect, that's all. I wish I had made that decision a few years ago and saved myself the time, but better now than 10 years from now."

"Well, aren't you going to at least finish first, since you've already put two years in?"

"Why, and waste more years? No, I'm going to start again, just as if I was a high school graduate."

"They won't let you do that, will they?"

"I met with my faculty advisor yesterday. He has a colleague in the medical school who he will talk to. He thinks they can enrol me as a first year medical student starting in the new year without me having to sit for exams again."

"And what if you don't like medicine?"

"Then I will have gambled and lost. I won't switch again. I think I can succeed in medicine, and I think that I'll enjoy it at least a little more than architecture."

Hany just looked at me. "But you haven't taken any biology classes for years now. Aren't you worried about being behind?" My decision, I was learning, was far out of everyone's reality. I was answering questions like this a lot. I did not myself know if I could get caught up on the sciences, but hard work and applying what brains I had had not let me down before, so I was counting on them to pull me through this time.

Still, it saddened me that this close childhood friend was looking at me now as if I was slightly mad. "Ensha Allah," I said, "God willing, it will be alright."

Our talk turned then to updates about mutual friends and classmates, and in this way, we slowly eased into the effortless exchange that we had known for so long. When the sun glowed orange at dusk's onset, and the outlines of the buildings around us darkened, we looked at our watches, and got up to walk back down their street, our rift mended, if not forgotten.

8

Cairo
1972

They say that you remember scenes from your past like flashes from an old video reel, and it was just so with my memories of my wedding day. I remembered, for example, my friend Atef coming through our apartment the morning of the wedding, holding in his hand the rings, two traditional gold bands with each spouse's name and the wedding day's date engraved on the inside. Atef had strutted around the apartment, as if this marriage was his own personal achievement, which, I suppose, it was. Atef had, after all, been the one to introduce me to my bride Aida. Atef and I were classmates in medical school, me being the slightly older student Atef had met his first day on campus. Atef had been my main study partner, other than Hany, who studied with me, more for my benefit than for his own, until he graduated a couple of years before us.

One day, when Atef and I were studying in the library, I had looked up to see my old friend Aziz joking with a young woman. I vaguely recognized her as Yasmine, the student I'd missed that study session with on the morning Amira had gone out with Hany. Aziz and Yasmine would be in their last semester now, on the verge of completing the architecture program. I approached Aziz to say hello, and after the surprised pleasantries had been completed, Aziz asked me how I was finding medicine. I responded honestly: I loved it, but it was a lot of studying. I asked him about himself, and Aziz told me where he would be working, and then, briefly, introduced — or rather, reintroduced — Yasmine and I. A few minutes later, I had gone back to my table to continue studying with Atef.

Atef enjoyed my company, I think, because I knew my way around campus and could tell him the best corners of the library in which to study. I enjoyed the friendship of someone who didn't always compare my life in medicine to the life I almost had as an architect. Atef was Aida's older brother; I had met Aida early in my friendship with Atef. We would often study at Atef's house in the afternoon because it was a closer walk from the university. Aida was still a couple of years away from starting university then, so at first I had thought of her as just a little girl, much like I thought of my own sister, Amira. But I distinctly remember one evening, three or four years after Atef and I had become classmates, when we were studying unusually late for an organic chemistry exam the next week, and Aida had returned home with her parents from the engagement party of a cousin. Aida had gotten dressed up for the occasion, getting her hair pulled up in that complex and sophisticated way that women of every age did for formal events. Her dress was made of a material that, even to my inexperienced eye, looked elegant and not inexpensive. It wasn't her hair or the fabric of her dress that had caught my eye, though. It was the fact that, in the intervening years since I had relegated her in my mind's eye to the pigeon hole of little sister, Aida had grown up into a young woman. She carried herself differently, and the expression in her eye was different, almost more world weary.

Atef must have caught a change in my demeanor towards Aida that night, because he made it his mission in the next few months to create circumstances where we could and did speak privately. He would liberally sprinkled tidbits about Aida into our conversation, and I'm sure he did the same with her. I would sometimes wonder, in later years, if we would have ever gotten married had it not been for Atef. I loved Aida of course, and respected her, but, if asked, I could never have given a reason for choosing to marry Aida, beyond the allure she held of a beautiful young woman who had just discovered her womanhood, and one who shared the same experiences of a middle-class Cairo youth, coming of age in the '60s.

Aida was in the humanities college studying French. She explained to everyone who asked that she had the grades to follow her brother into medicine but that she despised blood and that, besides, reading French novels had been her favourite pursuit since she had been old enough to do it. I had found this an endearing quirk at the time, though I would wonder in later years whether it wasn't in fact an unwillingness to test deeper waters. When we had emigrated years later, she was initially the one who had been most excited about it: the chance to develop some new language skills, meet new people, see a new way of life. It was, she kept saying, an adventure. But then, when we had decided to stay abroad, she had withdrawn into the familiar, restricting her social circle to other immigrant mothers, or the occasional mother of one of Dalia's friends. When presented with an opportunity to befriend someone new, in the way that sometimes happens at work or social functions, or even volunteering through a church or school event, she declined opportunities to meet the unknown. Over time, instead of growing any meaningful roots in our new home, she favoured creating a bubble of a life in which lived other Egyptian expatriates.

But that was all in the future and unknown to me that day, as I stood in my wedding suit. I looked at the friends congregating in the church and saw faces from my neighbourhood and from university, my friend Hany among them. He was beaming with joy. "So," I had teased, "when is it going to be your turn?"

Hany had blushed at that, demurring. He had just finished his medical training and was back in Cairo after having spent most of the past two years in Upper Egypt, completing his medical training in the smaller villages that doted the Nile banks. The month before, he had gone on an official visit to see my mother and I and to ask for our blessing for him to start seeing Amira. Amira had just finished her first year of medical school. Though it would be a few years before our mother would consider allowing her to marry, Amira had been excited about the prospect of spending more time with Hany. Now, I glanced over to see that my sister had noticed Hany's blush and was herself trying to hide a shy smile.

9

Cairo
1970

"I don't know why he didn't ask you," Yasmine was saying. We were sitting in our small kitchen, some bread fragments and smears of feta cheese on each of our plates from breakfast. As was our habit on workday mornings, I was doing the crossword page of the paper, and she was reading the front page headlines.

Rather than saying anything, I just stared at her. She poured herself a second cup of tea, as she always did, dipping her spoon, just once, into the sugar bowl I'd just smoothed over. She stirred in the sugar and took a sip of tea.

She tried to resume the newspaper article she'd been reading, but then looked back up at me. "What I'd like to know is why you're reacting this way about it. You work at a big firm that mostly does commercial and government buildings. Even if he had asked you, you probably would have turned the project down.

"Then I get a little residential project, and you're upset. Why, Tayib?"

Rather than answering, I got up and put my tea cup and plate in the sink, rinsing them briefly. After a moment I turned back around to face her. "I have a right to know how long you and Hany have been talking. Where do you meet? How long have you been talking?"

"Be-esmellah, is that what this is about? He called me at work last week sometime and told me about the project and asked if I'd be interested. When I said I would, he said he'd talk to the client and get back to me. Then yesterday he calls and asks me if I'm free to meet the client with him at the Nile Hilton."

"The Nile Hilton."

"Yes, the Nile Hilton, where you have gone for work meetings no less than 10 times."

"Lots of men take their girlfriends there too."

"Don't be ridiculous. What kind of a person are you suggesting I am? And isn't he supposed to be your friend? Is that really what you think of your friend? Weren't you telling me just last week that you hoped he and Amira might be getting more serious about each other—that Amira had feelings for him?"

"All women have 'feelings' for him," I said, not hiding my sarcasm. "But he doesn't deserve my sister."

"Tayib, do you realize how completely irrational you're being?"

Rather than indulge her in that question, I asked, "why, of all the architects he knows, would he contact you?"

"Maybe because I'm the wife of his very good friend and he wants to help my career. Maybe because designing homes is what I do. Maybe because I'm actually good at it."

When I wouldn't answer, she continued.

"Which is it, Tayib? You're jealous of me because he asked me and not you, or jealous for me because you've come up with the ridiculous idea that he's after me?"

63

"Or is it the other way around?" I asked, realizing as I said it that I had not admitted this fear even to myself before now.

"Now you're insulting my integrity," she replied, her beautiful eyes blazing into me. "We are done talking. I'm getting ready for work." With that, Yasmine got up and left our small kitchen, leaving me staring at the bowl of sugar by her tea cup, its perfect surface broken by a single dip, crystals scattered around the spoon lying beside it.

10

Alexandria
1976

"Do you ever think about living in Egypt again?"
Amira was asking her sister-in-law, Aida.

Aida looked up from feeding 15-month old Dalia.
She fed her another spoon of the moulokhaya and rice,
remarking how this soup, with its rather slimy texture
and unique flavour, could be so universally liked by
babies. "We think about it," Aida answered finally,
"especially when we're missing you—it's hard without
family. But I'm just not sure that we could come back.
We've got spoiled," she said with a wry smile. "I can
drive there without having a heart attack, because
people actually follow traffic signs and stay in their
lanes. And there's so much more room there. We'd
have to be millionaires here to have an apartment as
big as our regular little house there. Of course, we're
not in the city itself—you know that? We're in one of
the areas just outside Sydney—a suburb, they call it.
But it's nice because Tayib can get to work in his car,
and the schools are good, for when Dalia gets older."

Just then, Dalia, as if hearing her name, gave a loud
pound on the table in front of her, kicking to be let out
of her chair. Aida put her on the ground and watched
her half toddle, half crawl out of the kitchen.

"You haven't given any more thought to whether
you'd emigrate?" Aida asked in return, treading
cautiously. Amira shook her head. It had been a year

since Hany and Amira had decided they could not marry. Hany had his heart set on emigrating out of Egypt—and had even considered Australia, where Tayib and Aida could have helped him settle in, but his visa had not come through. Before the visa application had failed, Tayib and Aida had repeated hopefully that Hany and Amira could get married and move to Australia, bringing their mother Iriny to live close to both of her children.

But even if Hany had gotten the visa, Amira had been quite vocal that she did not want to leave Egypt. Herself just a year out of medical school, Amira had seen the change in her brother and his family since they had emigrated just a couple of years ago. She couldn't quite put her finger on it; she just knew she didn't want that change for herself. Tayib and Aida never seemed to be fully at ease anymore, as if they were still awaiting something, some undefined destination perhaps—or rather some undefined destiny. Not for her, that journey. Amira thought the world had enough hardships and losses to endure without the self-imposed hardship of life as stranger in a foreign land. No, she would stay—and besides, her mother needed someone close by to care for her as she got older.

Still, the loss of a future with Hany had crushed the joy with which Amira had sailed through university. She and Hany had taken every opportunity to be together during those years, during which she—and likely he too—had built their dreams of the coming years, of a life in which the other was the central character. That future had crumbled down in ashes when Hany had finally secured a position at a hospital overseas and Amira had made the painful decision not to go with him. She had spent the weeks after that decision either in bed, or being coaxed to eat by her mother. Eventually, though, she had forced herself to resume the small everyday normalities: getting showered and dressed, going to work, doing the shopping at the markets for her mother. She resolved over the coming months to rebuild her future. It was her decision not to go with Hany, she knew, and if emigrating was more important to him than she was, then it was the right decision.

"Have you heard from him?" Aida asked, correctly reading what was on Amira's mind.

"No," Amira responded. "And I think that's probably best."

Just then Dalia came toddling back into the room, triumphantly holding the end of a roll of toilet paper. The rest of it trailed behind her all the way down the hall from the bathroom.

"Dalia! Why!" her mother exclaimed in frustration, jumping up to begin re-rolling the toilet paper.

Amira repressed the giggle that had been about to emerge. There were so many moments like this that she imagined recounting to Dalia when she was older. She herself had loved hearing funny stories about the things she had done in her own childhood. But then she saw how Aida responded to her daughter's antics, efficiently erasing their effects and reordering her surroundings so quickly that the stories barely had time to be remembered. Maybe, Amira thought, this was another thing about Sydney that suited Aida: life must appear so ordered; she could choose to ignore its undercurrents of chaos.

PART THREE

11

South Pacific Ocean
2008

The world was entirely still when she opened her eyes. They were at port: Noumea or Isle of Pines or wherever. It didn't really matter to her: she was somewhere in the South Pacific; not so much a destination so much as a stop on this meandering float on the ocean, as far as she was concerned. Still, she decided she ought to get off the ship and enjoy the solid ground — solid sand, rather — under her feet for a few hours.

She quickly dressed, applied sunscreen, gathered together a hat, sunglasses, her book, and towel, and went down for some breakfast before debarking. Since when, she wondered, did "debarking" become a real word? What was wrong with its proper antecedent, "disembarking?" It reminded her of the time she had flown on an American flight and the attendant had announced that they would be "deplaning" in a few minutes. Really, just because you announce it confidently over a loudspeaker system, it doesn't make it a real word in the English language. But then again, she answered herself, why was that any less a valid way for a word to enter a language than by repeated use in text messages, or even graffiti. Hadn't she recently read somewhere that "sciency" was now a word in the Oxford English Dictionary? Now there's a word she never would have considered putting in one of her briefs.

She sipped tentatively at the coffee, happy to find she'd come down early enough that it still tasted like coffee, and not warmed up water with burnt grounds floating in it. Tomorrow, she thought to herself—just as she had thought every morning since this cruise began—she'd wake up a little earlier and go for a run around the track before breakfast. But not now; it was too late and she wanted to enjoy the beach. 'Maybe it won't be so bad to get back to my regular routine,' she thought. 'I don't feel like myself when I don't exercise…mostly because it's part of my routine, and I live by my routines.' But she wasn't living by routine life at the moment, and had yet a few more days in which she didn't have to live her life. Still, all this free time and lack of exercise was doing strange things: making her question things and think about things she hadn't thought about in ages.

All these strange thoughts about Liam, for example. She knew Liam loved her and she loved him. They knew each other as well as any two people can, and they were so easy with each other. To her, he was comfort, and safety, and contentment. Why all these doubts about why she hadn't brought him along? They were, after all, free to have their relationship be anything they wished it to be. A nagging thought entered her mind: maybe what she meant is that their relationship should be anything she wished it to be. 'No,' she thought, 'our relationship is ours to place expectations on, not our families' or anyone else's. When I get back to Sydney, I'll have a chat with Liam about this, and we will pick up exactly where we left off. Life will resume as normal.'

Did she want life to resume as it was, though? Wouldn't that put her right back in need of another vacation in a few months? OK, maybe not a vacation; surely she's proven that she was made of tougher stuff. Maybe just more weekends away; she and Liam could maybe fly up to the Gold Coast for a couple of days. Surely she won't soon be as burnt out as she was when she got on this ship. And anyway, having stressful periods is just part of life. She could handle them. In fact, she thrived under them. A life with no stress was a life wasted. It's not a life she wanted. But yes, maybe a little more balance won't do any harm.

She was through security now, and walking down the pier. As was so often the scene at these ports, a cluster of tour guides greeted the passengers, offering to take them around the island. She was in no mood to talk, so instead kept her eyes focused elsewhere until she found herself at a quieter line of kiosks. Stopping at one, she bought a two-litre bottle of water, and headed to a quiet spot on the beach. The shore could have floated off a postcard: the sand was blindingly white, turning to a light aqua colour under the pristinely clear water. Further out, the ocean turned a blue so deep and tranquil it made her chest tighten. It reminded her of the lost peace and assurance of childhood summers, and their loss caused an ache somewhere inside her. She exhaled, and focusing on the present, pulled out the sunscreen she had bought. As she reapplied it, liberally as instructed by the bottle, she remembered the suntan oil that she and her friends would use when they went sunbaking on the beach as teenagers. Her mother would be furious that she had allowed her skin to get so dark. She could never give her any justification for this, other than that it was ugly to get so dark. It didn't matter how many times Dalia explained that only in Egypt was tanned skin considered ugly. In Australia, everyone thought her bronzed skin beautiful. It was one thing Dalia could find that was truly attractive about her: her nose had always seemed too masculine to her ("strong" is how she once heard it described), and her eyes were brown and ordinary. Her mother's response was always that they — meaning Dalia's Australian friends — were just saying they liked her tan to be polite, and that besides, what Australian boys was she trying to look beautiful for? Now, thinking about how much had changed made Dalia smile; the public health campaign to prevent skin cancer had certainly worked on her. She dutifully applied a strong sunscreen anytime she was going to potentially be outside for more than 15 minutes. That task done, she sat down and arranged her water bottle and bag to be within arm's reach. At least for the next couple of hours, the only company she wanted to keep was that of the characters in her book.

12

Cairo
1956

I looked up from my book when I heard a sound at
my door. I had finished my homework for the day, and
was prepared to tell my mother so if she started
scolding me about reading again. It wasn't Mama at
the door, though. It was our neighbour and friend,
Tunt Salwa. Her face was pale and her expression
shocked. It frightened me. "What's wrong, Tunt?" I
asked.

"Tayib. Come here, habibi."

"Where's Mama?"

"She's downstairs at the Yacoubs." She paused.
"Tayib, why don't you wear something you can go out
in?"

"Why? Where are we going? Where's Baba? Where's
Amira?"

"Just get dressed, habibi. We'll go downstairs to see
your mother. I'll wait right outside your door."

I got dressed as quickly as I could, though each limb
felt impossibly heavy. I didn't want to go. Maybe if I
just took long enough, Tunt Salwa would leave and I
could go back to reading my book as if she'd never
come. Nothing bad was happening, I told myself.
Everything was fine. I was just going down to be with
Mama. Everything would be just fine.

But Tunt Salwa didn't leave, and eventually, dressed,
I stepped out of my bedroom door. None of this meant

anything yet. Maybe something had happened to a
relative of someone I didn't know very well from the
building. Someone my mother knew and was upset
about. "Do I need my shoes?" I asked.

"Yes, habibi. Do you need help tying them?"

I had tied my own shoes for years, but I didn't
answer. So we would be leaving the building — it
wasn't someone in the building then. I didn't want to
leave. Everything was fine as long as we were here. But
I knew I couldn't question Tunt Salwa, so I bent down
and tied my shoe laces. She offered me her hand, and
we went downstairs, where the Yacoubs' door was
cracked open.

Even before I could see anyone, I could hear the
keeling sound of a woman crying. It was, I
immediately realized, my mother. Tunt Salwa, still
holding my hand firmly, turned into the living room.
For a moment, all I could see was black. Black shirts,
black pants, black dresses, black skirts like a wall in
front of me. That's how I knew that someone had died.
When did everyone have time to change their clothes, I
wondered? The sight of it alarmed me. But I still didn't
know what this was. Was it a grandparent, perhaps?
That would make sense; my grandparents were really
old.

Tunt Salwa nudged her way through the visitors,
pulling me along towards my mother. Her face was
almost unrecognizable. The serenity, the alertness that
it always held was gone; in its place was utter
devastation. It frightened me. Once she saw it was me
in front of her, though, she immediately wiped her
eyes and took me by the shoulders, trying to quiet her
own sobs. Her hands on me were desperate, as if trying
to reassure herself that I was really there, and that I

was alright. She was trying to be calm, I could see, but it was too late. "Tayib," she said. "I need you to be a big boy. We have to go to the hospital now. Your father and Amira are there. Do you think you can come with me?"

One of our neighbours — I didn't notice who — said to her, "Iriny, maybe you shouldn't take him with you. Keep him here with us. He's just a boy; the hospital is no place for him." But I gripped my mother's hands, and so she replied and said, "thank you, but really I think it's best if he comes with me."

Another neighbour, Ostaz Makram, said he would drive us, and so my mother and I were ushered downstairs and into the waiting car. I was terrified. Someone had died, and my father and Amira were in the hospital. Which one of them one of them was actually in the hospital? Was it because they were sick? Dead? Was only one of them dead? I didn't know, and I couldn't bring myself to ask my mother. The car ride to the hospital seemed interminable. When we finally pulled up to the main entrance, I froze, and felt my mother do the same. Whatever was beyond that door would wipe away our life as we knew it, and as long as we were still out here, I didn't have to face it. I didn't want to go in. I looked at my mother. Her hands were trembling and her breath was shaking. "Yala, ya Tayib. Let's go inside."

By sheer force of will, I made myself get out of the car. Inside, Ostaz Makram went up to the desk and talked to the nurse; his question and her answer drowned out by the sounds of other conversations, of orders being called out, and of other patients and families conversing in the lobby. He came back and led us to the elevator and up to the third floor. There, a doctor—or someone in a white coat, anyway—came up to us and asked, by way of confirmation, "Madame Salib?" When my mother nodded, he asked us to follow him. As we walked, he explained that my father and Amira had been walking past a shop where some work was being done on the gas line. Someone must have dropped a lit cigarette in precisely the wrong spot, or maybe a pilot light had been left on somewhere accidentally. Whatever had caused it, there had been an explosion, and the two of them had been passing right in front of it when it happened.

We reached a closed door. In it, the doctor said, was one of the patients: "your husband," he said to my mother. "He received the worst of the explosion, and we have tried to revive him, but I am afraid nothing has worked." She inhaled deeply, as if this is the news she had been expecting, but still hoping it had somehow been a mistake. "Would you like to go in and see him?" the doctor asked. She nodded, ever so slightly. I felt a hand on my shoulder; it was Ostaz Makram.

"Tayib, habibi, why don't you and I wait out here for your mother?" I hesitated, wondering if Mama needed me to go inside with her, but she gave a small nod to Ostaz Makram, squeezed my shoulder, and went inside without me. As the door closed behind her, I could see a white blanket covering what I supposed dimly was my father's body, and at the head of the bed, some flesh colored lumps and blood that I could not even distinguish as any particular part of him. Once the door had closed, there was a moment or two of silence, and then a loud, desperate wail as my mother called out my father's name, over and over. Not for the first time that day, I was so frightened. I wanted Mama back out here with me; I wanted her to tell me everything would be alright. If she could just come out and put her arm around me, I knew that everything would be alright.

I was vaguely aware of Ostaz Makram's hand on my shoulder. I stood, half holding my breath, half letting my mind wander to stupid, insignificant things like the pattern of the tile on the floor until, finally, she came out. I got up and ran to her, wrapping my arms around her waist. Instinctively, her arms went around me, all the while shuffling us towards a chair, where she dropped down. The doctor, who had stepped discreetly away while she had been in the room, came back and sat next to us now. "Madame Salib," he said, "I know that this is a very big shock and a very heavy burden."

"Amira," she interrupted. "Where's Amira? How's Amira?" I couldn't tell if she wanted all the bad news at once, rather than to be knocked down a second time by Amira's loss, or whether she was just now remembering that Amira was somewhere there too. Probably both.

The doctor sighed. "She's just in this next room," he said. "She suffered some burns, but her father, and a partial wall between her and the explosion, shielded her from worse injury. Her burns are severe, but she is young, and we think she will recover."

"Can I see her?" my mother asked.

"Of course," he replied. "But as you saw with your husband, you should be prepared for the shock of seeing burnt skin." He paused and looked at me doubtfully. "I don't know if you want your son to come in with you…"

I spoke up, my tight throat making my voice squeaky. "I can go in. She is my sister, and I am going to be 10 years old this year."

The doctor's eyes flickered between kindness and pity. "Ok, little sir," he said, "but I want you to know that your sister's skin was very badly hurt. It's ok, though, she will heal. You just have to give her time, and take good care of her until she does. Ok?"

I nodded.

"Let's go inside," said the doctor.

Amira's eyes were closed. Machines beeped rhythmically, numbers floating on screens. Her head was bandaged, and so were her hands and arms, I saw. Her skin, just outside the bandages, was shiny with some salve they must have applied.

"We have her sedated," the doctor said now. "There are enough burns covering her body—mostly her arms and back—that she would feel a lot of pain if she was awake."

"Can't you just give her painkillers?" asked my mother. "I'd like to talk to her. Can't we let her wake up?"

"In a few days, Madame Salib," he replied. "But given the severity of her burns, and for a child her age, this is what is best for now."

There was a faint knock at the door. It was Ostaz Makram. "Iriny," he said, "if it is alright with you, we are going to start making arrangements for the funeral." I heard my mother's breath catch. Had she, like me, managed to forget for a moment about Baba in the next room?

"Can you wait just a few minutes?" she asked. "I'd like to be there; I just need a few more minutes with Amira." He smiled kindly and nodded.

She and I leaned back on the window ledge of the hospital room, watching Amira. The doctor had left, whether to give us privacy or because he had other patients, I was not sure. I was not sure how long we sat there, either, both of us looking at Amira, listening to the machines, waiting for any change in her. But there was no change. She lay there without expression, without moving. Only the machines gave any indication that she was alive, the heart monitor beating regularly, the chart showing that oddly shaped but rhythmic rise and fall of her heart rate.

Ostaz Makram knocked again, this time with the doctor right behind him. "Iriny," he said, "why don't you stay a little longer and we'll come get you and Tayib when it's time for the funeral. It's just it's getting a bit late, and we need to contact the cemetery and arrange for the car."

"Can't we wait until," my mother began, but then she stopped. I knew what she was about to say. Tomorrow—couldn't they delay until tomorrow? But of course they couldn't. Funerals always happened the day of the death, unless it was too late and too dark, and then they would happen the next morning. But there were still a few hours of daylight left in the day. She must have realized the futility of asking, because then she said, "that's fine. Thank you, Ostaz Makram."

She began to look at Amira again, then looked back up. "Wait, I should be the one to pick out the casket, and get the clothes he will be buried in." She looked back at Amira. I knew what she was thinking: how could she leave her? The doctor must have sensed this too, because he interjected.

"Amira is not going to wake up for some time. We have her strongly sedated. I or my colleagues will be

79

checking on her regularly. If there is any change at all, we will call you or send someone for you. You can leave us some phone numbers, and tell us where the funeral will be so you can be sure we will reach you."

Our neighbour, Ostaz Makram, thanked the doctor and told him he would write down the contact details for him. My mother took the moment to look back at Amira. Tentatively, she put her hand down on a part of Amira's arm that was unbandaged, and then she took in a deep, shaky breath. She looked over at me and gave me a small smile. I smiled back at her. This seemed to give her comfort, because she reached for my hand, slowly stepped away from the bed, and said, "Yala. Let's go."

Later, I would remember the next hours and days as a blur. From the hospital, my mother and I were taken back to the apartment, where all four of my grandparents had now arrived. Neighbours, family, and friends had filled every room. During the time we had been at the hospital, arrangements had been made to have someone at the hospital with Amira at every hour, even during the funeral, so that we would not feel like Amira had been left alone. Food covered every surface in the kitchen and filled the fridge. While Mama excused herself to go pick out clothes for Baba's burial, some kind hand grabbed my shoulder and made me sit down to eat. I ate mechanically, not thinking I was hungry, but registering by how quickly I swallowed that my body must have wanted food. At some point, I heard my mother start to sob again, and saw her best friend and her sister both rush into the bedroom. I started to get up to go after them, but someone blocked my way, telling me everything would be alright, and asking me if I wanted to go out to the balcony, where a handful of neighbour children, many of whom went to my school, were playing checkers. I loved checkers, and despite the shock of the past few hours—or maybe because of it—I soon found myself engrossed in the game.

When I looked up after what seemed like a short while later, I noticed that the apartment inside was much quieter. There were just a few adults inside, talking quietly while they tidied up the apartment and put food away. More platters seemed to have appeared since we had gotten back from the hospital. But where was Mama?

I went inside. "Where's Mama?" I asked.

"Habibi, everyone's gone to the funeral. They will be back soon."

"But why didn't anyone tell me? I wanted to go. I need to be with Mama."

"It's ok, Tayib. You are too young for a funeral. And your mother is in good hands. All of the family and her friends are with her. She will be back soon."

I didn't answer.

"And you know what? You will need to be a big boy, because your mother is going to need a lot of help while Amira's in the hospital. Do you think that you can be a helper to her?"

This sounded a little silly to me. There were so many adults here, cooking and taking care of things. My mother clearly did not need another helper. Did they think that I was still some toddler who could be tricked into obedience by being told to be a good little helper?

Tunt Salwa walked into the room just then and saw the scowl on my face. "Tayib, what's wrong?" she asked. "Everyone went to the funeral without me," I answered, wishing I didn't sound so much like a little child.

Tunt Salwa paused. "Do you know what happens at funerals?"

"They are going to dress Baba up in a suit," I replied. This is what I had gathered from snatches of conversation about the funeral preparations.

"That's right, habibi. And then the priest says a prayer, and everyone says goodbye to him so your father can go to heaven."

"But I wanted to say goodbye. And how could Mama have forgotten to take me?"

"She didn't forget you, habibi. It's just that funerals are not for kids. You know something?" she said, switching subjects. "Wait here for one minute." She got up and went to the next room, where my father's desk was. On it was a framed picture of my father from about 15 years ago, when he was a young architect, newly graduated from university. He was in a suit, his hair parted and combed perfectly, the expression on his face both serious and relaxed. The perfect portrait. Tunt Salwa picked it up and brought it back to the couch and sat down next to me.

"Why don't we have our own special goodbye to your father?" she asked. "You can either say it out loud, or in your head. If you want, I will start."

I looked at the picture. I had always loved this picture. My dad looked so handsome in it, and so reassured and so solid. 'Nothing in the world will shake me,' that expression seemed to say. But of course, something had just shaken him. It had shaken all of us. My dad had died, which meant I would never see him walking around our home again. It suddenly dawned on me that this picture, and the few others we had of him, were the only way I would see my father from now on. But this was my father, who was always so strong and reliable, and not at all like the truly old people, who were supposed to die first. How could he have died? How could he have made such a terrible mistake?

Tunt Salwa asked gently, "what do see when you think about your father?"

I wouldn't answer. What I wanted to say is that my father had betrayed me. The man in the picture was my father; he was supposed to always be there to watch over me and my mother and sister. I couldn't imagine it, only the three of us at home. It seemed to me we would spend the rest of our lives just waiting for him to come home.

It was then that the tears began to spill from my face. It was all too much. I wanted to bury my face in my mother's embrace. I wanted Amira home. Why couldn't they be home, where at least I could know they were safe, not being burnt by some explosion?

Tunt Salwa put her arms around me, hushing me while she rocked me back and forth. "It's alright," she said. "Whatever it is you love about him you can always love about him. You will see. Just because you won't be able to see him does not mean that you can't always love him."

That made no sense. If you couldn't hug someone, if you couldn't talk to them and listen to them, how could you love them? My father had just disappeared from our lives, leaving us without so much as a chance to say goodbye. I realized in that moment that you could continue to love someone after they were gone, but that this love would be a stone in my heart for the rest of my life, turned from a source of joy and security

when my dad was alive to a presence of grief,
constantly hard and cold.

13

London
2008

It had now been 10 days since Layla had sent her letter back to the mysterious Dr. Abdelmallek. In the age of email, she'd repeatedly wondered, why didn't he just give her an email address to write back to? Maybe, she assumed, he was just old enough that he found email too difficult, or maybe he wanted to reassure her that he really did live in Lisbon; he wasn't some strange stalker lurking around the corner from her.

In any case, she had no idea how long it took for mail to get to Lisbon from London, but she was sure the letter must have arrived by now. She had deliberately kept it short and to the point. Thank you for writing, I would like to hear more from you; perhaps we can correspond by telephone or over email, please send me your information, that kind of thing. For some reason, she was not comfortable sending him her email or phone number, and while this delayed making contact by a bit, she didn't know what else to do.

She looked now at the quiet heads of Maggie and Tado in the stroller in front of her, contentedly looking around as Layla walked them to the park where she often met with some other mothers and their children on Tuesday mornings. It was a beautiful day, a rare London summer day without a cloud in the sky and the temperature almost too warm, but not quite. Layla loved days like these. The warmth reminded her of

Cairo, without the humidity and dust. On the right street and at the right time of day, it might also be just as noisy as Cairo, but she enjoyed this too.

She remembered that it had been a day just like today when she had met Peter. She was in university, and had just left a coffee date with a friend in Medan el Tahrir. She was picking up a book for her father at a shop nearby before heading home. She had happened to glance up in time to see a young man, most likely an international student at the American University in Cairo, looking around as if disoriented. It seemed like she always saw a student like this whenever she was in this square. These people came here and often found themselves in an urban center much louder and more crowded than where they had come from. The desire to immerse themselves linguistically and culturally turned out to be a necessity rather than a choice. Layla's university was several kilometres away, so she didn't socialize much with these students. She consequently didn't know whether any of these students welcomed the immersion experience or were overwhelmed by it. These thoughts were drifting through her mind when she noticed that today's student had made eye contact with her and seemed to be making his way towards her. "'An eznek," he said in halting Arabic, "fein el Metro?" He wanted to know where the Metro was. Clearly this was a man who did not find the bustle of the sidewalks to be overwhelming enough.

Layla smiled and responded, in English, "It's just around that corner. I can show you if you like. Come with me."

He nodded with a grateful smile and followed her. The stares of shopkeepers here were fewer than they would be in more traditional parts of Cairo at seeing an Egyptian girl walking with a Western man. She asked him how long he had been in Cairo. "About six weeks," he said, with what sounded like a British accent. Then he repeated, "hawaly sett asabeeya." His accent could use some work, she thought, but at least he is trying.

She decided to play along. "Gayt leh le Masr?" Why did you come to Egypt?

He shrugged, "Leh la'ah?" Why not? But then when he began to talk, it was with an earnestness that belied his initial casualness. "Ana ba zaker Araby, we ayez aba ostaz...how do you say "history" again?"

She smiled. "Tareekh."

"Tareekh," he repeated. "Ana ayez aba ostaz tareekh. Masr ahsan makan a zaker Araby wah tareekh."

An aspiring history professor, she thought, who was studying Arabic. So many of the foreign students who came here seemed to fall into one of two categories: those who wanted to understand Arab culture (as if it was one monolith!) and thought this was the most comfortable place to do so, and those who were history nerds, like this fellow.

"Esmak eh, hadretak?" She probably should have asked him his name earlier.

"Peter, Peter Tavistock. We enty, esmek ey, hadretek?"

"Layla. Layla Salib. Ahlan wasahlan."

"Ahlan wasahlan," he repeated, grateful for the cue. "Pleased to meet you," was not something they had covered recently, if ever, in his Arabic courses.

They were at the entrance to the Metro now. "Listen," Peter said in English, the effort of Arabic apparently too much finally, "I hope this isn't rude, but

I haven't met many Egyptian students yet, and I would love to get together again, even to study or practice my Arabic. I didn't even ask you if you are a student or what. I'm sorry. Maybe you are very busy or you don't have time to talk to international students who can't speak very well. But I would love to meet again. Most of the students I've talked to are other international students, and we communicate in English, which is not what I came here for. But like I said, that's not your problem. I just thought it wouldn't hurt to ask, and maybe..." he trailed off, clearly not knowing how to conclude his awkward request.

She had noticed his eyelashes then, as he had looked down. He was kind of cute, actually. The truth is she didn't think it was for her to coach some international student with his Arabic, but the poor guy seemed kind of desperate. She wondered if there was something wrong with him, socially. The AUC campus was teeming with Egyptian students from rich families who could afford the outrageous tuition, and moreover wanted the pedigree and connections that a degree from the university would afford. Why hadn't he befriended any of them?

She smiled. "Certainly," she said. "Do you have a piece of paper? I can give you my email address." Peter reached into the pocket of his backpack and pulled out a pen and flier of some kind, offering her the blank back of it.

Layla thought now, as she came upon her fellow mothers in the London playground, where her life would have gone if she had demurred instead.

14

Sydney
1991

"Dalia!"

No answer.

"Dalia! I know you can hear me!"

"What, Mama!"

"Have you looked at the time? We are leaving in 15 minutes. Are you even dressed yet?"

"Can't I just wear my jeans?"

Exasperated, Aida walked down the hallway and opened Dalia's door. Dalia looked up from the cassette tape insert she was reading. "Everything I Do, I Do It For You" was playing on her stereo. She'd just bought the tape the day before, and had been listening to it nonstop since. "You can wear those jeans if you have to, but you can't wear that shirt. It looks like you stole it from a street thug — don't roll your eyes at me."

Dalia normally worked on weekends. Half the reason she had gotten the job, Aida knew, was so that she would have an excuse to avoid weekend get-togethers like the one they were about to attend. This particular day, Dalia's boss had phoned the house and said Dalia didn't need to come in that day. She hadn't had time to make any other plans.

Aida looked at the sun streaming in on her daughter's dark head now and had a sudden flashback, to a bright morning many years ago, Dalia's little hand clasped in hers as they walked to the neighbourhood playground. The distant sound of traffic was quieting now that rush hour was over for the morning. As she walked, Aida tried to remind herself how grateful she should feel to have such a modern and safe playground so easily accessible to their apartment. Dalia, not yet four, could amuse herself endlessly there, and there was an easy camaraderie among the mothers who would often gather there, as they watched their kids play and chatted easily amongst themselves. In a country where she still felt like a visitor, even after almost seven years, Aida had appreciated this small semblance of friendship.

A short time later, Aida's gaze was half turned, responding to a comment another mother had made, when her eye caught one of the younger kids losing his grip on the monkey bar. With a start, she lurched towards him to catch him, but he fell before she reached him. He landed with a thud, and immediately started to cry. Panicked, Aida started to scoop him up, shushing all the while, while scanning the faces around her for the little boy's mother. Nobody rushed forward, but eventually his mother did saunter forward, telling him he was alright and taking him from Aida and standing him up. Brushing him off and seeing that he could stand on his own, she said, "You're alright. Want to go back and play with your friends?"

"But shouldn't you check him at least? Maybe he's hurt himself? A sprain or a broken bone—should you take him to hospital?" Aida had said to the mother.

The mother just looked at her and smiled politely. "If he's really hurt," she said, "he'll show it. But I like my chances that he's fine, and the quickest way to get him to forget about it is to get him back to playing."

Aida waited for another mother to come and correct this folly, to back up her opinion that he needed some medical attention, but no such support was forthcoming. 'How is it,' she thought to herself, 'that we carefully grow these precious beings in our bodies, and then nurse them and get up with them every night, all to make sure they grow and are healthy. And then it becomes ok somehow to release them to the world to do with them as it will?'

'Back home, mothers would not be so laissez faire.' She remembered thinking. 'But this is not back home. This is Australia.' Here, she knew, childhood was supposed to have bruises and even broken bones. And yes, kids generally turn out alright; they reached adulthood and had happy lives…But still, she couldn't quite make sense of this 'no worries' attitude. Aida knew that the other mothers must see her as overly anxious, and she knew that when it came to this topic, she was.

"I'm not an anxious person," she would tell Tayib later that night. "I think I'm quite relaxed about a lot of things. About what we have for dinner, or what the politicians are doing in Canberra. But about some things, it's just not right. This is my child, and her basic safety is my foremost concern."

It was strange, she thought, how on the one hand she wanted to belong — and more than that for her daughter to belong, to feel like she had a home, but on the other hand how she wanted her daughter to know a different sense of home, a different way of valuing the world and life. She often wondered if this was what the life of an immigrant was. Working so hard to make a new home for yourself, and yet yearning all the while for the home you willingly left behind.

To answer these questions, or perhaps to delay answering them, she and Tayib had, over time, got in the habit of gathering with the same few immigrant families once every other weekend, or every weekend if they could manage it. At whichever house was hosting, the table would be covered with all the dishes each family had brought. The food was familiar and comforting to Aida. It was also, invariably, delicious, which Aida knew because Dalia, a finicky eater, never once complained about eating it. And there were several other kids who were around Dalia's age. The boys always just wanted to watch an AFL game, and the girls would end up helping in the kitchen. Dalia didn't seem to mind helping, and she seemed to get along with a couple of the other girls, but when Aida asked her about who she was close friends with, Dalia always responded that things never went further than loud jokes and laughter. And with all the voices yelling loudly over each other, and the adults interrogating the kids about how they were doing in school and what their plans for university were, and the Arabic jokes that only the parents understood, Aida supposed she understood why Dalia said this.

Now, Dalia looked at her mother and tried one more time. "Do I have to go?"

"Yes, Dalia. What else would you do? Sit here for the rest of the night and play this song over and over again? Is this that Adam Bryan song?"

"Bryan Adams, Mama, not Adam Bryan."

"Same thing. Anyway, I'm not going to leave you sitting here at home by yourself. All we're doing is having dinner together. The other kids will be there too; you won't be bored. Now come on please. But change that shirt first!" Aida walked out the door, calling for Tayib to remember the drinks they were taking over.

Dalia looked down at her shirt, then went to the drawer. Any other shirt was going to be just as offensive to her mother's taste, or to her own, so she took the jeans off too and put on a simple brown dress.

In the car, Tayib asked, "Do you still need to stop at Wooly's, Aida?"

She did, and asked Dalia to come in with her so they could finish quickly. As they approached the service counter, they saw that there were a couple of people ahead of them. "Dalia," she said, "can you please go to the produce section and get some lemons, and also a loaf of French bread. But make sure the lemons are the ones on sale this week. I'll wait in this line."

Dalia returned a few minutes later, the lemons and bread in hand. Aida had just stepped up to the service counter. "I'm returning these crisps," she said. "When I looked at the receipt, I was charged full price for them, but they were supposed to be half price." The girl, who looked to be no older than 16, took the receipt and scanned it in. "There you are," she said, handing the money to Aida with a smile. As Aida thanked her and spotted Dalia, she asked her how much Dalia had paid for the lemons. She told her.

"Aida, would it really have killed us to just keep the crisps and save the time waiting in line? What was it, an extra two dollars? And thank goodness that cashier doesn't go to my school." Aida hated it when Dalia called her by her first name, but Dalia enjoyed annoying her. Today, she was rewarded with a look of daggers.

"Dalia, maybe when you have to work for all that you have, you will think twice about dropping a few extra dollars here and there for no reason at all."

"Maybe," Dalia muttered to herself. "Or maybe I'll value my sanity over a few gold coins."

15

Cairo
2003

Layla had finished work and was walking to her
mother's office to meet her for a little shopping before
they went to her parents' apartment for dinner. It was
late, and the sidewalks were crowded with pedestrians
with shopping bags, hurrying to get home. It was also
winter, so everyone was bundled up in wool sweaters
and coats; the faint smell of moth balls permeated the
sidewalk, along with the customary smells of old
cigarettes and meat roasting somewhere. It had rained
recently, and so the normally dusty sidewalks were
covered in a thin coat of mud. Layla tried not to step in
them as she got jostled by her fellow pedestrians, but
she noted when she looked down at her leather flats
that they were splattered with mud.

It was Peter's first year teaching at the AUC. He had
phoned Layla earlier in the day to tell her that he
would be working late again preparing for the next
day's class and would meet her at Tayib and Yasmine's
place, where her aunt Amira would also be joining
them. Layla loved shopping with her mother. Yasmine
had impeccable taste, and somehow just knew which
shops had the best prices for quality materials. Layla
tried now to remember the mental list she had been
making of the things she wanted to buy and wished for
the tenth time that she'd written it all down. Especially
in the past year or so, as Layla and Peter, being
newlyweds, were still buying furnishings for their
apartment and navigating the task of creating a space

that was both of theirs, Layla and Yasmine had more frequently made these trips. She knew Yasmine would leave work much earlier on those days than she otherwise would, but Layla suspected her mother loved the time together as much as she did.

Neither knew how long they would have this opportunity. Layla's research as a food chemist had earned her some recognition, and so the assignments she was getting were becoming more challenging and therefore more time-consuming. Between Peter's full schedule and her progressively long days, finding the time for things like shopping was becoming increasingly difficult. As a stress-reliever, Layla would sometimes go home and, if Peter wasn't yet home, work on a system for storing surplus things she'd bought so that she could easily check their stock before going out and buying something again. She imagined having her system showcased on one of those home organization shows that Peter had inadvertently introduced her to when he had insisted on installing a satellite dish with the countless television channels. If she was ever asked to come up with a new career, she'd sometimes thought, she would help other people organize their homes. How much of a market there would be for that in Cairo, of course, was questionable.

Layla reached the door of her mother's office building just as Yasmine was coming out. They greeted each other with a kiss on each cheek, and Yasmine, taking her daughter's hand through her arm, asked her how work was. Layla told her about the latest project and its challenges, Yasmine listening carefully. Her mother always asked questions about the details of the project and who was involved. Other than Peter, she was the only one who really knew in any detail this part of Layla's life. Her father would only ask if she was enjoying it, and upon hearing her answer, say that as long as she was happy, so was he. And it was true. Still, she appreciated that her mother, despite the many bigger stresses in her own work, took such great care to know the details of Layla's.

They were approaching one of their favourite shops now. It sold woven cotton bed covers, couvertas, in a dazzling variety of colours and patterns. The heavy cotton thread of these couvertas would stay breathable enough on summer nights not to stifle, but was woven tightly enough to hold in heat on Cairo's chilly winter. Layla thought fondly of the couvertas in her parents' apartment. They'd been there for as long as she could remember, and though faded and softer now, were just as serviceable as they had been when they had first been bought, at this same shop.

Yasmine was asking the shopkeeper about a sage green couverta she knew Layla had had her eye on, and feigned shock at the price—a first step in the bargaining process. Listening, Layla remembered a recent conversation with Peter, during which he had stated that she didn't have to spend money so carefully or bargain so eagerly. Neither of them had overly expensive taste, so there was always enough money for their needs—even a bit extra. Buying something every once in a while without shopping around for the best price would not break them. But Layla couldn't help but think this was wasteful behaviour. Why pay more for something than you had to? It's not like that money was going to an independent farmer or some local shopkeeper—a perfectly acceptable rationale, she'd noticed, to pay more for something among the expatriates that she had met through Peter. They were willing to spend a lot on certain items because they were locally made or supported local business. It saddened Layla how much she could find now that was made elsewhere and imported. When she'd been a child, no one identified things as locally grown or made, because everything was, and it was the luxury items that were imported in and bought at a premium. Now, whether most of those items were technically made here in Egypt or elsewhere, or whether manufacturers were owned by an Egyptian or foreign company, was largely irrelevant. The profits were going into the pockets of large multinational corporations, only to be funnelled to the top executives and shareholders, who frankly didn't need a dollar more than the millions they had.

She was brought back from her reverie by her mother's question. Did she want the couverta? The shopkeeper had agreed to bring the price down by a third. To keep Layla's choice open, her mother said, in the shopkeeper's hearing, that it wasn't the best price, but it would do. Layla smiled at her, shrugged, and said she'd take it. She couldn't wait to show it to Peter. While the shopkeeper wrapped it up, she and Yasmine chatted. Layla asked her if she remembered Faiza, her old school friend who had moved to the United States for a graduate degree in chemistry and, it looked like, would be staying there permanently. Faiza would be returning the following month for a visit to Egypt, and Layla and she were hoping to see each other before she went on holiday in Alexandria. Talk then turned to the upcoming trip to the Mediterranean Peter and Layla were taking together with her parents. They would be staying at the holiday home of an old client of Yasmine's. "Actually," Yasmine said suddenly, "I think it was an old friend of your father's who had introduced me to this client, who I've stayed close with. Strangely enough, though, I can't remember Tayib's friend's name. It must be at least twenty years or more since I've seen him. I think I heard that he emigrated. I wonder if your father even talks to him still." Their musings were interrupted when the call to prayer from a mosque very nearby drowned out their words. "Well, I hadn't realized it was so late," Yasmine continued when there was a break in the recitation. "Let's head home. I asked Zahra to make your favourite dish for dinner."

16

Sydney
2005

Dalia had tied the scarf over her head to keep the
wind from tangling her curls — they needed little
excuse to frizz into a bird's nest. The wind now flung
the scarf ends up to cover her face. She closed her eyes
and threw her head back, feeling the wind blow
against her neck and along her upturned jaw. She
breathed in and exhaled slowly. She was sitting in the
passenger seat of her friend Amy's convertible, with
the radio on loudly and the smell of sunscreen strong.
Dalia was giddy with an excitement she hadn't felt in
months.

The night before, she and her team had gone out to
dinner to celebrate: the case they had spent countless
hours on over the past year was finally over, and it had
ended spectacularly. What's more, the leading lawyer
had mentioned to Dalia that the partners would be
meeting soon to discuss promotions, and that her name
was on that list.

Tomorrow, she would think about that. But today,
on this cloudless, windy late summer day, what
mattered more to her was that she had been told to
take the day off, even though it was a weekday. Amy
was taking her to Manly Beach for the day. As they
drove by the Sydney Harbour, the sparkle on the water
was applause, telling Dalia she could conquer the
world. Amy looked over at her and smiled. They drove

along, singing loudly and out of tune to the songs on the radio.

An old song from her college days came on just as the wind again flung her scarf up over her face, and Dalia suddenly visualized the window valance at her parents' house, the heavy fabric shifting languidly with its faded paisley design. Her mother had so proudly put up that valance when they first moved to their house. Its deep colours were now faded from years exposed to the sun. Dalia was wiping her tears away, telling herself she wasn't going to sink into self-pity. It must have been her first year studying law at university. This was a time when she should have been carefree; discovering new pursuits and friends. Instead, she was having the same strained argument with her mother. Aida was reciting the same list of her friends' daughters who had become lawyers and either left the profession or seen their personal lives suffer from working too many hours.

For the what seemed to her like the hundredth time, Dalia went back to her main point. "It's what I want to do, Mama."

"What about being a journalist, Dalia? A newscaster? You would look good on television. You could even become an international newscaster."

Years ago, Aida had big aspirations for her daughter's international career, and had wanted her to study Arabic. 'How could an Egyptian girl not know how to read and write Arabic?' she'd argued. Besides, she had said, if Dalia enrolled in international studies and became a diplomat, or a foreign correspondent, Arabic would come in useful. Dalia had tried once, labouring to learn the unfamiliar letters' shapes, struggling when they shifted shape as their placement in a word changed. After that, Aida had not been able to convince her to study the even more strange grammar rules, no matter what justifications or incentives she offered. Japanese, or Indonesian, Dalia thought, were much more likely to be useful to her in the working world. Of course, she had not studied those languages either, following instead in her mother's footsteps — and the lure of the boy who for a short while had been her secret boyfriend in high school — and studying French. Once she'd settled on that, Aida had stopped pestering her about Arabic. She was pleased, Dalia knew, even if she never said so.

Dalia didn't quite understand it. She knew her mother thought the world of her, as most mothers do. Aida would tell her she was smart, and that she believed in her. But there was always a hesitation there, as if she was scared that if Dalia ventured too far into a world with which Aida was not familiar, Aida would not be able to keep her daughter's circumstances safe or predictable. It was only recently, as a young adult, that Dalia had come to realize that the world beyond Aida's circle had always been an uncomfortable place for her, even as she was intrigued by it. But it bothered Dalia. How could her mother know what she could become? Was it out of a doubt of her ability that she was urging Dalia to be so cautious, or was it to dissuade her from the great personal sacrifices she thought Dalia would have to make? What if Dalia was willing to make them?

"Maybe I'll just design jewellery," Dalia muttered then, just wanting to end the conversation.

Aida fixed her with a deadpan expression.

"What? It would be fun. And you yourself have said I have an eye for it."

"Fun is not what being an adult is about, Dalia."

It had gone on that way for Dalia's entire first year of university. She learned to change the subject of her studies whenever Aida raised it, until eventually Aida stopped mentioning it.

A few years later, Dalia would attend the wedding of one of her girlfriends whose family her family had spent so many weekends with over the years. Dalia had noticed how easy their camaraderie had been as they shared stories about the same strange things their parents said and did. Yet how different their choices had turned out to be as adults, and how different the paths that each had taken.

It occurred to Dalia, now that her team had successfully closed her first big case, that while she didn't have to justify her choice of law any more, she wanted to. She wanted her parents especially to understand that she was living this life because she had chosen it. Maybe it would take their seeing her achieving accolades and promotions to convince them that she was happy — that she'd made the right choice. Or maybe they would never be convinced, irrespective of what she accomplished. Dalia had eventually accepted that it was not a comprehension she could force upon them.

Amy was parking the car near the shops at Manly Beach now. On the sidewalk ahead, a small girl was skipping ahead of her mother, holding a bag of fairy floss, and Dalia smiled with the memory of how much she had loved that treat as a child. She and Amy headed towards some shops, their hands flipping abstractedly through racks of dresses and beachwear while they caught up on each other's lives. It had been months since they had exchanged anything more than the occasional short text sharing a joke or venting over small things only the other would understand. Dalia had met Amy during university, and even though their lives in the intervening years had taken different paths, she still considered her a close friend.

Passing a beachside pub, they decided to stop in for their first drink of the day, even though—or perhaps because—it was not yet noon. Amy excused herself to go change into a new dress she had just bought. While Dalia waited, she looked out at the waves' swell and frothy crash, inhaling that particular smell of the salt air, and watched surfers skim over the crests.

"I should be out there doing that," a voice said behind her. She looked up. A tan man in a faded polo, his hair wind-tousled, looked down at her, a big smile on his face. She must have stayed quiet a moment too long, because then he said, "What I meant was, I can give you some lessons if you like."

"Umm—" she began, distracted by how striking that smile was—and that voice!

"You know what—forget it. How about I just ask if I can buy you a drink instead? That's all I'm really after."

That shook Dalia out of her paralysis and she laughed. "Sure," she said, "but you might have to buy one for my friend too. We're having a girls' day—playing hookie from work."

"Are you, then? Well, that's alright. I'll buy you both a drink." He smiled again. "I'm Liam, by the way."

"Dalia," she responded. He had a gorgeous smile. They started talking, and Dalia was surprised to find that it was easy. Amy would say later that when she first came back to the table to find them talking and laughing, she had assumed Liam was an old friend of the usually reserved Dalia. The two friends learned that Liam was an amateur surfer whose boss allowed him to take the occasional day, like that day, off of work to prepare for surfing competitions, and that he worked for a tech company in Sydney's northern suburbs.

On their first date, which was the next evening, Dalia and Liam talked late into the night, sitting in a small bar not far from his apartment in Mosman. She asked him how he came to be a "computers guy," and he asked her how she liked being a solicitor. Because he seemed genuinely interested, she told him things even people who'd known her for years didn't know about her: about her dreams as a teenager of being a barrister and arguing for justice in court someday, and how she had once announced to her parents, much to their dismay, that if she had to choose, being a lawyer was more important to her than having a family. She told him how she had realised only after putting in those years of work and becoming a solicitor, that practicing law and fighting for justice were not the same thing. But she loved her job anyway.

They began seeing each other every chance they could. On the nights that they chose to stay in rather than find an open table at the restaurants they, and apparently the rest of Sydney, loved best, they would go to Liam's house. Dalia had attempted, just once, to cook dinner for Liam, and the result was an unspoken agreement that Liam would be doing all future cooking. Dalia did, however, do an excellent job cleaning up afterwards, and so it became their routine. He prepared scrumptious meals, and she would return the kitchen to pristine order afterwards.

17

London
2008

The late evenings had always been Layla's favourite part of the day. The dishes would be washed and the kitchen tidied up, the kids would be asleep, and Peter would be working on his computer. It was her time to relax without the guilt she'd feel if the kids were still up.

This was her moment to make a cup of tea and put a couple of biscuits beside it. She would sit back on some pillows and read in bed, or if there was something good on television, watch it with her feet propped up. That was on the good nights, at least. Lately, too many evenings were eaten up trying to tie up loose ends that had accumulated during the day. Layla knew she should work on this. She knew that it didn't have to be this way, that she let a lot more clutter in her life than she needed to. Why did she take time to flip through catalogues of stuff she didn't actually need?

And why did she read every single email, whether solicitation or article, that popped up in her inbox? She sometimes thought that she acted like an overgrown and overeager pupil, not wanting to miss a single word the universe had sent her. Did she think there would be a quiz on this stuff? Well, she answered herself, she never knew when a topic that she'd read about would come up in conversation with another adult, and she would actually be able to speak intelligently on it. It's just that it was often so interesting. This world had far too many interesting things if one stopped to notice.

Still, Layla recognized, her browsing took up time— valuable time. She didn't have to read so much about every topic, even if she was curious about it, and she didn't have to speak intelligently in every conversation. There would be time for more reading when the kids were older, and even more when, an eternity from now, she and Peter were empty nesters.

As for this preoccupation with sales and bargains, it was, of course, something she had inherited from her parents. They had never been poor, or anything less than comfortable when she had been growing up. But it was nevertheless deeply ingrained in them that one took care with money. You bought everyday necessities as inexpensively as you could, and spent money willingly, if still carefully, for something beneficial but not vital (extra education and travel had always fallen into this category). Only very occasionally did you spend money purely for pleasure. Those were the rules she had grown up with; they had served her well, and so she believed, despite any rationales she told herself, that there was no reason to stop living by these rules.

It drove Peter mad, sometimes, she knew. He came from a family that wanted little, but when they did, they simply went out and bought it. His parents' house was decorated with beautiful, tasteful things, but not many of them. Their kitchen pantry and fridge were always stocked for the next few days, and rarely more. Their closets, built in the previous century and thus tiny by modern standards, were quite enough for the clothes that they owned, many of which they had owned and worn for over a decade. There was something admirable about this, Layla thought, though she doubted she herself could pull it off.

There was just too much beautiful stuff in the world. She could not pass up a scarf with a beautiful pattern, or an appealing colour palette, especially if it was an attractive price. The same went for shoes. Layla would be ashamed to admit how many pairs of shoes she owned. Actually, she had preferred not to count.

The point was that she was feeling like the things in her life had started to drown her. She didn't want to go through the endless catalogues and mail every night. And if she could avoid it, she would rather not get on the computer at all after the kids went to bed. There were simply too many links to clink and too many articles to read. What did all these subjects really have to do with her life? With the illusion of time that the late evenings gave her, she would emerge an hour or two later from that rabbit hole and find that she had wasted yet another evening without the chance to do the things that actually felt like a reward for having survived another day successfully. The kids were alive and healthy — even happy and loved! Dinner had been made and left-overs put away, the house was — well, no hope for that. The house was as any house occupied by toddlers would be. "Lived in," isn't that what they called it these days? Everyone had enough clean clothes for the next day, at least. Nothing more really had to be done. She wanted to sit in bed with a cup of tea and a good book: was that too much to ask? Layla ignored the question that preceded that: were the accomplishments of her day really worth celebrating?

She was an intelligent, college educated woman. She never would have predicted that she would be a stay-at-home mother (was that still the socially acceptable label?), even less that she would be happy doing it. But most days, she was. There was a satisfaction in being there in those moments when her children leapt in their understanding of the world, and in seeing their sense of security with her. There was a satisfaction in providing nutritious meals for them and for Peter. Even walking around the house after bedtime and seeing the vestiges of the kids' play of the day gave her happiness — though those same scattered toys were the cause of much muttering and cursing by Peter as he tripped over them in the semi-dark. True, she missed adult conversation. She missed the challenge of using her brain to solve problems more complex than how to calm a screaming toddler. But, as she often reminded herself, there would come a time for that. You could have it all, they said to women these days, just not all at once. She liked that.

Now, Layla thought, what she needed to do was raise her standards for what she bothered to take in. More mail would go straight to the recycling bin, and more emails would go to the trash unread. The world wouldn't fall apart, and neither would her little corner of it. She would start tomorrow. She would stick with it for a month, because she had read somewhere that it takes a month for a habit to form. And when she successfully kept up this information asceticism for one month, she would allow herself the treat of buying a new book. Maybe a crime novel would be fun. It would be a fun read, anyway. With a pretty cover.

18

Cairo
1957

I have very few memories of my father. There is one memory that has remained very clear still, though whether I remember it because it was stored in my own memory, or whether my mother has told me the story so many times that I only think I remember it myself, I'm no longer sure.

At the time, utilities like the electric bill were paid in person. One day—I was maybe eight or nine years old—my father gave me a handkerchief, folded and tied up at the corners. "Go," he said, "to the office on El Sayid Street where we always see the line out the door. In there is where we make our electricity payments. Go and tell them our address and give them the money that is in this handkerchief."

I remember feeling important, but also a little nervous. My father had never asked me to do something with so much responsibility before. But I knew the office my father was speaking of; it couldn't be more than a half kilometre away. I remember thinking that this should be easy.

"Whatever you do, though," he warned, motioning to the tied-up handkerchief, "don't let anyone take this from you until you arrive at the office."

"Ok, Baba," I had responded. I had quickly put on my shoes, taken the wrapped up handkerchief, and gone downstairs and into the busy street. About halfway to the utility office, a man had come up to me.

He had a mole on his cheek, I remember, and was wearing a collared shirt and pants; I thought he must be an office worker on break from work. "Little boy," the man said, "Your shoe lace is untied. You should tie it before it causes you to trip and fall." I stopped looking at the mole on his face and looked down to see that my shoe was indeed untied. I bent down to tie it, and as I did so, the man added, "here, let me hold that for you while you tie it." Without thinking, I handed him the wrapped up handkerchief and tied my shoelace nice and tight. When I looked up to take back the handkerchief, the man had disappeared among the many people walking past. Panic quickly rising in my throat, I scurried forward a few steps and then back-tracked, trying to spot the man's shirt among the many people passing to and fro. A sickening feeling of nerves and bile was building in the back of my throat. My father had told me to guard the little package, and even in this little thing I had failed. I looked for a few more minutes, knowing even as I did so that the man was long gone. Eventually I gathered up the nerve to go back and tell my father what had happened.

When I did, my father's eyes flashed something — whether it was disappointment or simply an acknowledgment of what he expected, I couldn't be sure. But it left quickly, to be replaced by a short nod and a smile. "It's ok, Tayib," my father said. "I thought that might happen, especially since this was your first time, so I hadn't really put money in that handkerchief. It was a few worthless trinkets — that thief is going to be unpleasantly surprised when he opens up that package!"

My smile came out more as a grimace, relief and shame swirling in my chest. My father produced an identical handkerchief, wrapped up in an identical way, and gave it to me again. "This is the real payment," he said. "Now be careful and come back and tell me how it went."

This time, I put the handkerchief in my pocket, my hand tightly gripping it from the moment I stepped out onto the street until I reached the office. I gave the woman behind the counter our address and carefully handed her the coins, just as my father had instructed. The woman smiled and gave me what I imagine was a receipt. I skipped home, feeling triumphant in having taken this grown-up step, and succeeding. When I arrived home, my father had turned and, seeing the look on my face, smiled.

"Come on, Tayib," he had said, "let's help your mother by setting the table for lunch."

I remembered that triumphant homecoming sometimes when I would walk into our door after his death. Of those weeks — or were they months? — I remember the apprehension of coming home from school and finding that Baba still was not there, and would not be coming back. But inevitably, I would find someone there: an aunt or uncle, a neighbour, a friend sitting with my mother drinking tea, or if she had had a busy day, then standing together in the kitchen rushing to finish preparations for our dinner. As the months progressed, I would find her more frequently talking and taking an interest in the lives around her again, and less often wiping away tears when she saw me come in.

But before she — we — started to recover, there were weeks spent at the side of Amira's hospital bed. I remember clearly, as I sat there for the hours after every school day, willing her burns to heal and her memories of this time to disappear.

Sometime after Amira came home, and in the year after my father died, we moved to a new apartment. My primary school was now down the street from our apartment. At first, my mother would walk me to the gate of that school every day. As she got a little more comfortable with the outside world again, though, she would let me walk to and from school with the other kids, our uniforms forming a growing mass of navy and light blue as we moved down the street, and dissolving in the reverse pattern as school let out and we each got to our respective doors.

When my sister started school a couple of years later, I would take pride in holding her hand and making sure she got to the door of her classroom safely and on time. Amira was a sweet and kind child, her innocence and faith in others born of having a mother and brother who doted on her and loved her protectively, knowing how close she had come to being taken away from them. She was a pretty little girl too, and rarely did a day go by that someone — a classmate, a teacher, a stranger on the street — would not comment on what an adorable little child she was. Her scars from the explosion had not affected her beauty; they were mostly on her arms and back, and those she would keep covered pretty much for the rest of her life.

As she and I grew, it became clear that, while she had the intelligence to learn the concepts being taught at school and to progress with her peers, the increasing toughness that was required on the playground was something she lacked. It made my heart ache to see her sob at home because of some taunt from a child that day at school. I would find the kid the next day and warn him with threats (empty threats, if it came to it — I don't know if I could have actually hurt another person). My mother would talk to the school administrators and teachers, and they promised to do what they could, and they did. But Amira's sensitivity was such that anything short of genuine and constant kindness devastated her, and neither my mother or I could bring ourselves to break her innocence by conditioning her to expect unkindness.

So Amira grew to become a quiet child, with only two or three loyal friends who she would keep even through university and into adulthood. She always excelled in academics, but she also became expert at fading into the background, such that the school children outside her small circle of friends eventually stopped noticing her presence, and this was the way it would remain until she entered university.

Her experiences of school were in this way very different from mine. During my school years, I got the reputation of being one of the smartest and most hardworking students. And the truth is, I enjoyed learning, and enjoyed the challenges that my favourite teachers would give me to do in addition to our regular homework. It's not that I made a special effort to be well-liked, but in retrospect, I know I was. It might have been because I did not differentiate between the poor kids and the richer ones. Neither did I distinguish between the friends who, like me, finished maths and history homework with ease, and those who spent hours hunched over their notebooks every night. The only kids I kept my distance from were those who charmed other students into doing their work for them or constantly charmed our teachers into giving extensions.

When I was admitted into the college of architecture at Ain Shams University, my mother, quietly bursting with pride, cooked all of her best dishes and invited our extended family and some of our closer friends: the Naims, the Abdelmalleks, and the Yacoubs. I would remember that evening with fondness in later years. It, and the eve of Amira's graduation, were two of the very few moments since my father's passing that I had seen my mother without that worried furrow on her brow. Both times, I remember our mother laughing a lot. She seemed to bask in the glow of our guests' praise, both of her kids and of the food she had prepared. As for me, on the night of my graduation party, I was flying high: I had made it into the college of my choice, and the world lay before me, full of possibility.

19

Cairo
1996

The school year was nearing its end, and as had been their tradition since secondary school, Faiza and Layla spent the month before exams studying at Faiza's house every afternoon. Now that they were in university, their school days were shorter and their study sessions longer, which meant that they often digressed from their school subjects to subjects more immediately pertinent to the two best friends' lives.

"Do you ever wonder," Faiza was asking now, "why we went into chemistry? I mean, honestly. Our lives would be so much easier right now if we'd gone into, I don't know, fashion design."

"Faiza, you don't even like shopping. You were always making fun of our classmates who did. And besides, chemistry was what you were aiming for when we took our entrance exams. If anyone's to blame for us being here, it's you!"

Faiza looked at her best friend with a raised eyebrow. "Me? If I remember correctly, you're the one who has been saying since we were 14 that you were going to go work for Chipsy and create a version of their potato chips that was just as tasty but a lot less fattening. Don't you remember?"

"Ha!" Layla responded. "Do you know, I'd forgotten about that. I can't believe you remember that. That was my I-want-to-find-a-way-to-eat-a-lot-and-still-be-skinny phase."

"It's not a phase! Didn't I hear you say just last week that you were going to apply for an internship with Chipsy — or was it some other snack company — for the summer? I mean, what else were you planning to do when we graduate?"

"No, I suppose that's true…I've aimed for chemistry — food chemistry specifically — for so long that I think I've forgotten why." She paused. "Maybe I'll go to America instead for a graduate degree in chemical engineering, like you. Actually, no I won't. My parents would probably die."

"You're assuming I'll get in. Anyway, it doesn't matter. Neither of us is going anywhere if we don't pass this semester. Let's get back to studying."

"Yes, but don't you wonder," perseverated Layla, "what would have happened if we hadn't chosen chemistry? I mean, maybe I should have gone into architecture, like my parents. At least it's work that has some meaning, something to show for it. Architects are amazing, and with all the people my parents know, I could get a job at least. I wouldn't be begging Chipsy to let me spend the summer working for free. I mean, who goes into chemistry to make healthy snacks? What kind of a job is that? And I don't want to wear a lab coat every day! I'll be bored to death."

"What is wrong with you?" Faiza broke in. "Are you listening to yourself? I mean, if you don't want to go work for Chipsy or whatever, that's fine. But then what do you want? What do YOU want for yourself? When are you going to figure out that life doesn't repeat itself exactly in different people. Just because you grew up a certain way doesn't mean you have to make the exact same choices as your parents to have the "right" life, whatever that is. Life is not that…straight-forward,

Layla. You are your own person. Your life is not scripted for you. Eh dah! You are so amazing, and you could do so much, be so much! I absolutely believe that you could create the world's next healthy snack, if that's what you really wanted. And yet you insist on confining yourself to this little category that you think you're supposed to fit in."

"Wait, what category is that?" Layla retorted. "First you say I should go into food manufacturing, like I've planned, then you say I'm confining myself too much. Which is it?"

"You tell me," Faiza answered, quieter now. "You are following the dream you've had since you were 14. But now you wonder if it's the right dream to have, and if you shouldn't really have followed in your parents' footsteps. And I think by that you mean your mother's footsteps. I love and respect your mother, but you are not her! Not that that's bad. Yes, your mom is very elegant and very accomplished, but being just like her isn't the only way to be. Haven't you noticed that you're constantly measuring yourself up against her? I mean, I suppose we all do that at some point: compare ourselves to our mothers. We think we're better than them, then we think we'll never be as good as them. But you have never thought you're as good as her, let alone better than her. Haven't you wondered if, wonderful as she is, you could be just as wonderful, but in a different way? You may have her looks, but I've known you and her long enough to know you don't have her personality. And again, I'm not at all saying that's bad!"

Layla looked at her friend for a moment. Did she really compare herself to her mother that much? She hadn't noticed. But perhaps it was true that her mother's story had always been the ideal. Smart young woman, succeeding spectacularly at a time that very few women even worked in architecture. What wasn't to admire? And Lalya knew that Yasmine wanted the same thing for her. That's why she'd pushed her so hard, both in school and in life in general. Layla could still remember her mother's voice telling her that she was smart, but that she had to work hard and earn respect in this world.

She suddenly remembered weekday evenings when she was in secondary school. Her father would come home from work, and she, having rushed through her homework, would be waiting for him. She would sit with Tayib while he ate his late dinner and they would share stories about their day. Layla would ask specific questions about her father's architecture projects, and they would often look at pictures after dinner, both of current projects and of old Cairo buildings' architecture. They would imagine what people did in them, how they moved around in them, how they felt in them. Yasmine was sometimes present for these conversations, but in Layla's memory, her mother often was not. She too worked late, and would have left instructions for the housekeeper to prepare dinner. Even when she was finished with work for the day, she often had social functions in the evenings with her fellow architects, often attending alone if Tayib was still working.

Tayib would always hesitate to eat dinner alone when he did get home, so Layla would often eat again with her father. Layla was approaching puberty, her growing body changing out of the smooth roundness of childhood. In its place was an awkward plumpness. Her mother, noticing the weight, had started reprimanding her daughter, with increasing severity, for eating too much. "If you have to eat with your father," she'd say, "then restrain yourself from eating until he comes home." But Layla was hungry when she came home from school, and could not resist the milk and buttery biscuits their housekeeper, kind-hearted soul that she was, would put by her books while she did her homework.

It became a battle of wills. Tayib had tried to intervene at first, asking Yasmine to leave Layla alone, reminding her that she was still a growing girl and that she was sure to grow up as beautiful as her mother. "This is something you don't understand, Tayib, you leave it to me," her mother had said, not so much with anger as with a resolution to solve a problem that excluded her husband. "You don't know what it's like to be a female in Egypt, or how harshly we are judged. People don't take you seriously if they see you as a chubby girl preoccupied with eating. It will affect how her teachers see her now and how's she's treated when she grows and starts working. I want what's best for Layla, same as you do. We're responsible to teach her how to succeed in this society. She won't succeed as an overweight wallflower."

Layla had not previously thought of herself as an overweight wallflower, but when she stood next to her mother, who, even in middle age was as lean and graceful as she had been in university, she could not help but feel awkward and unattractive. Yasmine had asked her sister-in-law Amira, a physician who often counselled overweight patients on eating well, to suggest some snacks she could eat until her father came home. "I just don't know what to do," Layla had overheard her mother say to Amira. "I don't want to traumatize her; I know she's just a girl. I feel like I'm becoming this overbearing mother. I already feel guilty enough that I leave her alone so many evenings. Maybe this wouldn't be happening if her father and I were home more. But what can I do? We were girls once, and I wouldn't be where I am if my parents hadn't pushed me a little. She is capable of so much, and I don't think she knows that. I don't know what to do for her." Tunt Amira's snack suggestions had helped, but Layla remained plump.

It was by accident that Tayib and Layla had happened upon the solution. Tayib had left a box of blue prints and other jumbled remnants of old projects from the firm in his home office one afternoon. He had wanted to keep them in some semblance of order, but had not had the time to open the box. On a whim, he had asked Layla if she could try to organize the box for him, assuming she had time after she was done with her homework. Layla, eager to be helpful and curious about the box's contents, had quickly finished her homework then spent several hours over the next few evenings grouping the objects together chronologically, and then devising ways to store the items in a way that would keep them well preserved and stored neatly and compactly. When she had walked her father into the office to show him the results of her efforts, he had been genuinely pleased, and Layla glowed with the effusive praise he had lavished on her. "Layla," he'd said, "you have a real gift for this." Only later, when the housekeeper said something to her, had she noticed that, in her absorption with the project, she had entirely forgotten about her customary snack cravings. Tayib and Yasmine began to assign projects to Layla to organize cupboards, or go through old boxes, or occasionally to come to their offices to help with archiving work projects there. And so it was that, out of a need to occupy herself during the solitary parts of her evenings, or out of a desire to create some order in her surroundings, Layla had found a deep satisfaction in conceptualizing order and then executing it. Without a conscious effort, she continued to grow out of her awkward prepubescence. By the time she had reached university, no one would have ever known that the trim young woman confidently walking about the campus had ever been anything less than stunning.

Now, Layla wondered, as she watched her friend absorbed in her textbook, pen and notebook in hand, whether she had missed her true path somewhere during those years. Shaking the thought from her head, she turned instead to her textbook, and to passing the exams that loomed.

20

Cairo
2007

Layla grasped the knife and started slicing the garlic cloves. Her mother always chided her for doing this herself rather than keeping a bag of pre-minced garlic in the fridge to save time. And while Layla was always generous in her use of garlic, pertinaciously using more than a recipe called for, she didn't like scooping it out of the bag because she had no idea how much to use. She didn't mind the extra minute it took to slice it herself.

In the living room, she could hear Peter and her father discussing the merits of the bottle of scotch her father had brought over. Her mother's voice sounded, asking Tayib for some over ice. Now her mother was in the kitchen, asking for what seemed like the hundredth time when Layla was going to get someone to help around the house so that she wasn't always so stressed. Matthew had just been born the year before, and with two small children and a full-time job, her mother was reminding her, she had to have help. Layla sighed. This conversation would have to happen sooner or later.

"Actually, Mama, I'm going to have a lot more time to take care of the kids and the house."

"Why?" Yasmine asked with surprise. "Did something happen at work? Does it have to do with that project you just finished?"

"I suppose you could say something happened. I decided — ya'ni, Peter and I have decided — that we're

123

going to try having me not work for a bit and see what happens."

"What?! Is this Peter's idea? You mean you would just stay home? Doesn't he know how much your work means to you?"

"Mama—"

"I mean, what will this do to your career?"

"Mama. Listen. This was not Peter's idea, although obviously he had to be supportive of it. Look...I do enjoy my work and I know I'm good at it—"

"Exactly! Do you know how rare that is? To have work that you enjoy and are good at?!"

"But...but, Mama, I just don't like the way things are going in my life. What energy I have left after work is barely enough to enjoy the kids, let alone keep up with the house stuff."

"Which is exactly why you need some help around the house! Think of how different, how much better it would be if you came home to a clean house and a cooked meal. You could have all the time in the world to enjoy the kids then."

"But that's exactly it, Mama. I wouldn't. Between how late I get home and how early they have to go to bed, there's not all the time in the world. Besides, Maggie's getting older now, and she has started to say how she wished her dad and I didn't have to work so much."

"Layla, she's three! You can't make such a big life decision based on the words of a three-year-old!"

"Why not, Mama? Why not?" Layla was feeling heat rising in her chest. "I don't want her to grow up feeling like her own parents had something more important than her keeping them away all the time. I mean, I remember being a kid and..." Her voice faltered. This was not the direction she wanted this conversation to go.

"And what, Layla?"

"Look, you remember that grant that Peter applied for? Well, we've gotten preliminary word that he's been approved, which means he'd need to live in London for about two years. We're thinking we will all move there, and it will be good timing. When we get back, the kids will be a little bit older, and I can decide then...about work."

"I see." The coldness in Yasmine's voice suggested that she did not, in fact, see. "Well, I suppose it's good that you have decided not to ruin your kids' lives the way your mother ruined yours."

"Mama! You did not ruin my life. I know you and Dad love me very much. I just...it's just that I've found myself at work, so many times in the past months, wondering what I'm doing there. I don't care as much anymore about these projects. I care much more about what's going on with the kids. It's not like you and Dad. You loved your work. I mean, really loved it. It's not that you loved me less; I know that. But I think you would have been, I don't know, unhappy without your work. I'm not like that; I don't feel that way about my job. So the question is, why am I spending so much time and energy on something I care so little about? Do you see?"

"I see," Yasmine repeated, with only a fraction more warmth. "But mark my words. You will come to regret this decision. You are a smart woman, Layla, and you will be bored to death cooking and cleaning and playing toddler games all day. And London? When were you going to tell us about this? Our only child is taking our grandchildren and moving away? Is this what we get for agreeing to let you marry a foreigner? No, it's clear that the opinion of your father and I has come to mean very little to you." With that, Yasmine walked out of the kitchen, calling to a startled Tayib that they were leaving. Layla followed her to the front door, asking her to wait. "Please give Peter our regards," was the only thing she said. The door shut behind them, Peter looking at her with raised eyebrows.

In the coming days, Layla had tried calling their apartment several times. Once, had she gotten an answer from her father, telling her that her mother was still very upset. "Why would you leave everything you've worked so hard for, Layla?" he'd asked. "You know I want you to be happy, and if you are happy, then so am I, but will you be happy? And I never thought you would choose to leave Cairo without even talking to us." Layla had tried to explain that it was temporary, that they could come visit, that it wasn't completely decided, but her explanations went unheeded.

After a couple of weeks of conciliatory messages on the answering machine were left unanswered, Yasmine finally called her. In a firm voice, she told Layla that she was disappointed in her choice and didn't support it, but if Layla insisted on moving forward with it, there was nothing she could do to stop her. And then she said goodbye. It terrified Layla that her mother would so completely reject her decision, but it angered her more to consider changing their plans just to appease her parents. Peter kept asking if they should reject the grant and stay in Cairo, but the truth was, Layla wanted to go to London; who wouldn't want an opportunity to live abroad temporarily? And she didn't think it was fair for Peter to give up this opportunity on the whim of her parents. When, months later, they did not even call on Tado's first birthday, she left them a message telling them that that they were leaving for London in two weeks, and that if they wanted to contact her, they could call her there. They did not.

PART FOUR

21

Sydney
2008

A bell over the loudspeaker system announced the
next group of passengers were to disembark from the
ship. The sound grated her ears, interrupting the
magazine article she'd been skimming. Just a few
minutes ago, the ship had floated by the Sydney Opera
House, which Dalia glimpsed from the window of the
ship's cafe. 'We're home,' she thought, feeling both
love for this city of hers, and fatigue in anticipation of
her day-to-day life. The coming weeks held the strain
of long workdays and the all-consuming nature of her
cases. Still, for the moment, she was tan and relaxed,
her feet were pedicured, and her mind relatively quiet.
She would hold onto that for a little bit longer. There
was still tomorrow before work started on Monday.
Maybe she and Liam could catch a concert, or just a
nice meal. They could even plan their next get-away
together.

Walking down the quay, her rolling bag rumbling
behind her, she saw the dozens of people at the end of
it, the glare making it hard to distinguish them. She
shielded her eyes and looked for Liam. Normally, her
parents and Liam would both offer to pick her up —
from the airport, usually — and she would divvy up the
rides so that no one felt slighted. But her parents were
currently in Egypt visiting family, so Liam had
dropped her off and was now picking her up. As she
got closer, she recognized his frame towards the back
of the crowd, shades covering his face. He had seen

her. He gave a wave, hesitant then overly enthusiastic. Something was wrong. 'Oh God help me,' she thought, speeding up and making her way towards him as he ducked between people, stepping towards her. When they reached each other, they hugged each other tightly, then he took her bag and they moved off to the side, away from the flow of walking passengers.

"Liam, what's happened?" she asked, wishing he would be surprised and say nothing was wrong.

"Your parents wanted to reach you." He was not one to buffer news.

"Why? What's happened?"

"Your dad called me because he couldn't get a hold of you yet. Your mom is in the hospital there. He didn't say exactly what was wrong, just that she would probably be alright."

"Well, that doesn't make any sense. Either he called because he's worried about her, or she really is going to be alright, in which case why did he go to the trouble of calling you rather than wait for me to come home?"

She had emailed her parents a copy of her itinerary, and she knew Dad would have known exactly when she was coming home. "Alright, well, it's 11am here now, which means it's the middle of the night there. We can't call for several more hours without waking them up. When did he call you? Where are they staying? Did he leave you a phone number?"

"Um, he called very early this morning…he probably waited up until he could call here without waking me up." Liam and Tayib had an affectionate, if still somewhat formal, relationship. "He's staying with his sister—said you had the number?"

"Yes, I have all the numbers he left me in my apartment...he didn't leave a number for the hospital, did he? Or even the name of it?

"No, he didn't. But he said it was a good hospital. One of the private ones." Liam paused and looked at Dalia. "What do you want to do, Dee? Maybe I can take you somewhere for some tea and then we can go back to your flat and call your dad?"

She knew she didn't want Liam to leave her alone, and something to eat sounded as good as any way to pass the time until she could call. She hadn't been able to stomach one more breakfast buffet on the ship, so she had actually been quite hungry before hearing Liam's news. Now, when they sat down, the only thing she reckoned she could keep down would be a cup of tea. Liam looked at her quizzically when she ordered it. "You're not getting a flat white?" he asked. She drank a flat white, nonfat, with half a pump of caramel syrup every day.

"I can't stomach coffee right now," she said. Tea had always been more of her comfort drink anyway, despite her daily coffee habit. It came, she supposed, from growing up with parents and an aunt who always had a mug of tea in hand, every morning and for every significant event: memorable family conversations, whilst celebrating an occasion, or while making a big decision. She pictured them all as they must have been at some point in the last hours, each sitting with their cup in hand. 'Please,' she thought, 'let this be a bumpy spot and nothing more.' Her mother, Dalia knew, didn't think Dalia needed her for anything. Dalia was successful professionally, financially secure, had loads of friends, and a faithful Liam who she told everything to. It's as if Aida had got crowded out of her daughter's life. Dalia wondered how she had allowed her mother to adopt this idea.

Her mind started going over what could possibly be wrong. Her mother had some hypertension, which was apparently normal at her age, but nothing more, and the medication she took kept it well controlled. She had been diligently taking her calcium pills for years now, along with an assortment of vitamins and supplements. She went for walks and swam every week in a permanent effort to lose weight. Not, Dalia thought, that she'd exercise in Egypt. Women, especially women over a certain age, did not publicly exercise in Egypt.

Aida had been losing a lot of weight recently, actually. Dalia wondered with alarm if it wasn't because of her efforts, after all, but a symptom of whatever was wrong.

"What time would it be there now?" she asked.

Liam glanced at his watch. "Just about 3am," he replied.

Dalia pulled out her mobile phone to make sure she had turned it on when the ship had docked. "Maybe Dad will be awake and try phoning," she explained to Liam. "He knows when I was supposed to arrive today."

"Why don't we head home?" Liam suggested. She nodded, and they both stood up, Liam's scone unfinished. They began walking back to the car. They could walk back to her apartment from here, and Dalia wished they didn't have her suitcase and Liam's car to worry about.

As if reading her mind, Liam said, "it's a nice day today. What do you say we walk to your apartment, and then I can pop back and get the suitcase while you settle in? You'll probably want to change your clothes or go through the post and all that..."

Dalia nodded, and, shutting the car's boot on her suitcase, she and Liam began walking towards her apartment. Liam put his hand around her waist, and Dalia leaned into him, matching her step with his. She had forgotten just how much she loved his nearness.

They walked in silence for a bit, and just as they were turning down a side street near her neighbourhood, she said abruptly, "if he called you, he is worried. Dad would have waited until I got back, and dropped this news into a casual conversation so as not to worry me, if it really wasn't serious I mean."

"He also said she's probably going to be fine."

"'Probably' isn't the same as 'is'," she said. "He didn't want me to worry, but he is worried. And if he is worried, we should be worried."

"Do you think they'll try to fly her back here for treatment?" Liam asked. "Would that be better?"

"I have no idea," Dalia replied. "Especially given that I don't even know what's wrong." After a moment's thought, she added, "but is there a possible scenario that doesn't involve me flying to Egypt?"

They were at her building's door now. They stepped inside, the lobby smelling at once familiar and new, as much did when one returned from holiday. Dalia and Liam strode across it and headed upstairs, saying hello to the concierge as they picked up the post that had arrived in her absence. Flipping quickly through it, Dalia saw with relief that nothing needed immediate attention. Walking had been a good idea, Dalia decided. It had allowed her to clear her mind. She would have to go to Egypt; the fact that her father had gone to the trouble of calling Liam was enough proof of that. But she didn't want to leave Liam again.

She reached for her purse, digging around for her key, which had migrated to the bottom from lack of use. 'Why would I have to leave him?' she thought, as they went into her apartment. She had forgotten about her last-minute cleaning, and was momentarily comforted to find it so calm and clean. Liam was right; she did want to sit on her couch for a minute, and if not change her clothes, at least absorb that she was home. Liam sat down next to her, and put his arm around her. She laid her head on his chest and put her arm around his torso.

"Liam," she said into his chest.

"Mm hmm?"

"Do you think you could come with me if I go?"

There was a pause. Dalia immediately thought, 'Selfish woman! He's probably got tons of work. Wasn't he in the middle of some big project right now?' When she looked up to apologize, she saw that he was instead smiling. Quite broadly, actually—a little too broadly for the occasion.

"I'd love to," he replied. After a pause, he added, "You're not worried about having to explain me to all your relatives?"

She had forgotten about that part of it. Well, whatever. She could come up with some explanation. She really wanted him with her. "They'll deal with it," she responded. "But are you up for it? They don't have Gloria Jean there," she joked, referring to his daily coffee stop. "And you'll have to be careful not to drink water from the tap. I will too—I'd forgotten about that part."

"You'll make me a Nescafe instant coffee every day?" he smiled back. It was one of their oldest jokes. A friend of hers had invited the two of them and some other friends over one day, when Dalia and Liam were in the first tentative steps of getting to know each other, and offered them instant coffee, since that was all he had. Like many Sydney residents under the age of — well, Sydney resident of any age, actually — their group of friends took great pride in picking the right coffee beans, and grinding and brewing them just so. Instant coffee was only a half step above what they served in waiting lobbies, as far as they were concerned. It was worse even than what the petrol stations served.

"If you're lucky I'll make you a Turkish coffee," Dalia said. She gave Liam's torso a quick squeeze and then bounced up. "I'm going to go start looking for tickets. I won't book anything until we've talked to Dad, but at least this way we'll be ready to go as soon as we know." She headed towards the corner of the living room that served as her office and pulled out her laptop.

Opening it, she typed in her favourite travel site. She remembered then that she'd have to call work. They'd understand, of course, but they wouldn't be pleased about her jetting off again, literally, before addressing whatever work was waiting for her from the past days' absence. She decided she would call once she knew more. Or email, rather, since no one would be at the office today. Correction — no one would be answering the phones, but she was sure a handful of people were there now, working whatever case was pending. Maybe she'd call a senior partner instead of emailing.

She had many of their mobile numbers, and that way she could address any issues before she took off again.

When would they leave, she wondered? This was crazy. She might as well not unpack. Well, not quite. A suitcase full of cruise attire would not offer much in the way of hospital attire in Egypt in winter. Speaking of which, she looked up to see Liam still sitting on the couch, swiping his mobile phone, a faint smile still on his face.

"You're sure you can manage getting off work?" she asked.

"Not a problem," he said. She didn't know whether this was true, but she chose to believe him.

"Done already, actually. Just emailed Bryan. Listen," he continued, "I'm going to go back to the car. Do you want me to bring your suitcase straightaway, or shall I swing by my place first and throw some things together?" She knew what packing meant to Liam, and she knew he'd be done in under 15 minutes. Early in their relationship, when she had thought it would be cute for them to pack together for their first weekend away, she'd quickly been relieved of that illusion. Whereas she laid everything out neatly and put everything in ziplock bags, he threw things together, and just didn't bother bringing anything that might spill, whether or not he'd need it. Yes, she thought, it made more sense for him to go now. "Go home first," she said. "And don't forget your passport!"

Liam nodded and walked over, kissing her on the forehead before he headed out the door.

Once it had clicked shut behind him, she turned her attention back to the laptop screen. She decided she should call the airlines instead. She picked up the phone and then stopped. What would she tell them? 'I know my mum is sick—I don't know how sick—so I'm going to go see her. And by the way, I'm taking Liam, who I'm not even engaged to, to meet my big, crazy family.' She shook her head.

Five minutes later, she was on the phone with a live person, and explaining that she needed two tickets, to leave as soon as possible, from Sydney to Cairo. She had a niggling doubt that it wasn't Alexandria, but at this point, it didn't matter much. The nice woman at the airlines agreed to hold the tickets for a few hours. The price was outrageous, but what did she expect on such short notice?

What time was it in Egypt now? 5am. Her dad was an early riser. He might be up, right? Alright, she answered herself. I'll pack and then I'll call. She went to her closet and began picking out some shirts. She packed some long sleeved shirts and pants, dresses and tights, and a couple cardigans for the colder evenings. They wouldn't be outside much, but even indoors they would need to dress warmly. 'I should call Liam and tell him—he probably assumes it'll be warm there.'

When Liam answered, she could tell he was home, probably packing too. "I realized I never told you what weather to pack for. It's winter there," she hurried on, "and lots of places aren't heated. So it'll probably get down to maybe 8 or 10 at night, and up in the teens or maybe 20 by day. Pack at least one good sweater."

"I'm on it," Liam replied. "Really, I don't need you to be worrying about me. I'm coming to support you, not give you more to worry about. I'm almost done, and I'll be over. Do you need me to stop and pick anything up on the way? Run out of anything on the cruise that you need replaced?"

Dalia named a couple of things and they hung up. Now what time was it in Egypt? Almost 6am. She'd wait 15 more minutes. At minute 14, she decided she was waking her father up. She didn't want to make this phone call; it would make real what had until now been just words. But neither could she wait anymore.

The phone rang only twice before Tayib's voice answered. He didn't sound like he had been sleeping. "Dalia," he said.

"Baba," she exhaled, reverting to the term for him she hadn't used since childhood. "What's happened? I'm sorry—did I wake you? I tried to wait until it wasn't too early. Are you ok? So what's happened to Mama? Why's she in hospital?"

She could hear him let out a big sigh before answering her. "Dalia, they are still running tests to determine exactly what is going on. A couple of days ago, she started complaining of back pain and saying that she was really tired. I'd noticed that she wasn't eating very well, but thought it might be that she wasn't used to the food here. And I'd noticed her back bothering her, but we both figured it was from sleeping on a cotton mattress after so long. Still, you know your mother: she's always so tough. And so when she started complaining, I insisted we take her to hospital. My cousin Sherif—you probably don't remember him, do you? Anyway, he brought us to a private hospital here—"

"Are you in Cairo?"

"Yes, Cairo. And the doctors have started running some tests. They have ruled out some things, and unfortunately, the possibilities that remain are more serious."

"More serious: what does that mean? And how's she feeling? Is she awake for all this? She can talk? She's not unconscious or anything?" Dalia knew little about medicine, but she pictured her mother lying in a hospital bed with tubes everywhere and her hands taped down.

"No, no, none of that. She has an IV in her arm that is keeping her hydrated and nourished, but nothing otherwise. She's perfectly aware of what is going on. She didn't want me to call you, in fact, because she worried that we would upset you over nothing." He paused. "But I thought you might want to know as soon as we knew, rather than hearing afterwards what we had learned."

"Of course, Baba," she said. He was right of course; she would have been furious if all she'd got was a report after this—whatever this was—was all over. "So what are the possibilities we are looking at?"

"She has a lump on her breast. The best we can hope for is that it is benign and just needs to be removed surgically. The worst that we can expect is that it is malignant, and that your mother may have cancer."

The word struck Dalia like a physical blow. Cancer was what happened to other people, to the 1 in 4 or whatever the statistic was that she saw on billboards. She herself had taken part in runs to raise money for one type of cancer or another, had donated when her friends and co-workers had organized fund raisers. But it was always in the abstract. It didn't happen in her family. They had no history of it.

This reassured Dalia. They didn't have a history of it. It would turn out to be benign. But still, it was surgery, so she should go and be with her mother. It would be fine. Her father was saying something.

"They also think that the reason for her back pain is because there's a growth on her spine causing pressure on her spinal cord. It's probably also what's caused the numbness in her fingers. We thought it was just age. The biopsy will be this afternoon, and then we will know more."

"Biopsy?"

"Yes, to see if it's what they think it is."

"How long will the results take?"

"I'm not sure. I hope not more than a couple of days."

"Liam and I will be there by then."

She could hear her father's reply pause for a minute, and she knew he was considering whether to give his opinion about Liam coming. "Are you sure you can take the additional time off of work?"

"Baba, I have way too much vacation saved up. If they say something about another week or so because my mum's in hospital, they can find another Dalia." She said this knowing it was pure hot air. They loved her, she loved working for them, and they would, she hoped, be very understanding.

"And are you sure you are ready to expose Liam to all your relatives? Are you ready" — she could see his eyebrows raised — "for the questions they will ask you about him being here?"

"Yes, Baba," she replied, giving, she knew, not nearly enough thought to what her answers might be.

"Your mother will joke that this is what it took to get you to finally visit Egypt again."

"We will tell her you tried to convince me not to come and I wouldn't hear of it." They both knew, in fact, that if he had tried to dissuade her from coming, she would have insisted, and it would have happened just this way. Neither of them liked to waste the time or energy on going through the motions. She gave him the details that the booking agent at the airlines had given her and asked whether they should go straight to the hospital or to her aunt's apartment, where she knew her parents were staying. He said someone would pick them up; it was unheard of that someone coming all the way from Australia should have to take a taxi. This time, she did insist that they would, hearing herself echo Liam's explanation that they were there to support, not cause extra work or worry.

Her father sighed, then, as if remembering something, added, "let me see what hotels are nearby, and I'll book a room."

"Hotel? Why?" she asked. "I remember Tunt Amira's apartment being quite big."

"It's three bedrooms," he conceded. "But it wouldn't be right for Liam to stay here, sleeping under the same roof as you, when you two are not even engaged. Remember, habibti, this is Egypt, not Australia. It doesn't matter, of course, he will be with us from the morning until bedtime. It's just for sleeping."

Dalia murmured an ok, told her father she'd try to call one more time before they left, and they said their goodbyes.

She really hadn't thought this through, had she? As she reflected on the last time she had been to Egypt— what had it been, six or seven years ago now?—she remembered how stifling it had sometimes felt. Not the actual congestion: she actually loved the crowdedness and noise of Cairo streets. But the rules that had to be followed, especially if you were a single young woman, and one unfamiliar with the culture at that. It left her feeling like she couldn't do anything without someone's permission. But this wasn't a visit, she reminded herself. They were there to be with her mother. They wouldn't see Cairo except out the car window on their way to and from hospital.

Just then, she heard a suitcase rolling down the hallway and heard Liam come in. Hotels or not, she was glad he was coming. She greeted him with a hug and filled him in on her mother's status and the flights she had found. While she called the airline back to finalize their booking, Liam poked around her kitchen, presumably to prepare dinner.

"Liam," she said when she got off the phone, "my father says he'll book a hotel room for you. I'm sorry, I didn't even think of it. They're really conservative there and so you can't stay in the same apartment as me so long as we're not married — or at least engaged or whatnot. He says it's just for sleeping at night. I hope you don't mind? I'm sorry."

"Stop apologising," he said. "I don't mind, so long as I'm with you while we're awake." Then with a twinkle in his eyes, he added, "Besides, maybe this will give me a chance to meet some other Egyptian beauties."

"Ha!" replied Dalia. "Then I better not teach you how to say, "'you're beautiful' in Arabic."

"You already did, remember?" he said, pulling her in for a kiss. "Entee gameela."

22

London
2008

There it was. Layla's hands paused as she was flipping through the mail. A handwritten envelope, the same unfamiliar handwriting, the address in Portugal. Layla made herself go through the rest of the mail first, taking care of the banality of bill payments and keeping to her resolution of immediately recycling catalogues and other advertisements. She "needed," literally, nothing.

The kids were, miraculously, down for a nap at the same time, and so Layla sat down and carefully opened the envelope, recognizing the familiar Arabic script from the first letter.

Dear Madame Layla,

I hope this letter finds you and your family well. I was happy to receive your response, and will be happier still to share what I know, or as much of it as you are willing to hear. As I said earlier, your father and I used to be close classmates and friends, but have been out of touch for many years now. After some consideration, I have decided to write you the story, so as to give you a chance to begin to absorb it before we speak about it. Nevertheless, I find myself hesitating to begin this story, for I hardly know where to begin or how it will sound to you.

I suppose the beginning is as good a place to start as any. When I was a child, my family employed a maid called Zaynab. One day, when I was about maybe 10 years old, Zaynab was finishing up her work when I saw her going to the living room, where my mother was. I followed her, and I

143

saw her pull out a charm from her pocket and show it to my mother. I couldn't hear everything from where I was hiding, but I heard enough to understand that she had bought the charm from a stranger the day before who had promised her it was solid silver and worth many times the price he was selling it to her for. My mother asked her who the man was or where he told her he had gotten the charm, but Zaynab didn't know his name, and all she remembered about him was that he had a mole on his face and was dressed in a shirt and pants. She had come to my mother because she did not know much about silver, but was hoping that my mother could help her find a reputable jeweller who would buy it.

My mother asked to see the charm, and looked surprised when Zaynab gave it to her. After a moment, I heard her tell Zaynab that she recognized the charm. It had been a present to the guests at the wedding of Is-hak and Iriny Salib. (You may know about this charm of your grandparents. It consisted of two very small frames, connected by a hinge on one side and a latch on the other. Inscribed on the outside were two intertwining hearts and the date of your grandparents' wedding.) My mother went on to say that, since there had probably been a few dozen of these handed out at the wedding, she doubted that they could be real silver, but that she was happy to have a jeweller look at it. Zaynab looked upset, for while she was a simple woman, she nevertheless disliked being cheated as little as anyone else. My mother asked her how much she had paid for it, and Zaynab told her one pound. That was a week's wages, I would later learn. It was not an amount she could so easily afford to lose.

I heard my mother tell my father the story later that evening. My father asked to see the charm. My mother gave it to him then stepped into the other room for something. Both of them seemed to have forgotten I was there, but I was able to see the charm my father held. In the frames were little papers, one of which had your grandparents' names and wedding date, and the other of which had a picture. It may just have been the stock picture that came with the charms; I never got close enough to see. In any case, my father looked closely at the charm and then started pulling out a piece of paper, folded up many times to fit into the frame. It had been tucked behind the picture. The letter was on very thin paper, and on it was very small handwriting. He kept the letter and returned the charm to my mother to take to the jeweller.

The charm turned out not to be real silver, as you may have guessed. (My mother, always having been very kind-hearted, gave Zaynab an extra half pound in her wages to help make up for what she had been tricked into giving that stranger.) But the interesting part of this story, of course, is the letter.

It was many years later, when I was a young man, and long after I had stopped thinking about that letter, that my father sat me down one day and showed it to me. It is in my possession now, and I will gladly show it to you when we meet – assuming you are willing to meet. To summarize, the letter was from your grandfather Is-hak to your father, Tayib. It said that if Tayib was reading this letter, then he had shown himself to be a boy of a maturity beyond his years, and that he (your grandfather) wanted to give Tayib a valuable present. The present was a large plot of land, in the agricultural lands in the Nile Delta region, which yields crops whose value is significant. The finances are tracked by a solicitor that has worked with your family for years. Your grandfather went on to write that he had chosen this gift because he wanted Tayib to choose his profession as an adult regardless of how much it paid; the proceeds of this land would be enough to make his life comfortable. The only condition was that he had to work anyway; if he didn't, the solicitor was under instructions not to give him access to the money.

You are probably wondering a lot of things right now. I had a lot of questions too. Like, when did your grandfather have time to write this, given that he died so young? And how did the letter end up in a charm? How did the charm end up in Zaynab's hands? Does this plot of land still exist? Did your father ever find out about it? To tell the truth, I have no answers to any of these questions. Neither do I think this is my story to finish, which is why I have sought to find you.

You may also be wondering why my father never returned this letter to your grandfather, Ostaz Is-hak. I have wondered this myself many times. I asked him, of course, when he first showed me the letter, but all he said about it was that your grandfather Is-hak had already died when my father first saw this letter, and that he assumed your grandmother already knew about the plot of land, so there was no point in showing her the letter and giving her more reason to grieve over her lost husband.

Perhaps you are wondering too why I never told your father about this letter. That is, of course, another story entirely, and one which I do think is best shared in person. I have enclosed my business card, which contains my phone numbers and email, although I must warn you that my email fluency leaves something to be desired. I nevertheless eagerly await your response.

Respectfully yours,
Dr. Hany Abdelmallek

Layla sat in stunned silence for a few moments, and then went back to re-read parts of the letter. 'What a strange story,' she thought. 'What a strange, strange story.' She could not, she found, entirely dismiss it as a hoax. She had seen, many years ago, the charms that had been handed out at her grandparents' wedding. And she knew there could not have been that many of them around, nor would a stranger have recognized them as belonging to her family. Still, it seemed so unbelievable that her grandfather would have chosen this charm as a place to put a letter of such significance. And if it was so significant, how did it get into that stranger's hands? And why, indeed, was Dr. Abdelmallek contacting her rather than her father? As far as she knew, her father had no enemies, nor could she picture Tayib holding a grudge against anyone for so long.

Layla heard the kids stirring. She got up and tucked the letter up high out of their reach. Whatever this story was, whoever this Dr. Abdelmallek was, Layla knew that she would not be able to put it out of her mind until she had found an answer. But for now, the playground beckoned, and she knew better than to resist the little hands that would soon be tugging her towards their world.

23

Sydney
2008

The whir of the plane's engine cut out as soon as
Dalia put her headphones on. They were the expensive,
noise-cancelling kind that she had bought as a treat for
herself a couple of years ago. They had bought a pair
for Liam at the airport early this morning, Dalia
swearing that they made all the difference on a long
trip. Her parents, she remembered, had scoffed at such
an extravagant expense. "They're just headphones,
after all," they had said. "Surely you don't need
symphonic surround sound just for a plane ride." She
had tried to explain that they blocked out the noise of
the plane engine too, to which her mother had said
flatly, "I like the noise of the engine. It's like that white
noise people pay to have in their bedrooms. It helps me
sleep."

And that had been the end of that discussion. Dalia
reflected now on all the things about which she and her
parents would never agree. They had lived as the
immigrant generation, where every dollar they could
save on necessities was saved, and not a dollar was
spent on what was not necessary.

It was not, Dalia thought now, that she disagreed
with their choices. They had saved scrupulously, but
had spent willingly on the things that mattered to
them. They had paid for her education and all the
expenses associated with it. She knew, although she
had never discussed it with them, that they had some

money saved up for her wedding, if she would ever get married.

But she herself would not save in the same way, she already knew. She paid to have her dry cleaning picked up and delivered every two weeks; the extra time she would have to find to do this herself was not worth the extra few dollars she paid for the convenience. Lately, she had also gotten her laundry done by the same service. It was a fairly good deal, since she was such a loyal customer, and it saved her heaps of time because the laundry came back folded and ready to be put away. She remembered that when she was just starting out in her career, it had been her Thursday night routine to fold laundry while she watched recorded episodes of *Home and Away* on a PVR. It had been ages since she had had time to watch that show at all, and when she had, it was always days or weeks after they aired. What did people do before there was the internet and PVRs?

It was, she thought, not for the first time, the irony of modern day conveniences. In her parents' time, people spent time and energy to save a little bit more money. Time and energy were the resources they could spare— well, at least time was. She wasn't going to pretend her parents weren't always tired. But today, money was the resource people chose to spend in order to try and free up the newest rarity: time. Now, everyone had access to take-away food, delivery services for everything, and even options to record TV and watch it at their own convenience. She never would have believed, as a child, that this is what adulthood had in store for her. And yet, people were busier than ever. On first impression, it seemed that life was easier in her generation than in her parents', but she questioned if

this was true. It was more convenient; that was
certainly true.

But she also remembered her childhood as
more...alive. Was that just because she was a child, or
was it that the timbre of life itself had changed? In her
memory, there was a social gathering of some kind or
another every weekend. If she could name the sound of
her childhood, it would be the sound of adults
laughing in the background, or yelling out the
occasional instruction or warning to a child, while she
and the other kids laughed and played. Yet as an adult,
she herself did not socialise as much. There was the
occasional work event, or dinner with friends of hers or
Liam's, but these events seemed to be treated by
everyone involved as occasional indulgences in a
schedule otherwise too full with more important
things. Her work, she suspected, took up more of her
time than work used to take up for people. Also, she
chose to prioritize different things. Rock-climbing and
boxing were things she did at least once a week, each,
and classes at her gym took up the other days. On
weekend nights, she and Liam often went to gallery
showings or to try new restaurants. She was lucky! She
lived in Sydney and could afford to enjoy the city. She
didn't ever want to be one of those people who missed
out on all their city had happening. She didn't want to
take it for granted.

Not that any of this mattered at the moment. Now,
she was on a plane to Egypt, with Liam, of all things.
To see her mother, who was in hospital. Her stomach
dropped with a thud; she had been keeping this reality
at bay successfully until now. Her father had said they
hoped the tumour would be benign. But without him
saying exactly this, chances were high that it would not

be benign. Dalia was terrified too by the fact that she knew almost nothing about Egypt's health care system, only enough to know that one generally didn't want to get seriously sick there. 'Couldn't this have happened when they were home in Australia?' Dalia thought. 'Or visiting Germany or something?'

"Liam?" she said now. His headphones were on, and he seemed entranced with the movie showing on his screen. At least, she thought wryly, those noise-cancelling headphones were working. She poked his arm, "Liam!" He looked at her with a start and took off his headphones.

"Where is it that we recently heard had cutting edge cancer treatment? Wasn't it Germany? Do you remember? I don't remember—maybe someone was telling us about it..."

"Oh, the thing about targeted radiation or something?" Liam answered.

"Yes, I think that's right." Dalia had no idea, actually.

"I think it was Germany," he replied. "But Dee, we are a long way off from needing to know that."

Dalia nodded and patted his hand. She turned her own screen on. They weren't actually that far off from needing to know. And why hadn't her father already started looking into options? For all she knew, she realized, he had. He would have had a few days, by the time they arrived, to digest the news and start making plans.

Why couldn't they know already? This limbo of not knowing how serious it was or what they could do about it was awful. Dalia willed her mother to be strong of mind and for her body to reject this thing, whatever it was. She would be fine. She always had been. It was just a bump in the road.

24

Lisbon
2008

Layla stood in the hotel foyer, nervously clutching her purse. She rarely carried purses anymore; it was always the diaper bag. She had had to search to find it, actually. She hoped she'd gotten all the dust off. She hoped too that she looked alright, and more confident than she felt. She didn't really need to look nice, she told herself, just worldly enough that this Dr. Abdelmallek would be dissuaded from trying to dupe her, if that is in fact what he was there to do.

She had flown in last night and would be staying the weekend in Lisbon. What was she thinking? She should have asked him to come to London. But in the end, Peter had convinced her that he could watch the kids solo for a weekend, and that she could use it as a mini getaway if this person turned out to be some sort of charlatan. She'd never been to Lisbon; she could explore the city, she had decided, and eat breakfast at her leisure, and finish a café latte while it was still hot.

So here she was, waiting in a hotel lobby for someone she'd never met before. At a few minutes before the appointed hour, an older gentlemen, wearing a suit and worn but polished leather shoes walked in, with the barest hint of a limp. She watched him look around and start towards the sitting area of the lobby. She noticed too that he had a bit of a stoop in his posture. He would be about the same age as her father, she thought, and it pained her again to remember how long it had been since she had seen him. The man looked over just then, and his eyes registered a question, and then recognition. He turned to start in her direction, but Layla was already walking towards him.

"Madame Layla?" he said, with the respect she did not feel he needed to show someone 30 years his junior.

"Yes. Dr. Abdelmallek?"

He nodded with a smile, and gestured for her to sit down. He took the seat at the adjoining corner of the end table. "First of all, I must thank you for coming all the way to Lisbon to meet with me," he said. "It is difficult for an old man like me to travel, but I imagine it was not easy for you to leave your family to come."

Layla smiled and said she was happy to be there. She did not, she felt, need to go into details about her family. He did not need to know more about her, at least, she decided, until she knew more about him.

"So have you lived in Lisbon for long?"

"Yes, I suppose so. We moved here about twenty years ago now. My sons—I have two—were still in secondary school. Before that, we lived in Italy for about seven or eight years. And before that, my family lived in Egypt, although I travelled a lot in those days, mostly to Europe and the Middle East. I would work in a given hospital for a week, or sometimes up to a month or two, and then I would return to my family for a short while before taking the next job. It became too much. But that was a long time ago now. Lisbon has been home for some time now, but we go back to Egypt maybe every year or two."

"How interesting," Layla said, genuinely intrigued. "And do you and your family now speak Portuguese pretty fluently?"

"Well, I suppose so. My wife and I both have a pretty heavy accent, I think, but we are understood. The boys speak it very well, although they still speak Arabic and Italian quite well also." He said this with no small amount of pride in his voice, and again Layla thought of her own father. Something about this Dr. Abdelmallek reminded her of him so much.

"And you?" he asked. "How long have you lived in London?"

"Oh," she started. "Well, actually, we live in Cairo normally. My husband teaches at the AUC. But he has been working on this research project with some colleagues that has us living in London for the meantime. Sometime in the next year or so, we expect to move back to Cairo."

"Ah," said Dr. Abdelmallek. "So are your kids keeping up with their Arabic as well as learning English, then?" He stopped himself. "Sorry, assuming you have kids, of course."

"Yes, we do have two kids; they're still pretty young. And we speak Arabic and English at home. I suppose they'll be able to speak both pretty well."

Dr. Abdelmallek nodded again and smiled. Then he said, "Thank you again for meeting with me. I had been worried that once you mentioned my name to your father, he wouldn't want you to speak with me, so I appreciate that you are here."

Layla looked for a sign to indicate whether he knew of their rift, or was perhaps simply asking after her father. But she couldn't read his face, so she nodded a restrained acknowledgement.

"Well, in any case," he continued. "Do you want to see the letter now, or did you have any questions for me first?"

Layla had thought about all the questions she had, but she didn't even know where to begin. "Well," she started, "I guess I'm curious how this charm ended up in your maid's hands. Did she ever name the person she bought it from? Did she ever say if he told her how he got it or why he was selling it to her?"

"I asked my father the same thing," Dr. Abdelmallek responded. "All he and my mother could get out of her is that the man was someone who seemed to know the area, but no one seemed to know who he was. And she never saw him again after he sold her the trinket. He told her it had been given to him by his mother, and that he needed the money it was worth. It's such an untraceable story; there's no way to verify it, but no reason to think it's not true. My parents don't think she was hiding anything. She was very distressed by the whole thing, and was otherwise a very naïve young woman…"

"And why didn't your father take it to my family when he first got it?" Layla hadn't meant to ask this so early in their conversation.

Dr. Abdelmallek paused. "To be honest," he began, "this is almost as much of a mystery to me as it is to you. My father, you have to understand, was, well, his judgement was sometimes clouded by his ambition." Here, his eyes went up to the far ceiling, as if he might find the right words there. "When I asked him the question, he gave me a vague response about it being too soon after your grandfather's death, and not wanting to upset your grandmother. But I have to wonder why he wouldn't then have waited six months or a year and then given it to her.

"I don't know how much your father has told you about our childhood. Your grandfather, Ostaz Is-hak was a very well-respected man. Everybody knew your family. And not just because they had money. No, your grandfather was almost like a judge in the area. He knew everyone. Whenever a dispute would arise between people: neighbours arguing over something, or some business transaction, people would take their concerns to Ostaz Is-hak before they got the police or the courts involved. And he usually solved it for them somehow. Whatever he suggested was deemed to be fair, and the matter would be resolved. It was quite remarkable, really. He was like a modern-day King Solomon. As for my family, we were comfortable enough, never had any problems. We were normal, and unremarkable, I suppose, in our normalcy. As an adult I've come to the theory that this normalcy was not enough for my father. He wanted prestige. And I think that when this letter fell into his hands, he saw it somehow as a card he could play when the moment was right. He probably thought the information in it would turn out to be profitable to him at some point, and he was just waiting for that moment. The moment, of course, never came.

"After your grandfather's death at such a young age — do you know, by the way, how many hundreds, maybe thousands, of people showed up for his funeral? It was, of course, a tragic loss to your family on a private level, but it was also a great loss to the community. I was only a boy, but even I remember that day. Do you know the mothers gathered us boys, who were friends and classmates of Tayib, in your family's apartment to keep your father Tayib company during the funeral? We were told to play with him to keep him from getting sad. Yes, we played cards — or was it checkers? — in the balcony, and every little while, one of the mothers would come with snacks for Tayib and the rest of us. It was an awful day, and because of that, memorable.

"In any case, after he died, your grandmother, although she did not continue to run the family business, did keep the family together and successful. I mean, look at Tayib and Amira."

Indeed, Layla's father had become a successful architect in his own right, Yasmine's overshadowing success notwithstanding. Through the years, Tunt Amira had also built a successful medical practice.

"That is, anyway, the best explanation I have for why he kept it all those years. I hope I'm wrong, but I don't know what other explanation there would be."

The waiter approached them just then, and they each ordered a coffee, to which Dr. Abdelmallek also added some pastries with unfamiliar names. Layla began to object, but Dr. Abdelmallek insisted that it was the least he could do, given that she was in his city.

"I didn't know that about my grandfather's funeral," Layla said, pulling the conversation away from what Dr. Abdelmallek's father's intentions might have been. She thought she should see the letter before asking Dr. Abdelmallek the even more delicate question of why he was having this conversation with her rather than with her father.

"I'm curious to see the letter," she said. "Would it be alright if I looked at it?"

"Of course," he replied. He reached into his inside breast pocket and pulled out an envelope, browned and brittling with age. He handed it over to her carefully.

Just as carefully, Layla took out the tissue thin paper, seeing the many creases where it had been folded to fit into the charm so many years ago. The ink was faded, and Layla had to adjust her eyes to the curves and accents of the handwritten Arabic letters. She began to read.

My dearest son Tayib,

You are reading this letter because you have succeeded in the task I gave you. Well done!

And if you have succeeded in this task, then you are beyond your years and are ready for some grown up advice. Here it is: the world is open before you, but you can only choose one path at a time. Never make a decision that you will not be proud of when you are old so you can look back with pride.

The task I have given you is small, and yet you have succeeded when others your age might not have. You are ready to be trusted with more. When I was a boy, my father left for me a large plot of land that has been used to grow some of the country's finest cotton for generations. The land is now managed by a trusted firm that our family has worked with for many years. Upon your reaching adulthood, this land will be yours to do as you wish. The annual proceeds of it are enough that you can live comfortably and do anything you want without regard for income.

There is, however, one condition. Our family has always believed in the value of work. It gives us purpose, and makes our days on this earth worthwhile. So, although this land generates enough money that you won't need to work, you must nevertheless work in order to receive it. So keep up with your studies and school; I know you are a very smart boy. When it comes time to choose a profession, choose something that you enjoy, without regard for how much money you make.

This freedom to choose the work you do is perhaps the best gift that I can give you, and I am happy that you have earned it.

With all my love,
Your father

Layla held the paper for a moment longer. It seemed unreal that this same paper had been held by her grandfather, who she had never met, and was now, these many years later and these many kilometres away, being given to her by someone she had just met. The connection to her past and to her family raised the hairs on her arms.

She looked up to see Dr. Abdelmallek looking at her. He was about to say something, but they were interrupted by the waiter bringing them their coffee and pastries.

"So now," he began gently, "I have a question for you. How is it that you did not know anything about this? And that your father did not object to your meeting me? Or that you did not object?"

Layla thought before she answered, wishing she had given more thought ahead of time to how to explain this. "It seems," she finally began, "that you are not the only one who has not spoken to him in some time. Although I must add that, in our case, it's only been since shortly before my husband and I moved to London."

Dr. Abdelmallek looked at her with sorrow in his eyes, but did not say more.

"Without making it too long of a story," she continued, "it has been about a year since my father and I spoke. Before that, he had mentioned, of course, his friends, but I don't remember him mentioning you. And I certainly don't remember any mention of a plot of land belonging to the family."

"Do you," Dr. Abdelmallek began, keeping his eyes on the pastry he had just picked up, "um, do you still keep in contact with your aunt Amira?"

"Yes, we talk on the phone."

"Do you think she might know about this property?"

"I don't know why she would," Layla said, "unless it's no longer a secret. My grandmother passed away a short while ago, so it is possible that the existence of the property was revealed to my father and her at that time..."

"So they are still close, your father and Amira?" Dr. Abdelmallek asked. It was a feigned disinterest—a question too awkwardly introduced to be a passing curiosity.

"Yes, they talk often." She smiled, thinking about her aunt Amira.

Dr. Abdelmallek smiled too. "Yes, well, that is good," he said.

"How about you, Dr. Abdelmallek?"

"Please, call me Hany," he interrupted.

"Ok, Uncle Hany" she continued. "If I may ask, what caused your estrangement?"

"Oh, it was a long time ago," he said. "When we were young men, just recently out of university. A misunderstanding, really, but then we saw each other so infrequently during those years that we never gave it a chance to heal, and then time passed, and we emigrated, and here we are."

Well, thought Layla to herself, I suppose that's as much detail as I gave him. Layla smiled politely.

"So why did you contact me? And why now?"

"Ah, yes," said Hany, and paused. "Layla, I am getting to be an old man, and there comes a time in your life...You reach a certain age, you see, and you want to finish any unfinished business, as they call it. My father left this for me when he died, and I didn't know what to do with it—my relationship with your father seemed too distant by then, so I just let it sit. And then life got busy, as it is wont to do, and it was easy to forget about it. When I did remember it, it was easy to continue to let it just sit; there were too many other pressing things to attend to. But then retirement came, and there were fewer things to attend to. And I don't want it to become my sons' issue to deal with when I die. I want to close this chapter.

"As for why you, well, I can just say that London is closer than Cairo." He smiled at this, as if acknowledging that it was not nearly adequate as an explanation. "The truth is, I don't know, after all these years, how your father feels about me, if he is still angry with me, and I didn't want the messenger—me—to distract him from the message. I hoped that if it came through you, he may be more likely to welcome the letter and any new news that it bears."

"Then you learn, of course, that I..." Layla began.

"Yes, well. I don't know what happened between you and him, but you are still his daughter, and I can't imagine that whatever it was was so bad that Tayib never wants to speak to you again. You'll pardon me for speaking so boldly; of course I know nothing about the details."

"Well, God willing it will be resolved," she said, reflexively responding with a polite and noncommittal answer.

Almost simultaneously, they both started. "So now what?" she began, while he said, "I wonder what you would like to do—"

They both smiled then, and she waited for him to continue. "I think it is right for your family to have this letter," he said. "But I'd like to make a request, if I give it to you." Layla raised her eyebrows.

"If I give it to you, will you make sure your father sees this letter and knows what I have told you? Despite our distance now, he was a dear friend, and I want to make sure he sees this letter. Can you promise me that?"

She nodded quickly and said, "Yes, I can promise that." Then, almost as an afterthought, she added, "Thank you for returning it to him." If she didn't give it to her father, she could, she supposed, ask Tunt Amira to show her father the letter.

Seeming to consider something, he added, "Would it be alright if I wrote him a letter of my own for you to give to him as well? I really did respect your father, and his family, and it is perhaps appropriate that I write him something directly."

"Of course," Layla said. "I'm here until tomorrow afternoon."

"Oh, that's good —"

"Not that you can't mail it to me if you need more time to write it."

"It should be enough time, I think." After a pause, "I was just thinking that if you don't have any plans for the day, I could at least recommend for you places to go in this city. It's quite beautiful, you know, if you know where to go."

"I don't have plans, no."

"Well, allow me to tell you about some places. Do you like to shop?" he asked. She did not normally like to shop, but the idea of doing anything without a list firmly in hand and a clock ticking down the minutes she had to herself was very appealing.

"I suppose so," she answered nonchalantly, "for some gifts and things." After a pause, she added, "Or if there are some nice sight-seeing spots, those would be good too."

Hany asked a passing waiter for a piece of paper and jotted down some places for her, opining about taxis and the best places to find them, and what prices to expect to pay. Then he said, "We should arrange a time for me to come by tomorrow to drop off the letter. Perhaps my wife and I can take you out for lunch? There are some restaurants in Lisbon that are not to be missed."

Layla was surprised to find herself readily agreeing. As she watched him walk out of the lobby, she noticed again the stooped back that used to, she was sure, hold up a much taller man.

25

Cairo
2008

I sometimes wonder what drew Aida to me all those years ago. The jaded side of me would say it's because I was a convenient choice: her brother had already vetted me, I had a respectable occupation that would allow us to live comfortably, and she knew as well as I did that I would treat her well, unconditionally.

But I'm not always that jaded. Watching her sleep now, her hair perfectly coiffed even on this hospital bed, I'm reminded of the early days of our marriage. I remember walking into our first, tiny rented apartment one day — that would have made it around 1974 — and finding Aida curled up asleep on the lounge. I was tired. I was still a medical intern, which in itself is exhausting, but to also be mentally translating all day between Arabic and this heavily accented English was completely draining. I had looked forward to sitting down to dinner with Aida as I was coming home. But looking from the front door, I had seen that the kitchen was empty, the dishes neatly dried by the sink, and no sign of a meal forthcoming on the stove.

That's when I had found her asleep. She looked so child-like, and so beautiful, when she was sleeping. For a moment, I was grateful to at least have somewhere to go every day. I wondered how she could stand being here, day after day, with no one to talk to until I came home. Yes, she went to the library, and the supermarket, but there was only so much one could do.

She had been so excited about coming on this adventure; was it still, I wondered, what she expected?

"Aida," I said quietly, rubbing her arm. "Aida, wake up."

She opened her eyes. Then they got big. "Tayib! What time is it?" Looking up at the apartment's only clock, she pushed herself up quickly. "Oh my goodness. It's so late! You must be so hungry! Tayib, I'm so sorry!"

I was hungry. And tired. "Habibti, why don't we treat ourselves to a dinner out? We haven't eaten out since we got here, and there is that little place on the corner we've wondered about since we moved in. What do you think?"

She smiled a small smile. "Ok," she said. "Let me just tidy myself up a bit."

Fifteen minutes later, we were walking into the small Italian restaurant. Most of the tables were already occupied with patrons, and the noise of quiet conversation and laughter, and the smell of garlic and tomato sauce made us feel both excited at the prospect of eating out, but also a little anxious about navigating yet another new custom. We stood hesitatingly at the door, wondering whether to seat ourselves, when a server approached with a brisk smile and showed us to a table.

As the server set down a bottle of water and some cups for us, Aida and I picked up the menus and began studying them. Deciding quickly, I put down the menu and looked at my wife. She took a little longer to decide what she wanted, but a moment later, she put down her menu too. "So how was your day?" I asked. "What did you do?"

"I woke up when you left this morning, and so I called Egypt before it got too late for them."

"How are they all?"

"They're fine, el hamdu le-llah," she responded. "But of course, we only talked for a few minutes — I need to remember to find out if there are better rates for calling Egypt. Anyway, after we finished talking, I just missed them so much. And there was so much I didn't have a chance to say. So I decided to write a letter, and before I knew it, it was nearly lunch time. And I had meant to go to the library this morning and pick up some more of those ESL tapes!"

Just then, the server came back. "You ready to order?" she asked.

We both smiled and nodded, giving her our orders in turn. I heard the sounds around us change, as they always seemed to whenever Aida and I spoke English with others, our accents creating a discord to the native Australian cadence. With each other, we slipped back into Arabic, despite an early resolve to practice our English by speaking it exclusively with each other. It hadn't lasted; speaking in our native tongue created a bubble of refuge that had become an anchor as we navigated our new home.

"So did you send the letter?"

"No, I'll go by the post office tomorrow and drop it off. I should have done it today, but after I ate lunch, I turned on the television to listen to the news, and before I knew it, I'd fallen asleep. So I really have nothing to show for my day!" She gave a sheepish laugh.

"How about you? I'm sure your day was much busier. Weren't you supposed to start that new rotation today?"

I had recounted my day to her, then added, "Oh, I almost forgot. They're having a potluck dinner at the hospital next week for all the interns and house officers. Families are invited, and everyone brings a dish. Do you think you can make something?"

The following week we had attended that potluck. After agonizing over what to make, Aida had settled on mousaka'a. The eggplant dish was one of her favourites; she had learned from her grandmother to perfectly season the mince beef that went in it with buharat and a little nutmeg. The table where we were directed to put the dish was laden with cheese and fruit trays, biscuits and cake platters, and the occasional mysterious dip. Aida put her dish down, then took my arm as I began introducing her to the various staff, some of whose names she'd heard me mention in my stories about work. I found that I did not have to keep any conversation going for long; as soon as I introduced Aida, she would start asking questions, or making jokes. It was clear she enjoyed talking to these new people, and to their spouses, some of whom, like her, had not yet found work. At the end of the night, she had accumulated quite a few phone numbers, and the accompanying promises to have coffee or dinner together. When we came to retrieve the mousaka'a dish at the end of the evening, it looked almost untouched. "No matter," Aida had said to me lightly, "all the more for us." By her smile, I knew that she wasn't upset. Still, when I think about it now, she always brought a dessert trifle to future potlucks with work colleagues or neighbours,. Ironically, her mother had taught her this British dessert when she was a child.

I don't know why I would think about her potluck contributions over the years as she lay here in the hospital bed. Perhaps I was realizing that her love for me meant everything right now, and it was not a love born just out of familiarity and of what I could provide for her. Aida was lying here in front of me with this thing inside her, and none of us knew yet what would happen. What if I lost her? Could it really happen? I wouldn't imagine it. I couldn't endure the iron grip that grabbed my heart when I would try.

When we were first married, and still now, when our busy lives gave us a few hours of time alone together, we would talk about topics that we both loved and that we didn't often talk about. They would remind me that, behind the bubbly, chatty persona and the perfectly done hair, there was a mind that could spar and analyse with the best of them. I could not imagine living without those conversations. I would not imagine living without her.

Instead I wonder, if we had stayed in Egypt, how our marriage might have looked different. Australia had been good for Aida; we had known within six months of living there that we would not be returning to Egypt. Aida especially could not have gone back to a life that was as literally closed in as it was. Abroad, she had seen things and met people that had opened up the world to her in a remarkable way. Granted, she had eventually stopped seeking out new people and experiences, but wasn't that more a function of aging than of living as an expatriate? Had we stayed in Egypt, we probably would have lived somewhere close to her family, and she would have kept her circle of friends exactly the same as when she had been in school.

But was this a bad thing, really? When we would go back to visit Egypt, or even among our neighbours and friends in Australia, we knew people whose closest friends were the same friends they had grown up with. They had a shared history that went back as far as either could remember. They had a built-in community that banished any possibility of loneliness, or of questioning who one was. Their circles defined them.

Still, I don't know that this would have been a better choice. I would not trade my life for that life. Just as life abroad had opened up Aida to new experiences, so had it opened me up to new ways of thinking, of interpreting people and situations. And I like to think it has made our marriage richer. Our life as immigrants has given us a wealth of shared memories and experiences that has taught us more about ourselves and each other than I think we ever could have learned otherwise. When we had decided to try living abroad all those years ago, it had been just for us; we had no children to be affected by our decision yet.

But I too had decided I wanted to stay abroad, despite the sacrifice of seeing my family less frequently. I liked to think living abroad made me a more sympathetic person who understood the world as the complex little universe it was. Listening sometimes to how my more rooted friends and family saw the world, I would hear so much narrow thinking — if not also certainty. Now that certainty was something I sometimes envied in them. Still, my life was rich just the way it was, and I would not take that for granted.

And of course there is Dalia. Dalia certainly would not be living the life she now lives if we had stayed in Egypt. I wonder if my daughter is truly as happy as she says she is. She is very successful at her work, of that there is no doubt. And she enjoys herself, what with her travels and her gourmet meals at nice restaurants. She has a freedom I could only have dreamed of for my daughter. But would that be enough for her in old age? I don't believe that you should have children to take care of you in your old age; that is a very selfish way to look at the world, in my view. But some day, when you are retired and life is no longer crowded with the urgency of doing that it used to be, is there enough left to make you feel like your days have been worthwhile? Maybe there would be. If anyone could make it so, Dalia could. I imagine Dalia at age 70, living in a condo building that had outings for its residents, dressed as smartly as ever, perhaps still going out with that poor Liam once a week.

But then again, maybe Liam wouldn't always be that poor Liam. Maybe Dalia would finally see how devoted he is to her and marry the fellow. She could be happy married too, I think. Being married wouldn't mean she would have to have children and quit her job—although nothing would make me happier than to have a couple of grandchildren. But I would never say that to Dalia. That, now, would be selfish. Still, they could get a nanny; they'd be able to afford one, and Dalia could continue her work. But no, I know Dalia. She would approach motherhood as she approached every other endeavour in her life: she would read all the parenting books, then reluctantly give up her job so that she could be home with the children, because that is what good mothers do. I wonder how society could have regressed so much to two generations ago.

In my view, motherhood is as varied as kids are. Dalia, for example, would not be a good stay-at-home mother. She would be bored, bitter, impatient. But she would try. She would buy activity kits to keep the kids occupied, and when the kids lost interest after 15 minutes, she would despair. She would enroll them in activities to keep them occupied at all hours of the day, until they got so accustomed to it that any down time would prompt them to say, "I'm bored. What can I do now?"

No, much as it saddens me to admit it, motherhood would not be for Dalia. As I concluded this, I noticed a grumbling noise and realized it was my own stomach. Why would I be hungry — when was the last time I had eaten? I couldn't remember. I remembered Sherif's wife pressing on me a couple small sandwiches she had brought from home this morning and some piping hot tea. I might have taken a few bites to pacify her. Had I eaten yesterday? What a silly question. I couldn't remember, and anyway it didn't matter. I was fine. Maybe I would just go down to the corner fuul shop and buy something small. I would be back in less than 15 minutes.

When I got up, Sherif, who I had forgotten had come in and sat down a while ago, asked me where I was going, and offered to go buy the sandwiches in my place. But I said I needed the fresh air and asked him to stay in case Aida woke up while I was gone. He agreed, of course.

As I walked down the hall, I wondered at how, after these many years of separation, Sherif and I still had the familiarity of brothers. And yet. And yet there was something different in our relationship. We had known each other as children and youth, and we would do anything for each other still. But in the intervening years, each of us had grown our own life: had our own conversations with the people around each of us about politics and society and faith and God knows what else, listened to different news perspectives about world events, got used to living with different comforts and accommodations. We could so easily understand each other, and so comfortably ask things of each other, but the years had stripped away our ability to actually live in the other's shoes.

Now I had reached the shop and was paying for the sandwiches. They charged £1.50 L.E. each now! I remember when these sandwiches where 25 piasters. £1.50 L.E. would have fed my entire family easily back then. Well, I couldn't complain. This was still a fraction of what I would pay in Australia. I dwelled on this thought for a moment, in the distracted way that people do to allow insignificant thoughts to keep their mind from returning to the truly catastrophic things they must face.

Minutes later, I returned to the hospital room and handed Sherif a sandwich, insisting, as was the custom, that he eat with me so that I wouldn't eat alone. We ate in silence for a few minutes, listening as we did to the sounds of the hospital staff walking by in conversation outside.

26

Lisbon
2008

Back in her room, Layla tucked the letter safely away inside the journal she had brought with her, and then called Peter.

"Hi!" he began. "So you haven't been kidnapped at least. Or is this the ransom call for money?"

Layla reminded herself that Peter's British humour came out most when he was stressed. Jokes were how he directly but lightly addressed what was bothering him.

"Not yet," she began. She wanted to make a joke back, but she couldn't think of one. "He seems a perfectly nice old man, actually. He gave me the letter, and he put a condition on it."

"Ah, here it comes," Peter said.

"Nothing like that, Peter. He wants to make sure my father sees the letter and knows what he told me."

"Then why doesn't he bloody well give it to him, rather than put you in the middle of it?" Peter asked, to Layla's surprise.

"It's been a long time since they talked, and it wasn't on such great terms, apparently, that they last talked. I don't know the details—he didn't give any—but he did say he didn't want the fact that it was coming from him to distract Baba from the message of the letter itself."

"I don't understand why Egyptians have to involve everyone in everything all the time," Peter said. Layla knew he was speaking out of frustration about other things, mostly in his work. The politics in his

174

department at the AUC, for example, and the—in his mind complicated—in-law interactions that, compared to her interactions with her in-laws, were so layered and had so many unspoken rules.

"Well, anyway, if I don't talk to him directly, I can give the letter to Tunt Amira to give to him," she added.

"Well maybe it wouldn't be a bad excuse to call him," Peter began.

"I don't need a reason to call him," Layla snapped.

"No, of course not." Peter forged ahead, "But maybe he and your mum would be ready to talk again now? And this letter could be an excuse to just open the door."

"Well, in any case, there's time to think about that," he continued. "What are you going to do with the rest of your time in Lisbon? Did you ask the concierge about that bathhouse I'd heard about? A spa or massage or something might be a nice treat…"

"Maybe," Layla said. "For the moment, I'm going to go out and try to find some good coffee." To herself, she added, 'And I'm going to enjoy thinking in peace.'

The streets of Lisbon, it turned out, proved very good for clearing her mind. The smells emanating from the cafes, and the sights of people walking by, and of shop windows, was so new and yet in some unnameable way so familiar. With no one with her, Layla found pleasure in walking, covering blocks of the city quite quickly. It was mostly aimless walking: she would walk until a shop window or building would catch her interest. She enjoyed most wandering the narrow streets of Alfama, climbing its steep steps, and looking at the faded but numerous colours of the old buildings. Then in Mouraria, her eyes would look up to see wrought iron balconies, or lines of wash hung out to dry. The streets' and buildings' age fed her imagination, and she found herself creating lives for the people who used to live here, and those who lived here still. She chose to imagine that here, families lived tranquil lives. Working spouses never had to work late, and family members could always watch the kids and allow couples time to go out together, perhaps to one of the little cafes like that one there! Her stomach was growling with hunger, she realized, so she stopped at the café — or bakery, she didn't know what they were called here — and picked out a pastry to go with her coffee.

Peter would have loved exploring this new city with her. When was the last time they had done something like this? When they had been younger, newlyweds, they would vacation in new places walking around for hours like this and trying new foods together. They had been on top of the world then: their love young and uncomplicated by what the years would teach them about each other. Their cares were far fewer then too: Peter had a secure, if poorly paid, teaching position waiting for him, and Layla was enjoying an only slightly better paying job with Chipsy. Their relationships with family and friends were simple and easy. Their love was still new and exciting. Life, in short, was good.

Layla wondered when things had changed and how to rekindle that sense of adventure and fun. It's not as if they could plan those short trips to new places any more. Travel wasn't the same with children. Nothing was the same with children. She loved Maggie and Tado with all her heart, and could not imagine her life without them, cliché as that sounded. They made her life infinitely richer, and yet more limited. But kids had also changed her and Peter's marriage. How could they keep that feeling of closeness to each other, and the excitement they used to feel over seeing each other?

She knew, of course, that at this stage, love was no longer going to have that giddy, irrational joy of new love. She missed the experience of loving the young, earnest PhD student Peter had been those many years ago. Why was that? It was because, she realized now, there was so much unknown about him then. They could talk forever, and make each other laugh, and each could take pleasure in the new admiration from the other.

In those early months, all she knew about his past were the few stories he had shared. She hadn't met a lot of his family yet. She hadn't lived with him to know about his extreme dislike of eggplant, or his uncanny ability to recognize tunes and songwriters after just a bar or two, or his annoying habit of leaving all his clothes in laundry baskets, so she never knew what was clean or dirty. And of course, she thought with a smile, she hadn't known what he would be like in bed. They didn't discover that particular pleasure until after they were married. He would have been willing—eager—to earlier, of course, but he knew what the cultural principles were that she had grown up with, and, to his credit, never pushed her to defy them, much as he might have wanted to. As she remembered it, he might not have had to push very much. Layla had known after a couple months that he was the man she would marry, although she was happy to let him determine when they would marry, and even what kind of a life they would live afterwards. Goodness, had she really been so young once? So trusting that life would just work out? But it had, hadn't it?

Well, mostly it had. They were still mostly healthy, mostly secure in their careers — his career, rather — and all that. But there was, painfully she thought, this separation from her parents. Layla understood her mother's disappointment in her career — or rather noncareer — choices; it was, at least, consistent with the message Yasmine had given Layla her whole life about having a successful career without compromises.

But her father's reaction had angered her. She remembered again their last phone conversation. Tayib initially kept asking how she thought she would be happy if she wasn't working, and she had eventually given up trying to make him understand that she had no interest in living with the kind of stress her parents both brought home from work.

It was Peter's grant and their move to London that had seemed key to Tayib. Since it was Peter's career that would advance by Layla choosing to leave her work, Tayib had, unlike her mother, accepted her decision.

It angered her; it really did. This was the same man who had told her as a young girl that she was as smart and capable as anyone, and could choose for herself whatever life she wanted. She had believed him. She had chosen, and he had not been happy with her choice. But he had been happy with Peter. Peter was the only reason her father hadn't pushed harder for her to keep working. Her father loved and respected Peter. Peter had made a respectable choice of professions, and clearly loved Layla fully and faithfully. As Tayib saw it, Peter would be responsible for Layla's choices, however foolhardy he might think they were.

She found it ironic that the same man who had
instilled in her a sense of self-sufficiency when she was
growing up was now so willing to see her defer to her
husband, putting aside how great he thought Peter
was. For the first time, it occurred to her that life in
Egypt as a woman was indeed a paradox. At least in
the cities, women were respected as equally intelligent
as men, were valued for the roles they played in public
and private life, and were, for the most part, free to
enter most professions. But in the private sphere, their
roles were still very fixed. Their husbands and children
came first. Husbands' careers came first, husbands'
wishes were honoured. Women could be trusted to
manage offices and companies, but had to defer the
decisions of the family to their husbands. It was
infuriating really.

Was that entirely fair, though? Compared to many of
her friends' fathers, her father was actually quite open
minded. He had let her read whatever she wanted
starting in high school, and travel to Europe when she
was in university. He had talked to her, asked her
questions, asked for her opinions. Her friends'
conversations with their fathers were more like
interrogations. Those fathers would ask who they had
seen that day, what they had decided to study, and
then proceeded to give their opinions, both about their
choice of friends and course of study. And they
expected those opinions to be followed.

Even if Tayib had been that kind of father, could
Layla really fault him? He had grown up in this
culture, had known nothing but this culture. How
could she expect him to be otherwise? After all, wasn't
the only reason that she herself knew or expected
otherwise was that she had married Peter, and had

travelled enough to see how other people lived? No, she answered herself, the reason she knew otherwise was because her mother had lived out an example of defying those expectations. And now Yasmine was ostracizing Layla for making a decision that, at least on its surface, seemed to throw away all the independence her mother had fought so hard for.

She couldn't win. Her mother disapproved of her decision to give up working and her father attributed her decision to Peter. The fact that she, not Peter, had decided she would leave her position, and that she still believed it to be the right decision, did not seem to factor into the equation.

Layla sighed now and brushed the pastry crumbs off her lap. If she was being honest with herself, she knew that the silence between her and her parents was born, on her part, more out of a frustration with all these irreconcilable paradoxes her life held than it did with their actual reactions. She remembered how old Dr. Abdelmallek — Uncle Hany — had looked, and recognized with a small twinge of panic that her parents were also aging, and that she might well regret the lost time with her parents.

When she got home, she resolved, she would call them.

27

Cairo
2008

The peculiar smell of the Cairo airport, of stale refrigerated air and body odour and faint cigarette smoke and of perfumes and spices from faraway places, assailed me as I walked through the arrivals entrance with my cousin Sherif. Dalia and Liam would be arriving soon. I had a moment of panic: I hadn't mentioned that Liam would be coming with Dalia, nor had I thought about how I would introduce him.

The airport had gotten a computerized screen, I noticed, listing arrival times and baggage carousels, that I thought must be fairly new. I remembered, suddenly, the Sydney airport. It was 1974, the first time Aida and I had arrived in Sydney. We were walking towards the baggage claim, carried forward by the stream of passengers around us. Up ahead, there was a split-flap display with the domestic departures listed. Rockhampton, Cairns, Darwin, Rarotonga, it listed. These were places I had never heard of. Even the smells of baking bread and of coffee wafting out of the airport cafes smelled slightly different here, and I felt a knot start to form in my stomach at my foreignness amongst it all. When Aida and I had told our families that we were thinking about going to Australia, everyone had been shocked. "But it's so far," they'd all said. The more encouraging ones had said that they knew someone in Sydney or Melbourne who could help us when we arrived. As far as Aida and I knew, though, Australia consisted entirely of Sydney and

Melbourne, where other immigrants would provide familiar comforts. It appeared now that this place was much bigger, and much more strange, than we had realized.

I had been, of course, curious about what life might look like in this new country. So many of my friends and acquaintances had emigrated to Australia or the United States. My life in Cairo had stretched out ahead of me interminably. It would be a life full of small frustrations and challenges that would never amount to anything greater than simply getting by. And Aida had been so excited about the prospect of going on this adventure that I would not have had the heart to deny her, even if my reservations had been greater. If the stories we had heard about other emigres were to be believed, life in Australia would also be full of challenges, and often bigger hardships. But the possibilities and rewards were greater than anything I could dream of in Egypt: it was too compelling a possibility to ignore.

Aida, it turned out, was the perfect partner for the venture. She would joke later that I had married her for her foreign language ability. Indeed, in our first few months in Sydney, it was Aida who would spend hours at a time practicing English with me. It was not her second language, she would acknowledge, but English and her beloved French were both Latin languages, and besides, she was a quick study and would go to the library and review ESL books while I was at work. She would also have pronunciation coaching sessions with me until I acquired enough of an Australian accent to be understood by even the least cosmopolitan of my patients.

When our daughter was born to Aida and I a few years later, Aida had insisted on naming her Dalia because it was a name that Australians could pronounce, but was also a common name among Egyptian girls. She had not wanted to name our child a name like Kylie or Georgia, as our other immigrant friends had done just so that they could fit in with the other Australian girls. "Dalia" was also, Aida mistakenly believed, a French name, and Aida was nothing if not a true believer in the superiority of the French language.

As if materializing out of my thoughts, Dalia appeared now through the customs gate. I recognized my daughter's head, hair pulled back in a pony tail, Liam a couple of steps behind her, each of them dragging a suitcase behind them and wearing the dazed expression of travelers who had been in transit for a full day. After Sherif and I embraced the two of them, I asked them if they were hungry. Dalia insisted that they wanted to go straight to the hospital rather than to her aunt's house to rest first. We walked them back to the car and left the sprawling airport car park. On the broad street leading away from the airport, and watching the hectic traffic stream by, I took a deep breath. I had been anticipating Dalia's arrival, and yet I dreaded it. I needed my family together to face the biopsy results, and I needed Dalia here to feel that my family was complete and that my world was rooted. But having Dalia here also made it too real that something had merited she make the trip. One of the things we would have to decide soon is whether Aida would have a better chance of recovery here or in Australia. My relatives had assured me that the doctors at this particular hospital were all trained abroad and that the reason it was so expensive was that they stocked the most advanced equipment and medicines. It certainly seemed state of the art; the rooms were very clean and the decorations on the wall both modern abstract and comforting, the way hotels were decorated these days. Still, I knew nothing about how healthcare worked here; I was having to rely entirely on the judgement of my family.

And in any case, would Aida be well enough to be transported elsewhere? The doctors kept saying that the initial operation, to ease the pressure on her spinal cord, needed to be done quickly. Well, now that Dalia was here, she and I could decide. What if there were better options elsewhere, and we wouldn't be given all the options here? It was impossible to know what the best thing to do was. I needed Dalia's level head to help me decide. At what moment had our relationship shifted from father and daughter to two-like minded adults, I wondered? I wasn't sure, but I suspected that it had been years ago. Dalia, despite her seeming frivolities, could always be relied upon to keep a cool head.

I turned just then to look at her in the back seat, looking out the window. She looked at me and I could see behind her smile the anxiety that she must have been carrying since she got off her cruise. Her eyes asked what news I might have, but I had nothing to offer.

28

Lisbon
2008

After she left the café, Layla had found herself trekking up and down the streets of Lisbon, barely registering the sights or people around her. Hours later, finding herself disoriented, she had asked directions and made her way back to the hotel, feeling as if she had just woken up from a vivid and upsetting dream. She suddenly found the idea of going home to London so soon almost stifling. She could not go back. She was not ready.

In her hotel room, Layla flopped her body down on the freshly made bed, inhaling the smell of soap on the sheets and of roasting meat from across the street. She hadn't even known she wanted to get away so much, but now that she was here, why did it feel like she was coming up for air after holding her breath underwater for too long? It was normal, wasn't it, to need a break from her tedious routine? Or did it mean something?

Layla was dialling the airline phone number before she could think about what she was doing. "I'd like to change my flight back to London," she was saying. "Well, I'm not sure when I'd like to come back. Can we leave it open?"

The cost would be an additional $250, she was told. 'Oh well,' she thought. I'll just watch our other expenses a little more closely next month.' Flight canceled, she called Peter to tell him.

"Hello," he answered on the second ring.

"Hi habibi. It's me."

"Oh! Hi! How's Lisbon?"

"It's great, really lovely. So much so, in fact, that I've decided to stay a little longer."

Silence.

"Peter, you told me to have an adventure, and I think you were right—more so than you realized. Having a break is exactly what I mean to do. It's just that two days—"

"When I said have an adventure, I meant treat yourself to a nice spa, do some shopping. I did not mean you should go missing for a few extra days, or however long you're thinking. Layla, what's gotten into you? I have work Monday, and the kids—"

"You can take the day off. Or ask Ms. Leed's daughter down the street to watch the kids. For goodness sake, Peter. I manage, usually on my own, all the time. I'm just asking for a couple days."

"When we moved here, that was the deal. You would stay home with the kids while I completed this research."

Layla didn't answer. Apparently not liking how his answer sounded, Peter continued.

"You had this weekend! And couldn't this be something you decided a little earlier, when we would have had time to make arrangements for the kids? The kids, Layla! What's gotten into you? What's happened over there? Did that man say something else to you that you're not telling me?"

"What?" It took Layla a moment to realize what man Peter was referring to. "No, no, nothing to do with him. I'm sorry, Peter, I know this isn't like me, and I know it puts you in a difficult position, a stressful one even. I'm sorry. But I've already changed the tickets. Please try to understand.

"Look, our lives have changed so much in the past few years, even in the past year, and I guess it's that I never have a chance to think for longer than 5 minutes before one of the kids needs me, or I have to go get some other stupid task done. Do you know how nice it has been to just finish a thought? I just need a little more of that. I need to think about the decisions we've made recently and if I'm happy with them."

After a few moments' pause, Peter answered. "Well, you're right. I don't understand. I don't understand why you couldn't come home and get a babysitter for a few hours to go finish your thoughts in London. What's wrong with bloody London? And what bloody decisions are you talking about?" The word "bloody" made frequent appearances in Peter's language when he was upset.

"Are you listening to yourself, Peter? Since when am I expected to be at your beck and call? When did I lose the right to make adult decisions?"

"When we had kids, that's when. If you ask me, it's not very adult of you to decide to leave them without care for a few days while you do God knows what wandering around the streets of Lisbon. Or are you about to tell me that you're actually jetting off to Paris or something?"

"I am not leaving them without care. I am leaving them in their father's care. Or have you forgotten that they are just as much your responsibility as they are mine?" Layla couldn't believe they were having this conversation. She took in a deep breath. "Look, I am not abandoning you, and I'm not crazy. I just really need some quiet time."

There was a long silence on the line, and Layla could almost picture her husband starting to respond, then stopping again. Finally, he said, "Will you stay at the same hotel? How can I reach you if I need to?"

"Yes, I might as well," she replied; she hadn't actually given this much thought. Then the budget keeper in her spoke up. "If I find a less expensive hostel or something, I'll be sure to let you know the contact details. And I can call you every evening so you know I'm alright."

"At least every evening," Peter's voice was almost petulant.

"Fine."

They hung up tersely, and Layla looked around her hotel room.

What had she just done? Here she was all of a sudden, with the next day, and the day after that maybe, stretched out in front of her, completely unplanned and free of obligations. Peter was furious, and she could see, in a way, why he would be. But she had surprised herself by her own indignation back at him. Since their move to London, hadn't she in fact acted like she was indeed at his beck and call? Maybe even since they had had kids — since they had gotten married even? And hadn't she in fact avoided making any decisions without him in the years they'd been married? But wasn't that what marriage was all about? Yes, Layla told herself, but only if it was a two-way street. He'd made plenty of decisions without her. Not big ones, granted, but changing travel plans on little notice? Surely he'd done that before. And she'd been alright with it. So why couldn't he extend the same flexibility to her? Sure, the kids were hard to handle on one's own, but she did it all the time. All the time. She remembered now how proud he had been of himself for offering to care for them this weekend so that she could go to Lisbon. He was the new-age dad who could handle the kids solo for a weekend. Well, here's a taste of real parenthood, not just a weekend's worth, Layla thought, startled at her own resentment.

Where was this venom towards Peter coming from? It was, she had to acknowledge, anger at herself, not at him, for allowing this shift in their relationship to occur. He only thought it a big deal to watch the kids on his own because she made it such a big deal. It was always her who arranged everything for the kids: scheduled playdates, planned their grocery shopping, enrolled them in activities and classes, made sure they had enough clothes in the right sizes for the upcoming season, brushed Maggie's hair every day. She researched potty training options. She made doctor's appointments. Honestly, how had this happened? If she left the kids with him even for a few hours on an evening or weekend, she made sure to have the food prepared and everything he might need laid out.

Layla had, she realized, made Peter an accessory parent without even noticing it. And he had let her. That's why she was angry with him. He had passively taken the minor role, the role of fun dad who played with the kids at bedtime and read stories. He wasn't doing any of the hard work involved.

But he was working, Layla reminded herself, so that she could buy those swim lessons and clothes without stressing about money. Layla thought about how archaic that thought would sound to all her British friends. But it was what she had heard growing up her entire life: the father provides for his family, and the wife runs the household. It is what she had heard, yet it's not the example her parents had set.

Without even realizing it, Layla had followed the role she thought a wife was supposed to adopt. The thing is, no one had ever taught her to run a household, unless she counted her mother's example, which was essentially to outsource all the tasks. But Layla had never chosen to be the wife who runs the household. She had chosen work, then Peter, then a family. Running a family household was like this behemoth that had crept in and dwarfed the simple life she thought she had chosen. 'Grow up, Layla. It's part of being an adult,' she told herself. Well, for a few days, for this little moment, she wouldn't think about it. She would be an adventurer once more.

She looked at her watch. It was almost time to go downstairs and meet Uncle Hany and his wife. Layla wondered what his wife would be like. Uncle Hany had told her they would come by the hotel to pick her up; she couldn't even remember if they were hosting her at their house or whether they were going to a restaurant.

She had packed some of her nicer clothes, with the subconscious assumption, she now realized, that she would be eating her meals without needing to cook or clean up, and that she wouldn't be chasing around marker-wielding toddlers or cleaning up messes. She was pleased to find that the clothes still fit her — or rather fit her again. She looked in the mirror: not bad for a mother of two who had never been an athlete and didn't exercise regularly (she liked to think picking up children, and cleaning and laundry were forms of exercise, but she doubted the health experts would agree).

Downstairs, the hotel lobby was bustling with the weekend crowd, and Lalya could not find a place to wait that would give her a view of the entrance. So she went outside. It was a glorious day. Unlike the last two days, which had been humid, this day was cool and sunny. The outline of the buildings around her were drawn clearly against the blue of the sky.

Layla watched people going by, trying to guess which ones were tourists and which were Lisbonites. Is that what a Lisbon resident was called? Or was it Lisbonian? In any case, Layla thought, it's not hard to tell them apart. The residents wore the dress and expression of working residents in any large city: even on a weekend, they had a determined look to get where they were going, the sights that tourists had come to see having long since lost their sheen for these residents. They travelled lightly, the women keeping a casual but alert hand on their purses.

The tourists like her, on the other hand, actually took the time to look around. Unlike the residents, they were spending this day outside their "real" lives, the tasks and worries of their lives hopefully at bay for the moment. Layla was finding that out here among the bustle of people and the smell of coffee roasting somewhere and petrol fumes from the cars, forgetting was remarkably easy to do. She almost wished now that she didn't have this lunch to attend. She didn't want to make conversation with people she barely knew, nice as she was sure they were. Then she wondered again what Uncle Hany's wife was like, and if their children would be there, and her anticipation returned. Hearing about other peoples' lives meant she could put off thinking about her own for a little longer.

This was a rare chance to relax, she thought, thinking of the tension with Peter it had cost her, and she wanted to maximize its benefit. It's funny, Layla thought, she'd never had any particular interest in seeing Lisbon, but now that she was here, she was almost giddy with the idea of exploring this city, with its hilly streets and old buildings.

Her thoughts were interrupted by a car pulling up a few metres ahead and Uncle Hany stepping outside to beckon to her. She smiled and started walking towards the car. Inside, a woman in the passenger seat turned around to introduce herself. She was wearing sunglasses, but Layla could see that her face was perfectly made up, and some classic women's perfume — Layla couldn't name which — filled the car. Her hair was perfectly coiffed, and her smile was big but disinterested. Just as she was about to speak, Hany introduced her as his wife Yvette. Yvette nodded a curt hello, and Layla tried to return the greeting a little more warmly.

A missed beat, and then Hany said, "We were thinking of taking you to this lovely restaurant in the old part of Lisbon. It's called A Travessa, and it's near the Museu da Marioneta. Have you ever had Portugese food before? No? I think you'll like it. You'll find a lot of shared spices and ingredients with our Egyptian food, but yet it's very different. You'll see."

"That's wonderful," Layla said. "Thank you so much for this. I am sure you have other things you could be doing." Hany replied that they were happy to host her, while Yvette gave the same practiced smile. Layla went on. "This is such a beautiful city. Do you live close by?"

Hany responded, "We live on the southwestern side of the city, so not far from here. Yvette is from Alexandria you see, so she wanted to be as close to the ocean as possible. Before I retired, my clinic was also on the west side, so I could drive to it in less than twenty minutes. I suppose I could have taken the bus. I would walk to the bus in the winter sometimes, when it wasn't too cold outside. Lisbon winters are rather mild."

"What kind of medicine did you practice?" Layla asked, more to make conversation than because she actually cared.

"I was a dermatologist," Hany replied. "My specialty was treating burns."

That would explain his wife's seemingly perfect complexion, Layla thought, then immediately chided herself. What she said out loud was, "My goodness, that must have been interesting work. But sad too, sometimes, no?"

"It was mixed," Uncle Hany replied. "It was wonderful when we could restore a patient's skin to the point that you couldn't even tell there were any scars there, but yes, it was sad when all we could manage was to make the skin functional again: face, hands, wherever the burn was, to make it so that they could blink normally, or open and close their hands, or move their arm, without pain. People look at you differently when you have burn marks. It was sad to see the patients' whole demeanor change when they became disfigured."

Layla remembered her aunt Amira's burns. They had happened when she was a child, in the accident that had killed Layla's grandfather. They would be the kind Uncle Hany was describing as functional. Tunt Amira could use her arms and hands just fine, but if she was wearing a short-sleeved shirt, which she rarely did, you could see the ugly spider web of scars on skin that, even after all these years, was shiny and papery smooth. Layla wondered whether to mention this now — surely Uncle Hany would have known about Amira's burns, but she decided not to.

Hany was pointing out the neighbourhood they were driving through. It was nice enough, she thought. Polished shop windows of designer names, shoppers walking in and out, some triumphantly carrying their purchase in the stores' specially designed bags. This could almost be any city in Europe, thought Layla. She would not come back to this area in the next few days; surely Lisbon had more unique flavours to offer.

Soon, though, Layla found the car winding through an older part of the city. They parked the car and got out, Hany and Yvette leading her down a narrow alley to an unpresuming door through which they stepped. Inside, the host greeted them warmly and led them through the candlelit dining room to their table. The three were seated and ordered a carafe of wine to go with their meal. 'This,' thought Layla, 'is a treat. Wine for lunch!' She couldn't remember the last time she had done that. It seemed to warm Yvette to the task of conversing as well, and Layla decided she must be a shy person when she meets someone new. They chatted amicably about life in London and life in Lisbon, sharing stories about things their kids had done, the older pair sharing stories about what their kids did when they were older, as if telling Layla what lay in her future. She always found it interesting how parents of grown children reminisced about their children's youth, seemingly forgetting how absolutely all-consuming and exhausting those early days were.

But that's the way memory worked, wasn't it? Even in the years that she had been a mother, she could tell herself those early months had been difficult, but she didn't feel it anymore. What she remembered were the sweet moments, like when Maggie had first told her that she was glad God had sent her to Layla instead of to another mother, or when Tado made that hilarious face he made when he knew he had done something and gotten away with it. By God, those moments. Those memories would flood her heart with such joy and love for her kids. It was only when she became a parent that she truly understood what it was to love a child. It was an all-encompassing, primal love that made life and relationships pre-children pale in comparison. Not, thought Layla, that she didn't love Peter, or her parents, or Faiza or her other close friends. She did; they were essential to her happiness. But there was an essence to her love for her kids, born perhaps out of the fact that they had, quite literally, been born of her body.

Maybe it was the wine, Layla thought, but she was filled with a sense of wellbeing. The talk at some point turned to what Egypt had been like when Uncle Hany and Tunt Yvette were growing up. They had not known each other as children, him growing up in Cairo and her in Alexandria. Layla found it comforting to listen to their memories of how people dressed, what movies had been popular, how old they were when phone lines were first installed in their homes. These were all echoes of her own parents' stories. It had been a different Egypt back then, less developed materially, yet more advanced in social thought. People treated each other more kindly, more patiently. Religion and class mattered, but not enough to dehumanize people who differed from you.

It was not so in Layla's childhood, or even now. Like so much of the world, so many Egyptians focused on their material advancements. They compared what kind of apartment each had, and what kinds of furnishings they had filled them with. They bought foreign cars with power buttons for everything. People whose parents had only ever had one bank account and had their family's wealth, however small, literally in the family jewels, now talked enthusiastically about stock market investments and buying rentals in new real estate developments along the Mediterranean. It made Layla sad somehow, as if something had been lost.

Layla was brought back to the present by a look of discomfort crossing the face of Tunt Yvette. She tuned in to what Uncle Hany was saying. He was recounting his university days, and how he had tutored his cousin and some of her friends, Layla's own Tunt Amira, among them. The group had been several years behind him in medicine. Perhaps, Layla thought, this Tunt Yvette was one of those women who tolerated no talk or memory of other girls from her husband. Some women were like that, Layla thought, noticing that Yvette's dish remained virtually untouched.

Layla, on the other hand, had tucked into her dish quite heartily. It was, as Uncle Hany had promised, exceptionally good. She would have to jot down the name of this restaurant so that she could bring Peter back here someday. Whatever the tension was between them now, it wouldn't last forever. One day, she would show Peter, and maybe even an older Maggie and Tado, this new city that she was discovering, and it would become part of their own family's memory.

29

Cairo
2008

Faces Dalia hadn't seen in years surrounded her and Liam, exclamations and hugs filling the narrow hospital hallway. So much for deciding how to introduce Liam, she thought, as she watched Liam's dark blond head bend down to receive the greetings. As exclamations, hugs, and kisses were exchanged, Dalia surprised herself by remembering the names of relatives she hadn't seen in probably seven or eight years.

Greeting their way through the cluster of family, Dalia and Liam, followed closely by Tayib, reached the door of Aida's hospital room. Tayib put his hand on his daughter's shoulder, and Dalia took in a slow breath, as if mentally bracing herself for what condition she might find her mother in. But when she walked in, she was surprised to see that her mother looked, well, almost normal. She looked tired, and as if she needed a brisk walk in some fresh air, but otherwise fine. Dalia was reassured by this: how sick could she be, looking as she did? It was foolish, she knew, but surely there was some glimmer of hope in such signs.

The chatter and energy of all her relatives filled the room, and Dalia and Liam were showered with concern about how tired they must be, how long the trip was, and declarations that they needed some food and drink, at which point two or three relatives were dispatched to get them a meal and strong tea. Dalia asked haltingly for some water, and this request was enthusiastically added to the list, a couple aunts opining about which shops had the coldest drinks and tastiest sandwiches.

After what seemed like a long time, Dalia thought that, in fact, all she wanted was for everyone to just give her and her parents some privacy to talk. Seeing, from the still eager chatter, that no one would be leaving anytime soon, she eventually pulled up her chair to the bed and took her mother's hand. Aida, who seemed to have been dozing, opened her eyes and focused her gaze on her daughter. Dalia saw there pain and fear, but also affection. "Mama," she said softly. "Mama, how are you? What are you feeling?"

"Well, you know," Aida responded, smiling.

Because she could think of nothing else to say, Dalia added, "I'm sorry I didn't get here sooner."

"No, no," her mother shook her head, with effort. "There's no need to worry yet. Your father shouldn't have told you and gotten you so worried." Seeing Liam in the background, she added, "Hello, Liam."

Liam came forward and gave her an awkward smile, trying to be warm but never having succeeded at developing a real rapport with Aida. And now there were all these watching eyes, Dalia wished her mother would stop being so aloof with him. She knew it was because she held the highest standards for her daughter's partner. 'He meets them, whatever they are,' thought Dalia as she looked at Liam, who was handling this situation with more grace than she might have done in his shoes.

Soft drinks were brought in and passed around, the sound of conversation not abating. At last, an older woman in a white coat cracked open the door to the room. "Mr. Salib," she said, "a moment, please." Tayib looked at his wife, and then at Dalia. Dalia could tell right away that this doctor would be the one to bring the news. "Excuse me," she said in halting Arabic, "we can clear out the room so that you can speak to my father and mother here. I think my mother would like to hear from you directly."

The doctor stared at her with disdain. "And you are their daughter?" she asked.

"Yes, excuse me doctor, my name is Dalia," Dalia responded. It seemed she had unintentionally offended the doctor. But she couldn't silently sit back and watch as her mother got put in the back seat of her own health care decisions. Dalia looked around and noticed the doctor wasn't the only one shocked by her suggestion. The visiting relatives looked equally taken aback.

"Well, it is not the normal practice in this country," the doctor continued, looking pointedly at Dalia, "for the doctor to discourage visitors. I can come back at another time and speak with Mr. Salib and his wife."

"We beg your pardon," Tayib now said to the room apologetically, "I'm sorry, it's just that Dalia's used to the patient hearing directly from the doctor. She doesn't mean any offense."

"No no, of course not," spoke up Sherif. "She's right, Aida, you should hear from the doctor. Why don't the rest of us go get some fresh air."

"Actually," spoke up another cousin, "it's getting late. I will see you tomorrow, God willing. Excuse us, everyone." Her words were friendly enough, Dalia thought, but that curt nod in her direction suggested that she had indeed taken offense.

The doctor, still at the door, stepped aside now as each relative said goodnight with a kiss on each cheek and, one after another, filed through. Liam leaned into Dalia's ear and said he'd be out in the waiting room. With his departure, there remained only Tayib, Aida, and Dalia. "Will you understand me if I speak in Arabic?" the doctor said now to Dalia, not unkindly.

"I'll do my best," Dalia replied. "It's most important that my mother understands. If there's something I don't understand, I will ask." Dalia wished they would just get on with the conversation.

The doctor pulled out a folder and opened it. "I'm afraid the results of the biopsy are not good," she began. "We had hoped for a benign tumour that we would be able to safely remove, but this tumour is not benign."

"So it's cancer?" Dalia asked, saying the last word in English.

"Yes, I'm afraid so," said the doctor, then added quickly, "now the next question is how likely it is that we can remove it all, and for you," she looked at Aida here, "to recover to complete health. Your health is good otherwise, and that will be a big advantage."

She paused here to look at each member of the family. Tayib was looking intently at her, holding tight to his wife's hand, but he was saying nothing. Aida was looking at the doctor and then at Tayib alternately, as if waiting for the good news in this to come. Dalia was looking down, stunned.

"Cancer of the breast," the doctor began. She stopped then began again, "The thing about this type of cancer is that, since it has spread as it has, we must decide and act quickly. If it was still just in her breast, then we could take it out, provide a course of chemotherapy to make sure it doesn't spread, and then keep monitoring it. And we will do that still. But this has metastasized to her spine, so before we do anything else, we need to remove the tumour there before it causes any damage to her spinal cord. The symptoms Madame Aida has shown—the back pain, the numbness in her fingers—are from increasing pressure on her spinal cord. This requires that we do this surgery as quickly as possible, and keep her as stable as possible until the surgery in order to avoid any permanent damage to her spinal cord."

"So either way, she's having surgery soon," Dalia said.

"Yes."

"How…how safe is this surgery?" asked Tayib.

"We would have an excellent neurosurgeon performing the initial surgery," replied the doctor. "But as with any surgery near the spinal cord, there are risks."

Dalia couldn't be so direct as to ask this doctor's advice on whether they should have the surgery somewhere overseas—even she wasn't oblivious enough to think that wouldn't offend. So instead she asked, "and, this surgeon, is he experienced? I mean to say, how often do surgeons here perform this type of surgery?"

The doctor seemed to understand the hidden question beneath it. "There are a few neurosurgeons who perform this surgery fairly often. But for Madame Aida, I might recommend Dr. Rifky Abdelmallek. He will look young to you, but he is quite skilled, and he was trained in Germany, where they have very advanced cancer care. He has performed similar surgeries many times."

Dalia made a mental note of this; there was that Germany connection again.

The doctor, perhaps misunderstanding their silence to mean they were unhappy with her proposal, continued, "Of course, you could be transported elsewhere for the surgery, but we would strongly discourage that, at least for the spinal surgery. You live in Australia, is that right?"

"Yes," Tayib said, finding his voice. "But..."

Dalia continued for him. She understood her role as the overly direct young woman who couldn't be blamed for the offense she was causing: she was not really Egyptian. "Is it—I mean would it be—safe to transport her? Is she stable enough?"

"She will be quite stable after the surgery, we hope," the doctor continued. "But with the location of this tumour, there is a very real risk that any wrong small movement could cause some damage to her spinal cord. The tingling in her fingers that she has reported suggests that it is far too close to her spinal cord for us to recommend a transfer. The key really is to decide quickly. Every day matters at this stage." She took in a breath, as if she wanted to say more, but then decided against it.

They sat in silence for a moment, each absorbing the news, and the decision before them.

"Well, if you would like," the doctor finally continued, "I can go see if Dr. Rifky is around so he can come in and speak with you directly. Perhaps that would be helpful."

Tayib nodded, and with a smile at her, said, "Thank you, doctor."

After the door had shut behind the doctor, Dalia looked at her parents. They both looked so worn out. The last few days must have been incredibly hard on them. A wave of sadness overcame her. This was not supposed to happen to them. They didn't deserve it.

Aida was the first to speak. "Tayib, what do you think?"

Tayib sighed, as if lost as to how to answer.

"I mean, you have that friend who is an oncologist. You worked together when you had that clinic together in Kensington. What's his name? Dr. Nagasaki?"

"Dr. Nakazawa," Tayib replied, not for the first time correcting her. "Yes, yes, I could get copies of the tests and images they've run here and see what he thinks. That's a good idea."

He made no moves, though, so after a moment, Dalia asked if they would mind if she went to check on Liam. They both shook their heads distractedly.

Walking down the hallway, Dalia passed a kiosk, staffed by a bored salesperson, and selling an odd assortment of tourist-oriented Pharoanic kitsch, and teddy bears and other gifts, presumably for patients. In Sydney, this might have struck her as funny, but she was too distracted by the news and preoccupied with finding Liam to take notice. She found Liam in the hallway, scrolling through his phone and trying to ignore the occasional stare, usually from a young woman. He was quite the looker, Dalia thought to herself with a smile. She would have to tease him about this later. But at the moment, slaying this tumour was the only thing on her mind. If they played their cards right, it would be gone, and life could go back to normal. If not...well, she wasn't going to go there. Not unless she had to. Not yet.

He looked up as she neared his chair. In a few sentences, she told him what the doctor had told them. He seemed to take it more like she thought she was supposed to. His face paled, he gripped her hands tightly. Then he said, "what do you need? Oh, I forgot. Someone brought these sandwiches up for us. I lready had one—I'm sorry, I was starved. They're quite good, by the way." Then he shook his head. "Listen to me go on. Other than these sandwiches, what can I do?"

"I don't know," she said. "I don't know what to do myself." Then after a moment she said, "Can you just stay here for a bit?"

Just then, she saw a young doctor walking by. He seemed to eye her appreciatively, as men did here. She had noticed more than a couple appreciative looks from some of the men on the plane as well. She knew she was not beautiful, but she was, as Liam had told her once, "striking." Her eyes were a deep brown and looked penetrating when her attention was focused. Her skin had bronzed deeply from the cruise. She didn't smile back at the doctor now, yet she couldn't take offense to it like she would have back home. She found it pretty flattering, actually. But then he caught sight of Liam, who, standing now, towered over her and pretty much everyone else in the room. A curtain dropped over his friendly look, and he gave them a nod as he walked on.

Liam, barely registering his presence, was in the middle of answering her. "Of course I can stay here. Are you sure there's nothing you want me to do in addition? I can maybe start doing some internet research on breast cancer. Or I can call my uncle who's a GP. He might know someone…"

"No, that's alright," Dalia responded. "My dad's calling an old colleague who's an oncologist back in Sydney." Then she added, "but maybe some research wouldn't be a bad idea. I'll come get you in a bit, alright?"

"Yes, of course," Liam said, giving her shoulder an encouraging squeeze.

Back in the room, Tayib was in the corner, talking to another doctor and asking for copies of the test results. Aida was looking sickly at the tea and biscuits an orderly had put in front of her. "I'm not supposed to eat anything," she said, smiling at Dalia. "That orderly — didn't look much older than sixteen — must have got his orders mixed up. Do you want it?"

Dalia shook her head.

"How's Liam?" her mother asked.

"Oh, fine. He looked shocked at the news. Says he's going to do some research on breast cancer."

The word hung for a moment between them. Dalia continued, "Did you and Baba decide anything?"

"Decide? No." Aida didn't speak for a moment. "I can't take the pressure of making a decision, on top of receiving this news. I can't. It's too much."

"Well," Dalia said, "maybe we can hear what Baba's colleague has to say, and then hear from this Dr. Rifky, and then decide."

As if on queue, the older doctor who had talked to them earlier walked in with another doctor. Dalia recognized him as the young doctor from the hallway. He was all business now, his attention focused on her mother, and then on her father. He began professionally, expressing regret over her illness, reassuring them they would do everything possible to get rid of the tumour safely, and that they had state of the art medical care here. 'Overachiever,' thought Dalia. 'He's exactly the type I hated being around in university. All the professional schools had at least a handful in each class, usually a lot more.' She tuned back in to the conversation he was having with her father. They were talking now in technical terms, Tayib asking for details about how the surgery would be performed, what tools and procedures would be used. She rarely saw her father in a professional light. It was disorienting, a little. As they talked, though, Dalia could tell from her father's expression that he was reassured by what the doctor was saying. At that moment, Liam knocked on the door and popped his head in. Dalia gave him a smile to invite him in, and he came over and stood beside her, giving her mother a smile as he came. Dr. Rifky stopped and asked, "Is he a family member?" Tayib replied, in Arabic so Liam wouldn't understand, "he's my daughter's fiancé." Dalia raised an eyebrow, but she knew it was the simplest explanation they could give, and they needed no distractions right now.

Dr. Rifky nodded an acknowledgement, and turned back to continue speaking with Tayib. His expression was both arrogant and, what, insecure? Dalia decided she did not like this man. He may be a good surgeon, but she would not be striking up any unnecessary conversations with him voluntarily.

Liam was going over now to her mother. "Hi Aida," he began. "How are you feeling?"

"Fine," she responded, "especially given that there's apparently something here" — she patted her chest — "that's trying to kill me." It might have sounded like a sarcastic remark, but Liam and Dalia both saw in her expression a determination not to give this thing any more weight than it already had. 'Poor Mama,' Dalia thought. 'She's not accustomed to life not being easy on her.'

Dr. Rifky was at the door now, murmuring, "Excuse me now — let us know if you need anything at all."

"Well," Tayib said, coming up to them. "He's a delightful young doctor. OK, maybe not delightful, but he does seem to know what he's doing. And, strangely, I knew his father a long time ago. We were good friends, actually. His name is Hany Abdelmallek. He graduated a couple of years ahead of me in medical school. Is living in Portugal now, apparently. Now, let me go see about getting those reports. I wonder if they will have them electronically, so I can send them to Dr. Nakazawa."

"If not, I can scan them in and send them electronically," said Liam. "I'm sure there'll be a business centre at the hotel where I'm staying. Here, let me come with you."

As they started walking out, Dalia could hear her father say to Liam, "Yes, I'm sorry about the hotel, Liam. Things here are different, you see — "

"Completely fine," Liam interrupted, adding lightly, "no worries at all. I understand. And look, it might be for the best if we need their scanner anyway."

Dalia felt a surge of love for this man. Had it been only 72 hours ago that she'd been on that cruise, wondering whether Liam was really all that important to her? She could be so reckless, sometimes, she thought. So ungrateful for the life she had.

30

Lisbon
2008

On Tuesday morning, Layla got up early and went downstairs for an early coffee and breakfast at the hotel restaurant. As she ate, she read the book she'd taken from her nightstand at home, where it had been collecting dust. The day before, she had wandered around aimlessly, lingering longer than necessary at kiosks selling trinkets, stopping for a coffee or some food when she was hungry, listening to conversations she couldn't understand around her, and simply revelling in the fact that she did not even have to check what time it was.

Now, Layla took a map of the city from the hotel concierge and began the day's exploration. She soon found herself in the Belem neighbourhood, and came upon a huge structure, stretching the remaining length of the block in front of her. She couldn't tell quite what it was: an old manor or museum, perhaps. Or a gate enclosing something? A garden? A church? Were there large churches in Lisbon? Wasn't this primarily Moor country? Her history lessons failed her. Her eyes went to a sign outside the main entrance. This was the Mosteiro dos Jerónimos, or, translated, the Monastery of the Jerónimos. Though it was still early morning, Layla could tell from the number of bus parking spots outside and signage that this was a popular tourist stop; cars and buses were already beginning to arrive.

Layla thought she'd better go in before it got too crowded.

Inside was a magnificent courtyard, surrounded by aged columns, the intricacy of which took her breath away. The style was Late Gothic Manueline, and Layla immediately thought of her father, who would drop bits of trivia when they would visit old buildings. She wondered if he had ever seen or studied this building. Yasmine, Layla was pretty sure, would not have studied it; her tastes leaned more modern. Still, she was sure her mother would have at least appreciated it.

Ahead was a set of doors that could only have led to a church. Walking through, Layla found herself in the sanctuary, the stillness covering her like a blanket. She had always loved the silence of old churches. As a child, she would sometimes stop at the church in her neighbourhood and sit inside. If she was lucky, the only people around would be outside, sweeping the walkway or talking together quietly, and she would have the sanctuary to herself. It comforted her to think about the many thousands of souls who had sat here, decades and even centuries before she or anyone she knew had been born, looking at the same light coming through the windows, the same images on the walls. And probably asking themselves the same questions she had asked. They were always her age, these imagined souls, their surroundings and circumstances different but their preoccupations and worries the same.

Now, she sat down and took a deep breath, as if clearing the street noise still in her ears from a few minutes ago. She thought about her kids, and her heart tugged with a longing for their sweet smell, their little arms wrapped around her. She thought too about catching Peter in a tender moment with the two of them; a new window in her heart opening to the person he was becoming. Her love for him, she was learning, would change dimensions as they lived and aged together. She felt a sudden pang remembering how, early in their life together, the two of them had loved to travel and explore new places, just as she had done through Lisbon's streets just minutes ago.

She remembered an earlier trip, solo — during her university years, actually — after which she had impulsively decided to write a book. It would be a novel about, fittingly, a traveller. She had had the summer to work on it, and she had gone about the task with a fervent gusto. A cousin who was visiting had marvelled at the volume of chapters which Layla had said she was producing every week. Layla had jokingly responded and said, "Yes, well, I can only write that fervently because I know it doesn't have to be evaluated yet."

Her mother had passed through the room just as Layla was saying this. "Yes, well, are you going to have it evaluated?" she had asked. Yasmine had been uncharacteristically quiet about Layla's endeavour all summer long; this was the first she had said about it.

"What do you mean, 'evaluated,' Mama? No, I'm not turning it in for a grade."

Her cousin had said, "Layla, I'm sure Tunt Yasmine just meant to ask if you plan to get it published."

Layla met her mother's silent gaze for a moment before answering. "We'll see. I'm not anywhere near that stage yet." Of course, Layla also didn't have the slightest clue how to go about getting it published, but like so many young people her age with a love for the written word, she wanted to try her hand at it, and sort out the business of getting it published at some vague point in the future.

Layla thought now that maybe she ought to dig it out of whatever box it was buried in. Or maybe once the kids grew a little older. She immediately felt a stab of apprehension. Did she really expect to publish a book? Did she really want to? What could she say that would resonate with others?

Everything and nothing, she thought with an ironic smirk. Her life experience was, in the end, so universal and so mundane. She had young children. She struggled to balance keeping her marriage vibrant and her career on the up and up (so much for that at the moment) and, above all, giving her children a happy childhood. Or, at the very least, to raise them to be well-adjusted individuals capable of leading productive, satisfying lives. Her struggles with toddler tantrums and meal ideas were just the beginning of the long road ahead, a road that many had travelled before and would travel after her, many most certainly more successfully than her. Her worries over the kids' developmental milestones, or her own sadly diminished sex drive, were nothing out of the ordinary, nothing worth noting.

Did she really want to write a book? No, Layla acknowledged. What she wanted was to do something of significance; something that had worth to others. The book had been a passing fantasy, a costume tried on during university, like so many others were, and discarded. Still, Layla found it strange that she herself had been and was still so undecided about her career when her mother had been so much the opposite. A pioneer of sorts: a female architect in an era when very few women went into architecture, or any of the maths or engineering fields. From what Layla could see, she had had a successful career. Did Yasmine ever question her choice? Had the sacrifices been greater than she had let on? Layla mused that they had never talked about this.

It was time, she thought again, to reconnect with her parents. It cost her too much: she missed conversations with her father, and doing things with her mother. She wanted her children to know their grandparents. Even if Yasmine would not accept her decision to leave work, she wanted to be a normal daughter, who had a normal, loving relationship with her mother. She wanted them to be able to have an uncomplicated afternoon together, cooking a meal, or going shopping like they used to.

For now, though, she continued to sit in the stillness of the sanctuary, allowing its stillness to comfort her. She casually observed the tourists who walked through, wondering where they had travelled from, and if any of them had left behind fuming husbands.

31

Cairo
2008

By the next morning, all was decided. Dr. Nakazawa
had agreed with the plan of the doctors at Dar El
Fouad hospital, adding that if Aida wanted, she and
Tayib could safely travel home to Australia and pursue
treatment there after the first surgery. Time really was
of the essence, apparently; the doctors wanted to
operate that very afternoon. After Dalia and Tayib had
talked with their relatives, who through their
connections had reported several successful surgeries
at the hands of this Dr. Rifky, they were feeling
confident to move forward. Aida, for her part, seemed
paralyzed by all the conversation around her. When
Dalia would ask her what she wanted, she would
answer that this was all happening so fast and that she
wished she had some time to absorb the diagnosis, or
what surgery meant. But then she would add with a
brave smile that maybe it was better to just dive in and
not give herself time to feel afraid.

The doctors had started emergency radiation on the
spinal tumour as soon as it had been diagnosed the day
before. Dr. Rifky had walked into her mother's room
just this morning, while she and her father had been
there talking to Aida. The young doctor reminded
Dalia of a popular athlete, come to bask in people's
admiration. Except of course he hadn't proven himself
yet, as far as Dalia was concerned. She prayed that
whatever confidence he had was merited. He was
reminding Aida now that she was not to eat anything

213

(as if she'd eaten in days!) and that they would be doing one final scan before the surgery. Then he began opining about the tumour, that while it was significantly sized, it was not the largest he had seen, and that the last scans showed that its edges were fairly well defined, meaning that it would be more likely that they would be able to remove all of it. Tayib started asking questions: medical questions that Dalia only superficially understood. Dr. Rifky's tone when responding was so condescending that Dalia stopped listening to his response. Finally, what was probably only minutes later but felt longer to Dalia, he excused himself.

"What an arrogant prick!" Dalia exclaimed once the door was shut. "I'm sorry, Dad, he may be a great doctor, but I really don't like him."

"Dalia," Tayib looked at his daughter with tired eyes, "it's just for this surgery that he will be involved, so it doesn't matter what a...prick...he is."

Dalia tried not to smile. Her father rarely swore, let alone in English slang.

"What matters is that he is an excellent surgeon," Tayib continued. "After the surgery, we don't have to see him again. Or maybe we will and you can tell him to his face what you think of him then. But let's just get through this. Please. Neither your mother nor I can take more uncertainty. Let's get this surgery over with, for her sake."

Dalia looked at her father, and then at her mother, who seemed like she was only half-listening to this conversation. Her father was right, of course. This man was indeed arrogant and condescending. But as Tayib had said many, many times, it was for God to judge man and grant forgiveness, not him. Still, Dalia couldn't understand how her father could remain so calm, so placating, in the face of such arrogance.

Then, Tayib said, "Dalia, it might be best if you keep your distance until after the surgery. I wouldn't want you to give our young surgeon a piece of your mind, and you know as well as I do that you're very close to doing just that."

Dalia looked at him with surprise. She needed to be at the hospital, surely. She couldn't leave during the surgery. Her father needed her here. How could she leave? And what if something were to go wrong? What kind of a daughter would that make her?

Tayib continued firmly. "Look, my cousin's apartment is just a few blocks away. Why don't you stay there? Maybe Liam can stay with you. And I'll call if I need you to come back; it would take you less than 5 minutes to walk back. Please, Dalia."

"But you can't wait alone."

"Dalia, has there been a minute we've been alone at this hospital? You are forgetting my cousins who have not stopped dropping in since you arrived. And Atef has been here since seven this morning. Of course, he is worried about his sister, as lots of people are. That's the point--I won't be alone! Not even if I wanted to be! Not that I do want to...Listen, Dalia, I promise, I will call at the first sign of anything out of the ordinary. OK?"

Dalia gave a resigned sigh.

"And actually, you can do something for me while you are there. When they emptied out our family's apartment years ago, a few boxes ended up at my cousin's house. He'd asked me, before all this happened, to look through them and see if there was anything I wanted. Could you look through and see if there's anything worthwhile in there? I doubt there will be, but it's worth a look. Could you do that for me? I'm sure he'd never say so, but those boxes must be taking up valuable space in the apartment, and I'm sure he'd be glad to have them gone."

Dalia, relieved to have a task, some way in which she could be helpful, agreed. While Tayib went to find Dr. Rifky to ask him another question about the surgery, Dalia spent a few last minutes chatting with her mother, and trying to distract her from the upcoming surgery. Her mother had never done well with needles or medications, let alone being sliced open. Dalia didn't particularly like the thought of it either, so the distractions were just as much for her sake as they were for Aida's.

Then, using the hospital phone, she called Liam back at the hotel and told him of the plan, asking him to meet her at the apartment. She then waited long enough for her father to come back and confirm that the surgery was still on. As she walked out, hoping not to run into Dr. Pricky, as she'd dubbed him, she passed a kiosk that had been set up in the hallway. The display was an odd assortment of ancient Egyptian artifact replicas, fluffy teddy bears, fake flower assortments, and other items that were presumably intended for guests visiting the hospital's patients. Dalia was too distracted to register this oddity.

Fifteen minutes later, she and Liam were ringing the doorbell of Tayib's cousin's apartment. He warmly welcomed them in. While his wife pressed them with tea and biscuits, feta cheese with sesame sticks, and fresh guava and watermelon, they talked about the surgery, which Tayib's cousin would be going to the hospital to wait out with Tayib, and about the weather, and about the shop on the corner that sold sugar cane

juice, their hosts telling them not to buy it there; they
didn't wash their cups well enough, and that after this
was all over, they would take them to a more reputable
stand so they could try aseer asab. Dalia remembered
loving it as a child, and had promised Liam that they
would have it before they left. All the frivolous things
they filled their thoughts with, Dalia thought at one
point, in order to try to reassure — or distract —
themselves while her mother lay in a hospital bed
nearby preparing to be sliced open. Dalia admitted to
them that her dad thought it would be best if she and
the surgeon stayed apart until after the surgery, which
amused their hosts. As their talk wound down, Dalia
mentioned the boxes Tayib had told her they had
kindly kept for them, and said she might as well go
through them while she was here. Tayib's cousin went
and got them while his wife continued to tell Dalia
stories about her grandmother.

The boxes were placed in another sitting room off to
the side of the living room, where the trees outside
kept the room dim, and Tayib's cousin excused himself
to go to the hospital. His wife also excused herself,
saying she was going to run to the market for some
vegetables, but that she would be back soon to start
dinner. On a day like today, the family would want to
gather together, she said.

Liam and Dalia found themselves alone all of a
sudden in an unfamiliar Cairene apartment, the sounds
of cars honking and people calling in the street below
muffled by the wooden shutters and retrofitted glass
on the windows. "Doing alright?" Liam asked, rubbing
her back.

"I don't know," replied Dalia. "As long as I keep
moving and don't think about the surgery, don't

question whether we made the right decision by staying, I'm alright."

"It will be alright," Liam said, and neither of them bothered to point out, though they both knew it, that this was more a hope than a certainty.

"OK, let's start on these boxes, shall we?" Dalia said. They opened the first one and began to go through them. Inside were assorted things, neatly piled. First were some old crocheted doilies, many yellowed with age and some starting to fall apart. Most of these, Dalia thought, would need to be thrown away, but she kept a few in case they meant something to her father. Her mother, she knew, considered such things not sophisticated enough to display, so she would never choose to put them around the house. Assuming, of course, that she came home, a voice said in Dalia's head. She quickly pushed aside the thought.

Next were some picture frames with old black and white photos in them. Some were wedding pictures, some were the enlarged portrait-style pictures of people who had passed away. Dalia recognized among them her grandparents' wedding photo, and one of her parents. Her grandfather's portrait was also there, and she remembered that it used to hang prominently over her grandmother's dining table. What must her father's childhood have been like, Dalia wondered, with he and his sister Amira looking up at this picture every night as they ate with their mother?

These photos they would obviously keep, as well as the frames that were still in good condition. They had plenty of space in their luggage; both she and Liam had packed so lightly. Next, Dalia moved onto a few pieces of what looked like valuable china, its painting delicate. Dalia herself had no taste for keeping such things in her home — they weren't very practical — but she loved looking at pretty china, and this set was indeed beautiful.

Below this was a bag of some kind. It was a large drawstring bag made of velvet, the kind used for jewellery. Stamped in Arabic script on the bag was, Dalia presumed, the name and address of the jeweller where it had come from. Dalia opened it up. Inside were perhaps a dozen charms, all of them identical. She pulled a few out. They had a hinge on one side, and when Dalia opened them, she saw two miniature frames on either side, one side holding what she presumed was a stock picture, the other a paper with what appeared just a few words — names maybe? — and numbers that might have been a date. Both papers had turned yellow and brittle. On the back was engraved, she thought, the same words and numbers. She read, in halting Arabic, the names of her grandmother, Iriny, and grandfather, Is-hak. There was a date there too: October 21, 1945. This must have been the date her grandparents were married. Were these engagement or wedding favours? They must have been, but Dalia thought the custom was to only give out sachets of Jordan almonds. Perhaps her grandparents were just decades ahead of their time, she thought with a smile. She would have to show these to her father.

Gradually, they went through the rest of the things. Dalia was making her best guesses about what her father might want from the boxes and what could be thrown away. At least an hour must have passed; she had heard their host returning from the market a little while ago. They were just finishing sorting what they would take and what would be thrown away when the phone rang, jolting Dalia back into the present. The

phone stopped ringing on the second ring, and Dalia
heard her name being called. Dalia jumped up and
went to where their host was holding out the phone to
her, trying to exhale slowly.

"Dalia," it was her father's voice, and she thought
she heard a note of jubilation.

"Yes, Baba, it's me. How did it go? Is it over?"

"It's over. Dr. Rifky says it went very well, and that
they are confident that they got all of the tumour and
that her spinal cord is fine. Mama is in recovery now; it
will be a few hours before she is awake and ready to
talk to us."

Their host was looking at Dalia for any sign. Dalia
gave her a smile and a nod, and got a big hug and a,
"thank God, thank God!" in return. Then she said to
Dalia, "your father must be hungry. Tell him we have
some dinner waiting for him. I am sure they aren't
going to let him see Aida for a while anyway. Tell him
to come!"

Dalia relayed the invitation, which Tayib,
surprisingly, agreed to. She remembered then that he
hadn't touched the breakfast someone had brought
him this morning, or much of last night's dinner, come
to think of it.

She went back to the room where Liam was waiting,
and in the moment of privacy that they had while their
host went back to the kitchen, sank into his chest,
feeling his arms wrap around her and inhaling his
beloved Liam smell, a smell that was part Palmolive,
part deodorant, and part laundry soap.

32

London
2008

On the morning of her departure from Lisbon, Layla was surprised and pleased to find that she missed her children. She didn't expect to miss them; after all, it really was just a few days. And anyway, didn't she always wish, when she was home with them, for just a few hours of peace? Here they were! But she was pleased. It proved, in some demented way — and to whom she couldn't say — that she was a worthy mother. She loved her children if she missed them. Well of course she loved them! Her restlessness was never about them; it was about whether she was happy with the way her life looked.

In any case, her departure date arrived just when she was ready for it to. Peter had eventually forgiven her for the surprise she had sprung on him, and her homecoming was sweet and perfect. The kids' chubby arms around her filled her with a sense that all was right in the world, and she found herself affectionately looking around at all the non-luxury, non-hotel knick knacks that made their house home. There was the tea mug that was the perfect size for which she had had to crochet a cozy so she could still hold it after the handle broke off, and Maggie's teddy bear that she insisted always wear a Minnie Mouse necklace, her many scarves hung in a small cascade of colour in their closet. These things were so familiar to her that she couldn't imagine home without them.

After the kids had gone to bed, Layla told Peter about her conversation with Hany Abdelmallek and about what she had done with the remaining days in Lisbon. He sat with her and listened as she told him about the meeting with Hany especially, his eyes showing surprise and questions, and finally, resolution.

It was time for the phone call to her parents; she had told herself she would make the call the very day she returned home. It was early evening in Cairo; her parents would not quite yet be sitting down for dinner. She dialled the number and waited for the double-ring of the phone. Peter used to say that when they were still engaged and he would call her from London and hear that dial, he would imagine that the phone was calling, "Lay-la! Lay-la!"

Now, her mother picked up. "Allo," she said, as if by stating it, she was not inviting any pleasantries.

"Mama, hello. It's me."

There was a moment of silence on the phone. Then, "Layla. I hope everything is ok?"

"Yes, everything is fine, thanks. We're in London."

"Yes of course you are. It's not as if you have a job here to return to." Layla could hear her mother stop herself. Then she continued, as if by doing so she could undo her jab, "Ok, I'm glad you're fine. The kids are ok? And Peter?"

"Yes, they're fine, thanks. How are you? And how is Baba?"

"Oh, we're fine. We're fine."

Yasmine didn't seem to know what else to say, so Layla continued. "Listen, can I talk to Baba? Is he there?"

"Yes, hold on." Then she said, "Layla, I'm glad you called."

Layla almost said, 'Why? So you can remind me how much you disapprove of my life?' But this was, she had resolved, a conciliatory call. So instead she said, "It's good to hear your voice." Hearing nothing in response, she continued, "I've been thinking about you and Baba a lot — and missing you."

"We haven't gone anywhere, Layla... we've missed you too."

Reconciliation, though, required resolution, even nominally, before there was peace. "Listen, Mama," Layla paused, not knowing how to continue. "I know you don't approve of my decision to leave work, but you are still my mother and I'd love to see you. Also, I don't think either of us wants the kids to be affected. Maybe you could come see them here in London." Layla knew, of course, that Yasmine would never come to London. Although she had retired, she still stayed active in the social world of Egypt's elite architects. Moreover, coming to London would be allowing herself to be hosted by her daughter and to depend on her — or impose, as she would see it. She would not do that.

"God willing," Yasmine responded vaguely. "Hold on; I'll go get your father."

Several seconds later, Tayib was on the phone. "Layla, habibti, my beloved daughter, how are you?"

Layla's throat closed up at the sound of her father's warm voice. "Baba, I've missed you. How are you?"

"Thank God, we're fine, we're fine," he replied. "And you? How are the kids? And Peter? How's his research going?"

"It's going fine. It's keeping him busy, but he likes it."

"And you? How are you finding London? Are the kids keeping you busy?"

"Always. Never a quiet moment with them. I hope you'll get to see them soon."

"I would love to, Layla. I've really missed those kids."

"They've missed you." There was a moment of silence as they each basked in the joy of hearing each other's voices.

"Listen, Baba. I'm actually calling because I've been contacted by an old friend of yours, and I have a lot to talk to you about." She paused, "Does the name Hany Abdelmallek ring a bell?"

"Hany. Yes, of course. Hany. We lived on the same street as kids, and we were close playmates, and classmates. We ended up parting ways; he went into medicine."

"You're not upset that he contacted me?"

"Upset? Why would I be? A little surprised, perhaps. I don't know why he would have gone to the trouble of tracking you down when I've been right here."

"He seems to think you two had a long-standing disagreement. Not that he seems to have any anger towards you now."

"Well why would he? No, I wouldn't say we had a disagreement. There had been a small incident with your mother, but that was years ago and I thought we had cleared it up."

This sounds scandalous, Layla thought.

"Nothing like that!" Tayib said, as if reading his daughter's thoughts. "No, it was a few years after we were married, and our careers, both mine and your mother's, were still just getting established. We were working very hard, both of us, to make names for ourselves. And, well, you know these doctors. Some of them have gone into medicine for the money and the prestige, and others out of some enlarged sense of altruism. Well, Hany, he was this second kind, almost to a fault. He had a patient who loved him and had mentioned that he was looking for a young architect to design his vacation home in this exclusive area outside Alexandria. Well, Hany thought he would do us a favour, and he recommended your mother."

Tayib paused here, remembering all those years ago. "I was furious," he said, a smile in his voice.

"Why?" Layla asked. She'd long since learned not to assume her father's motivations.

"Well like I said, I was young," Tayib said. "A part of me was jealous that my old classmate (all the girls back then thought he was so handsome and tall) was making a move on my wife, but I knew he wasn't. He really was trying to help us by helping her. No, I think that what made me angry was that he had not recommended me instead, and in a moment of anger, I resolved to stop speaking to him, and then I just never found the—what, humility?—to undo it."

Layla smiled.

"You see, I was not then the forward thinking father you have today," he said with a smile.

"Of course not," she joked back. Then she added, "but it doesn't seem likely that this would have caused such a rift. I mean, did Mama take the job?"

"She did, actually. We had a big fight about it—I doubt Hany ever knew about that—but then she took it. And it turned out to be instrumental in her career. Her reputation spread significantly from that one project. So what did Hany want? Why did he contact you?"

"Well, you're never going to believe this," Layla said, sitting down herself as if preparing. Then she told him everything, from the first letter that Hany sent, to meeting him in Lisbon and his recounting of his father finding the letter and showing it, years later, to Hany, to the letter from her grandfather that she now had.

"Unbelievable," her father said, after a pause. "I remember of course, those charms. We might even still have a few tucked away somewhere. I don't know how their family's maid would have gotten one sold to her, but it's very possible one was stolen, from us or from one of my parents' wedding guests. Unbelievable."

Then he remembered the most important part. "And this letter. You say you have it with you now?"

"Yes," said Layla. "Do you want me to read it to you?"

"Yes, sure," her father replied. "But I want to see if it looks like my father's writing. I have a few other things he's written. We could compare to make sure there isn't some mistake."

"Yes, sure," Layla said. "I can scan it in and email it to you. Or better yet, we could meet and I'll show it to you."

"A meeting would be good, Layla."

"Yes," she quickly agreed, and again, "yes, we have to meet." Finding the letter, she continued, "Ah--here's the letter."

She read it to her father then, and in the reading, imagined what her grandfather's voice must have sounded like had he been saying these words to her father. When she was done, she could hear only silence on the other end.

"I don't believe this," Tayib finally said. "Could this really have happened?"

"I was shocked by it," Layla responded. "But then again, I never met Gedo Is-hak. Is this the kind of thing he would have done?"

"Actually, yes," said Tayib. "It was." Layla could hear the smile, and also the longing, in her father's voice.

"Do you think Teta Iriny ever knew about this? Or Tunt Amira?" Layla asked.

"I highly doubt my mother would have kept something like this, so I don't think she knew. Neither would Amira have hidden this."

"Do you think—I mean, this would have been decades ago now. Do you think the firm is even still around? I have to wonder if this firm, or whatever it is, is still run by anyone we can track down."

"My family's been with the same solicitor firm since at least my grandfather's generation. Your mother and I still use them. I'll ask them; I'm sure that's who my father would have been referring to."

Layla marvelled at this. What else about her parents' lives and their affairs did she not know, even though they saw each other all the time—or used to, anyway? She wondered how much of this gap was because she didn't like to think about the things she would have to know after they were gone, or even when they aged, and how much was because they still saw her as too young, or too carefree, to need to know all this. How much of it was by her choosing, and how much of it was by theirs? She thought again about the way she'd insisted since she and Peter had decided to come to London that they support her choice. Was this not in itself a pretty childish reaction? Perhaps she had given them plenty of reason over the years not to think she was as grown up as her age would suggest.

A few minutes later, father and daughter hung up, agreeing to plan to see each other soon. Layla looked around her. A light was still on over the sink in the kitchen; it otherwise looked like Peter had gone to bed. After checking on the kids and turning off the lights, she found him reading in bed. 'Well?' his eyebrows were raised in question as she closed the door behind her and started undressing. She told him about the phone conversation, dwelling for a moment on her short conversation with her mother. Then she told him about her father's recollection of Hany and his stunned reaction to the letter. She told Peter that they had raised the topic of meeting soon, but not how that would happen.

"Do they have any interest in coming to London?" Peter asked.

"Baba might," Layla responded, then, after a pause, "but I don't think he or I could convince Mama to come. And he wouldn't come without her. Not because they have to travel together all the time, but because he wouldn't want to create any more tension between her and me, or look like he was taking sides, by coming alone."

Peter smiled at this. Layla was, of course, exactly right.

"Well," he said. "It's been months since we've been, and I've always got my faculty duties to keep up on. Maybe we can arrange for a short trip—a week or two back to Cairo—in the coming month. What do you think?"

Layla paused for a minute. She wanted to see her father, and she missed her hometown and her friends.

It would be great to see them. But it would be so much easier if her parents would come. Travel with toddlers made for lots of luggage and crying. She hated when practicalities got in the way of preferences.

"Let me talk to him and see first if I can't convince them both to come. But then again, maybe if we're going to need to meet with the firm or whatnot, it would make more sense to be there."

"We're coming up to a point in the research where they could probably do without me physically here for a bit. I have some research to do; the library at the AUC is just as conducive as here to getting it done. I'll talk to them about it tomorrow," he said with a smile.

As they turned off the lights, Layla thought how good it was to be back in bed next to Peter, with the kids just down the hall, and remembering the Lisbon smells and sights she had just left that morning, she offered up thanks, for Lisbon, for Peter, for the kids, for her life, just as it was.

33

Cairo
2008

Aida was recovering well from the surgery. The oncologist team who was now caring for Aida had said that with a second surgery on the breast tumours and a successful course of chemotherapy, her mother could recover. She might be one of the lucky ones; usually cancer that had metastasized so far was difficult to treat. She had to stay in the hospital several more days, just so the doctors could watch for complications from the surgery.

Dalia and Liam would spend the mornings talking with Aida and Tayib, or watching television or movies together. The two described to Aida and Tayib this one particular school they looked forward to walking by every morning — or at least they thought it was a school. One day, after smiling and waving hello to the same cluster of girls every morning for a few days, they finally approached the gate and struck up a conversation with the woman they assumed was a teacher.

She explained that this was no ordinary school. These were young girls whose families, if they were still alive, lived in Egypt's countryside. The girls were boarded here; a concept completely foreign in a country as family-centred as Egypt. They had come here because their families had wanted a better life for them, or because they had no family to speak of. To be admitted, each of these girls had had to pass an entrance exam; the mission of this school was to prepare Egypt's untapped intellectual resources, in the form of these unusually bright but underprivileged girls, for admission to the country's, and indeed the world's, universities. But alas, the woman said, the philanthropist who had founded the school and continued to provide money for its upkeep had fallen on hard times, and the principal was working hard with the board to find a way to keep the school open beyond the current academic year. Since that day, Liam and Dalia had stopped to talk to the girls for a few minutes as they walked to the hospital, often bringing the girls some snacks or small presents and patiently enduring the girls' giggles over their accents as they tried to chat with them in Arabic.

It reminded Dalia of a commitment she had back home in Sydney. Years ago, she had got involved in a mentoring program, and had never given it up, despite how increasingly difficult it had become to find the time for it. But she found that she enjoyed working with teenagers and hearing, through their accounts, echoes of the same tumultuous feelings she had had in those years. She was finding that the sense of good winning out, of obstacles overcome, that she didn't always find at work, she would often find here, with her mentees. But each year, she got older and they stayed the same age. She recognized the music they liked and the lingo they used less and less. Maybe it was time to give that up. The coordinator for it would be crushed, Dalia knew, if she left the program, but maybe it was time for a change.

34

Cairo
2008

The first morning back in Cairo, as had been their
habit for as long as Layla could remember, she and
Tayib met early out on the balcony. They watched the
street below them gradually fill with pedestrians and
cars, a glass cup of steaming, sweetened tea in front of
each of them. As a child, Layla's cup had held mostly
warm milk with maybe a teaspoon of tea. As she'd
grown, the ratio of tea and milk had gradually
reversed, until she no longer took any milk at all,
preferring it strong and sweet, like her father.

They had a meeting with the lawyers later that day.
When Tayib had called the firm a couple of weeks
before, they had said they did have some paperwork
for a plot of land, and that, in addition to Amira, whose
presence they said would be beneficial, they would
also call one of their retired partners who had been
practicing when Tayib's father had first made this
arrangement. "He must be in his 90s now," Tayib was
now speculating to Layla, "or at the very youngest, in
his late 80s."

Their musings were interrupted by an insistent tap at
the balcony door. Inside, a tousle-haired Maggie was
looking at them, demanding to be let out. They opened
the door for her, and she sat, alternately on her
grandfather's and her mother's laps, watching the
stirrings of the street below. It was amazing, Layla
thought, how the busier their surroundings were, the

quieter children became. Cairo streets were excellent for occupying the kids' attention.

After breakfasting on feta cheese, mortadella slices, and bread, everyone got dressed. Peter and Yasmine would take the kids to a nearby park while Layla and her father met with the lawyers. Layla and Tayib arrived just a few minutes before Amira. The three were greeted by a distinguished looking man in his 40s, one of the associates, and a meticulously dressed man who did indeed look no younger than 85. He explained that he had met with Tayib's father those many decades ago, and that when the firm had called him the other day to ask about this case, he had asked to come in. So struck had he been at the time about the unusual arrangement, and now, he said, he hoped they didn't mind his coming in, even though he was no longer with the firm.

Of course they didn't mind, and listened to him talk about how Tayib's father had actually made two arrangements, one in the instance Tayib got the letter that he got, and one in case Tayib didn't. The firm had the other letter.

"How would I have found this other letter?" Tayib asked, intrigued.

"We have it here at the firm," the old lawyer explained. He looked at the younger lawyer. "It was in the file, wasn't it?" They pulled it out and, with Tayib's permission, opened the brittle envelope and read it together. It was indeed, the same message, but it addressed Tayib the man, not Tayib the boy, making no reference to the task he was so smart to have completed.

"And when would you have shown me this?" Tayib said.

"Well, your father was never quite clear about that. You see, he was supposed to come in to finalize that detail and make some other, unrelated arrangements. But the accident that took him, God rest his soul, happened before he could come in."

"And how was I supposed to have found this letter that I've brought you, other than by this strange coincidence and through my daughter. I was supposed to have received it as a boy."

"I'm not entirely sure," the old man said. "He had mentioned something about putting a challenge before you, not expecting that a boy your age could meet it, but that's all he said."

Not for the first time, Tayib wished his father had lived into Tayib's adulthood, or even into his teenage years, where Tayib would remember so much more of him, let alone benefit from the guidance his father could have given. Ever since Layla had come to him with this news, he had felt like he was walking around his own past mostly blind-folded.

Layla brought it back to the present. "So now, what do we know about this plot today?"

At this, the younger lawyer stepped in, happy to have his role in this intriguing story. "This is where Dr. Amira comes in. Ever since your mother's passing, God have mercy on her soul, Dr. Amira has overseen the farming of this land and has continued to put the proceeds in the trust account we set up with your father, Mr. Tayib."

"And what can you tell us about this account? Other than my sister, who accesses it? Who controls it?" Tayib asked. Layla caught Amira give her brother of sharp look at the tone of his questioning.

"The account is with one of the bigger banks here in Cairo. We have been the trustees of it until now and have worked with the bank to invest the funds in it according to your father's directions. Now, we would turn its management and proceeds over to you—well, to Madame Layla, actually. It is yours to do with it as you wish. We are still happy to be the primary contact with the banker of course, if you prefer."

With this, the lawyer slid a small stack of papers across the end table towards Tayib and Layla. It was a recent bank statement of the account. Tayib and Layla's eyes grew big. Untouched, this account had grown exponentially over the years.

Tayib just stared down at his lap. He had never wanted for money as an adult, but neither had he ever had anything close to this amount. What would he have done had he known about this thirty years ago? How might he have lived his life differently? And why did his father make it so hard for him to find out about it?

"When would you have told me about this account had we not come to you with this letter?" Tayib asked again, a hard edge in his voice. He looked at both his sister Amira and at the attorney.

Amira opened her mouth to answer, but the younger lawyer spoke up. "Well, there's another piece to the instructions."

"Mr Tayib," interjected the older lawyer, "your mother, God rest her soul, knew about this plot and knew what your father had intended. Since you had not received the letter you now have, the plot technically passed to her when your father passed away, you understand."

"Yes...go on."

235

"About 25 years ago maybe, well after the time you and your sister, Madame Amira, had finished university and established yourselves in your careers, she had come to us and said that she did not think that either of you would need the money, so she did not want you to know about it. If you were to ever come to need it, or to find out about it and ask for it, she would have, she said, made it available to you. But if not, then she wanted it preserved for her grandchildren, with the same condition that they had to work in order to access it. In her will, she asked that Madame Amira take over the management of the account until the time came for her grandchild, Madame Layla, to take it over."

Tayib shook his head, unable to think clearly. "She never said anything to us. Why wouldn't she say anything? And how could you not have told me about this, Amira?"

"How would you have lived your life differently had you known?" the old attorney interjected quietly. "I do not ask you to answer that; just to think about whether your parents had perhaps had some purpose in mind when they arranged this. And Madame Iriny specified in the will that Amira should keep this account secret until the time came."

"But we were tight on money growing up. We were not poor, but neither did we have any luxuries. Why would she not have used it then?"

"She wanted it preserved for the purpose your father had set aside: for you to live the life you chose. He could not have known, when he planned this, that he himself would not be around to provide for your childhood more comfortably."

"And what about Amira? Does she have a similar account?"

"No," Amira answered quietly. Tayib looked at her.

"Madame Amira has a generous inheritance from an account established when she was born," continued the older attorney, "but no arrangement like this. You will forgive our generation, Mr. Tayib," said the old lawyer, "but back then we assumed that women would marry and have children...even if they worked, it would not be the family's primary income. Egypt has changed much in the intervening decades."

Layla heard this last sentence and was quiet. Had Egypt really changed that much? Her mother had pushed her toward the opposite life: that she have a successful career regardless of her husband, and yet Layla had chosen the older traditions. She had agonized about giving up her work, and she knew she was fortunate to have had a choice.

Had she agonized though? Not really; any satisfaction she got from her work projects was a hollow substitute for the kind of satisfaction she got from putting order and purpose to her own life, and given the chance, to others'. Layla remembered when Peter was finishing his PhD and was trying to organize the piles of documents and artifacts he was thinking he should keep. She'd sorted and asked questions, until his years of study and research had been neatly put away in two boxes. It had been very rewarding, and would have been, just as much, she thought, if he wasn't her husband.

She realized with a start that her father, aunt, and the two lawyers were concluding the meeting, her father thanking them and assuring them that they would be in touch soon once they had talked as a family. With a smile and a mumbled thank you, she got up also and caught up with Tayib and Amira. Together, they walked out of the office and down the hall to the building's main door, where, outside, the chaos and life of Cairo's streets greeted them.

35

Cairo
2008

The charms which Dalia found were indeed wedding favours from my parents' wedding. She showed them to me when we came together with a dozen other relatives for dinner after Aida's surgery. Over platters of grilled fish and corn, seasoned rice, feta cheese and pita bread, tomato slices seasoned with salt and cumin, and cooked lentils, Dalia's older relatives told her the story that I'd so loved hearing as a child.

In those days, the standard wedding favour was a sachet of melabess ("Jordan almonds," as Dalia knew them) wrapped in tulle and tied with a ribbon and a card bearing the bride and groom's names, or perhaps a ceramic figurine bearing the same card. But Dalia's grandmother Iriny had insisted that Is-hak and her wedding favour be unique. "Something people will actually use and remember," she'd repeated. And so the charms had been ordered. Sitting at the table now, my sister Amira added that our mother would still, many years later, reminisce about the favours at her wedding, especially if she actually saw a friend or family member wearing it. (Most didn't: they kept it on a shelf in a cabinet, a memento along with all the other sachets of melabess from other weddings over the years.)

The conversation turned eventually to news of other relatives and inquires about those not present. Aida's brother Atef and his wife were there, having sat with me through the surgery and now talking comfortably, visibly relieved. As the conversation wound down, Atef pulled me aside, telling me that he would head back to the hospital to sit for a little bit longer, even though Aida was presumably still in recovery. He said he would call me when he was leaving so I could go wait at the hospital.

The hour was growing late. As our host and a few of the women, Dalia among them, cleared the table, the room grew quiet again, those of us remaining remembering what event had gathered us together in the first place. As some began to leave, Amira went down the hall and summoned Dalia to come with her. She then motioned to me to follow them into the small sitting room where, hours earlier, Dalia and Liam had gone through those boxes. Indicating where we could sit down, she sat down opposite.

"There's something I need to tell you about," she began, after a pause that lasted just long enough to create a little discomfort.

"I have been waiting to tell you this for some time," she continued. "Tayib, you remember your old friend, Hany Abdelmallek, from our old neighbourhood?"

"Of course," I said, remembering too that Hany had practically been Amira's fiancé, until his decision to emigrate had ended their relationship.

"Well, there's something that he told me back then — something that he gave me, actually — that I never told you about."

I waited for her to continue, though I couldn't imagine what this story might have to do with our present circumstances.

"So when Hany was younger, a really strange thing happened in his family. Their maid came in one day with a charm — the very one from our parents' wedding, although she didn't know that — and asked Hany's mother if it was valuable. Some guy off the street had duped her into buying it, assuring her it was worth a lot of money. How he got a hold of it, who knows. But the interesting part of the story is that there was a letter tucked away in one of the picture frames. Hany's father kept this letter for years, and then gave it to Hany when he was maybe in university. Hany gave it to me when we were...well, when we were getting to know one another.

"Anyway, this letter turned out to be from our father and addressed to you, Tayib. It spoke of a plot of land that he was giving you because, by finding this letter, you had proven yourself worthy of this gift. Anyway, I showed this letter to Mama, and she explained that yes, she knew about the land, and that it had gone to her when Baba died.

"Apparently our father had owned a large plot of land in the fertile Delta region, and its crops and resulting investments had reliably produced enough income for a family to live comfortably on. Enough, actually, to live quite lavishly by Egyptian standards, but," here Amira gave a smile and nod to Dalia, "probably just comfortably by Australian standards."

"Of course, neither you or I knew about this letter when Baba died, and then the plot passed to Mama. Then when she died, she left very clear instructions that the plot was to go to her grandchild, Dalia, with the condition that she work in order to have access to it."

I stared at my sister. "Why," I said finally, "are you telling us about this now? Why didn't you tell me about this when Hany gave you the letter? In the name of God, Amira, it's been more than 30 years!"

"I know, Tayib," Amira said, a mixture of regret and defiance in her voice. "I almost told you. But you were in the middle of emigrating, and I didn't know what it meant, this letter—"

"What did it say?" I interrupted.

"That's the interesting thing," Amira said. "It said you were a boy who was wise beyond your years to have obtained this letter, and that because of that, Baba was gifting you with this plot of land. The catch was that, for you to have received the proceeds of the land, you had to work, even if you didn't need to. The money would free you to have any career you wanted, regardless of how lucrative it was, or not. That was his gift to you. You could live the life you wanted, without concern for whether you could provide for your family. Mama replicated that condition when she willed it to Dalia."

"And why didn't you tell me about it then?"

Amira sighed before answering. "I don't know, Tayib. I was in such shock at first. And as I said, you were newly married and making your plans for Australia. So I showed the letter to Mama. I wanted her to decide what to do with it. And do you know what she said? She said that she knew about this, and that the money would be there for you if you needed it, but that she didn't want to tell you then because she wanted you to make your plans without any obligations or influences. Baba had meant it as a gift to free you, not to bind you, she said. She worried that if you knew about it, you might have felt obligated to stay in Egypt. So that's why we never told you."

"And you've been managing this land all these years?" I asked.

"After Mama died, I took over the management of it. Let me tell you, I have learned a lot about agricultural practices because of this. But yes, every year, I have the proceeds directly deposited into a fund that's in our family's name — or I guess in Dalia's name, according to Mama's wishes."

Dalia, who had until now been listening with rapt attention to this story, suddenly sat up, exclaiming, "say again?"

"The proceeds of the plot belong to you, Dalia. Again, the only condition is that you continue to work."

We were all silent for a few moments, absorbing what had just been said. "Was there a similar arrangement for you, Tunt Amira?" Dalia finally asked.

Amira smiled at her niece. "I was well taken care of; our parents left me more than I needed. But no, there was no plot with which to provide for my family." After a light snicker, she added, "maybe it's just as well, then, that I never had a family for whom to provide."

"Anyway," she continued, "before Mama died, she said there was another letter that Baba had left with the lawyers in case the first one never turned up and he didn't have the chance to tell you, Tayib, himself once you'd grown up. I think that letter also concerns the plot of land, but it's sealed, and none of us have read it — Mama and I thought you should be the first to read it. I know we should have shown it to you years ago, but once Mama knew that you and I were both financially secure and wouldn't need the money from that land, she didn't think you needed to know about it and asked me to wait until after her passing to tell you. And now, you and Dalia's both being here in Egypt presented the first good opportunity."

After a moment, she went over to her purse, which had been sitting in a corner, and pulled out a sealed envelope, brown around the edges. "This is the second letter that Baba had given to the attorneys. It was with the paperwork from the attorneys from when Mama died. It was still sitting in my apartment. I have the other letter that Hany gave me in a bank safety deposit box. I'm sorry; I didn't get a chance to collect it before now, but of course I will give it to you before you leave."

Amira sat back down and looked at me. Dalia, too, was looking at me. I wondered what it would be like to see my father's hand writing, addressed to me, after all these years. Carefully, I opened the letter.

My dearest son Tayib,

I don't know when you will read this letter, but I hope that it finds you well and grown. The person who gave you this has likely told you about the inheritance that comes with it, but even more important is the advice I would like to leave you with. You see, my dear son, you probably already know — I hope life has been good to you and shown you — that the world is entirely open before you. But you can only choose one path, one adventure, at a time. Never make a decision that you will not be proud of when you are old. Aim to live a life that you can look back on with pride.

When I was a boy, my father left for me a large plot of land that has been used to grow some of the country's finest cotton for generations. Upon your receiving this letter, this land will be yours to do with as you wish. The annual proceeds of it are enough that you can live comfortably — if not richly — and do anything you want without regard for income.

There is, however, one condition. Our family has always believed in the value of work. It gives us purpose, and makes our days on this earth worthwhile. So, although this land generates enough money that you won't need to work, you must nevertheless work in order to receive it. So do something that you enjoy, without regard for how much money you make.

This freedom to choose the work you do is perhaps the best gift that I can think to give you, and I am happy to be able to give it to you now.

With all my love,

Your father Is-hak

I stared at the letter, my eyes watering. It had been so long since I had thought about my father's voice, but reading these words, I remembered that voice as distinctly as if my father had just spoken the words. I remembered too the abyss of sadness and terror that I had felt after my father died, every time I closed my eyes or found myself in a room alone. This letter was like something that had pushed its way out of the dimension of time, reaching in to enclose me with a feeling of security. 'You are loved,' it said. 'I have always looked after you, have always watched over you. You are my son, and I have always and will always love you.'

I took another deep breath. I thought about all the years that had passed since that dreadful day that we had lost my father, and almost lost Amira. It was a lifetime ago, and yet this letter had managed to cast itself across the years, to this place on this day, where my wife now stood on the boundary of the living. Time didn't matter. My father would always love me. Yet time was everything. The life we might all have led had my father lived would have been another life entirely. I ran my hand over the letter, feeling its frailness against my fingers, like a sand castle that, once dried, lost its form at the slightest pressure, crumbling back into the relentless sea.

PART FIVE

36

Cairo
2008

Dalia was exhausted. They had been in Cairo for just about a week, and the magnitude of everything that had happened these last days, combined with the jet lag for which she had made no accommodation, had finally caught up with her. She thought, not for the first time, that she ought to take a cue from Liam. Unlike her, he had begged off for afternoon naps these past couple of days.

But she could not unplug herself enough from the intensity of her mother being in hospital to even think about taking a nap. Instead, Dalia and her parents spent hours discussing whether to stay in Cairo for the remaining treatment or return to Australia. After the success of the first surgery, they trusted that the Egyptian doctors would be able to handle the next surgery and competently administer the chemo. It was, actually, partly a matter of finances: in Egypt, the private hospital fees would be paid out of pocket. In Australia, of course, treatment would be covered. It was also a question of where the family — especially Aida — would be more comfortable. After much discussion, Aida decided she wanted to return to Australia. If the chemo didn't work, she reasoned, she wouldn't second-guess her decision for treatment in Australia, as she would if she remained in Egypt.

When people asked her why she didn't remain in Egypt, Aida responded — truthfully if not fully — that she wanted to be in her own home and in her own bed. Dalia and Liam, on the other hand, had surprised her parents by telling them that they would stay another week or two in Egypt. Both of them were quickly falling in love with Cairo. They had both talked to their bosses. Liam's boss had told him to take off as much time as he liked. Dalia's had been a bit more vague; she had a lot of vacation time logged, but it sounded a little like the firm was keen to have her back. Dalia had organized with them that, once she returned to Sydney, she would take days off on the days of her mother's treatments and surgeries, relieving Tayib and making sure someone was always with Aida. In the meantime, she and Liam would explore this city that neither of them knew much about. They were exploring unfamiliar sides to each other, too. Liam would comment on how Cairo Dalia was ready to laugh and rib others with jokes, unlike his Sydney Dalia, always discussing something intense. For her part, Dalia was surprised to find that Liam, even though he physically stuck out everywhere he went, had gotten quite comfortable with Cairo's noise and pollution. He had practiced his customary greeting, in accented Arabic, that he gave to the fuul vendor every morning where he got his breakfast. He had taken a particular liking to the fuul, feigning shock that Dalia had never introduced him to this particular dish.

Every morning since they had arrived in Cairo, Dalia and her aunt Amira would leave Amira's apartment at the same time. Amira would go to work, and Dalia would swing by Liam's hotel and together, they'd walk through the city's crowded sidewalks, the smells of coffee and bread baking mixed in with cigarette smoke and diesel. They usually went to the hospital, but one day, she left him at the hotel, where he would spend the morning catching up on some work remotely.

Walking down the street, she was thinking about her own duties at work when she noticed, ahead of her, some figures ducking in from the sidewalk into a gate. As she approached, she saw it was a church. Without thinking why, she ducked in behind them and went inside. A liturgy was underway, and Dalia recognized by the prayers that it was almost over. She stood in the back, looking ahead of her at the sea of scarves covering the women's heads on the right side of the church, the men's dark heads on the left. Shoes, some lined up carefully, others kicked off and abandoned, could be seen by the back door and along the side walls. The scent of incense covered her, as if the very fragrance had warmed the winter air that followed her in. Suddenly, Dalia was transported to the hundreds of times she had stood in just such a liturgy, surrounded by these very sights and smells, the tunes familiar and uniform. It was only the language that varied; combined Arabic and Coptic in Egypt, the addition of English in Sydney. She remembered with a smile when she and the other teenaged girls would get shushed for whispering too long and too loudly during the liturgy.

There was movement as the congregants went to partake in communion, the flow of people in the aisles creating something that only those who had seen this ritual before could see some order in. Suddenly, Dalia felt a hand on her shoulder. Glancing to her left, she saw Noora, from the boarding school, smiling shyly at her. Dalia smiled back, glad to see her. They stood silently together until the service was concluded and the priests had come down the aisles spraying a blessing of holy water on them.

When the rest of the congregants filed out of the church, Dalia sat down in the back pew with Noora and a couple of the other girls who had come with her. The girls asked her what the churches were like in Australia, and then the conversation drifted to life overseas. Did everyone really live in big houses? They'd heard that everyone was rich: was everyone rich? Did her parents approve of her being engaged to a 'foreigner' ('fiancé' was the word she and Liam had used, out of convenience, to explain him)? Had it been hard to study law? (They didn't care that she was agonizing over whether to be a barrister; to them, the distinction didn't matter.)

Dalia found herself sprinkling her answers with praise of Egypt. At first, it was out of a practiced sense of diplomacy, but as she listened to their eager questions, she found herself saddened by their romanticizing of life outside their world. "You know," she said, "my mother always used to say that the thing she missed most about Egypt was her friends and her neighbourhood. There, no one just stops by the house to say hi. And you know what? I understand now what she means. You girls shouldn't take for granted the friends you have."

"The only people who stop to ask about us are the people who remember us and feel sorry for us. You are lucky to have family," Noora replied. "If you don't have family, this country is just like your country." The other girls shifted in their seats, their silence confirming this sentiment.

Dalia looked at these girls. At their age, her biggest worry had been whether she could buy a sweater she wanted. These girls' faces spoke of a childhood ended too soon. She tried to imagine her life without her family, without her mother. She hadn't allowed herself to really contemplate what it might have meant to lose her mother. She remembered with not a small pang of guilt how many times she had turned down dinner with her parents because she had work to do. 'And if you do have family,' Dalia thought, 'maybe any place is enough.'

Days later, over breakfast, as Liam was downing his second fuul sandwich and Dalia was sipping her cup of steaming, sweetened hot tea, Dalia announced she was ready to go home. "I could never live here," she told Liam, as if continuing a conversation they had never actually started. "I miss Sydney too much. I miss work. I miss my parents. I miss my apartment. I miss the foods we eat. Do you know I even miss the guy at that Thai takeaway place around the corner who always knows my order? I've loved being here, but I'm ready to go home, where I have a real place in the world, or at least my little corner of it."

"I bet you don't miss me having the television tuned to Rugby Union all the time," Liam joked back.

Dalia shook her head with a wry smile. She did, in fact, miss the comfort of that familiar sound, even though she would never admit it.

37

Cairo
2008

Machines were beeping, tubes were running along and across his body and his blood-stained face. Solemn-faced white coats and scrubs were moving around efficiently and urgently. On his chest, they were putting those electric paddles they always showed in the movies, his body springing upwards every time they sent a surge through. Layla just stared. This could not be happening.

Seemingly minutes ago, Tunt Amira, her father, and she had emerged from the street on which the solicitors' offices were located to find, in front of the park where they had left Yasmine and Peter with the kids, an ambulance and a gathered crowd. Layla had seen her mother looking worried, and her stomach had clenched. It was one of the kids. She started running.

But as she got closer, she saw that the kids were standing on either side of Yasmine, her hands clutching each of them close. Peter. Layla froze. Where was Peter? 'Oh my God,' she prayed, 'Peter. Where is he?' Then she saw the brown leather lace-ups that she had bought him last year on the gurney the paramedics were wheeling to the ambulance, and she screamed.

She had screamed loud enough to make her father next to her jolt forward, and together they had run over. Her mother had explained that they were walking back out of the park, and Tado had wriggled out of his father's hand and was running onto the street. Peter had caught him in time to lift him up, but a car coming around the corner had approached so fast that Peter, just a couple steps from the sidewalk, hadn't been able to jump out of the way quickly enough. At the moment of impact, he had thrust Tado sideways, landing him right in front of Yasmine as the car pushed him forward.

'Peter,' Layla thought now. 'This isn't happening. God knows I can't survive without him. He wouldn't allow this to happen.' She was glad the kids weren't with them at the hospital. Tunt Amira had taken them back to her apartment. Layla watched as a doctor came out, and listened intently as he told Layla and her parents something about internal bleeding, serious injuries. She was waiting for the only words that mattered. He's still alive. He will be ok. They didn't come. But neither did the doctor say that he wouldn't live, Layla thought. Finally, she interrupted whatever he was saying and asked, "Is he going to live? Please just tell me that."

The doctor looked at her with such sad eyes. "I'm sorry," he said. "I just don't know yet. He's fighting hard to stay alive, but like I said, his injuries are extremely serious."

"What can we do? Can I go in and be with him?" Layla asked.

"Not right now, I'm afraid. Try to be strong, be patient. We're doing everything we can." He gave her hand a small pat and turned around.

'How many times does he have to deliver that line?' Layla thought, watching his back as he returned into the room. After a few minutes more of watching, someone closed the curtain over the window, restricting her view of what they were doing. Her eyes glazed over and she kept looking ahead until her parents, one on each side, took her shoulders and guided her to a chair in the waiting area. People came and went, some devastated, some with nothing more than a hand wrapped in gauze. Finally, she dropped her head down to her knees and wrapped her arms around them. She kept her eyes closed. She didn't want to see the clock; she would drive herself crazy looking.

She forced herself not to think, and so must have fallen asleep, because the next thing she knew, someone was tapping her back, trying to wake her up. She raised her head. The same doctor was back, this time with a bloody surgical gown on. "Oh my God," she said. On one side of her, her father was already standing. On the other, her mother had her hand around her arm, lifting her up.

"It's good news, Madame Layla," the doctor said. "We had to go into emergency surgery to stop the internal bleeding. We found that the source of it was his spleen. It had to be removed. But the bleeding has stopped, and he is stable."

Layla couldn't believe this. "He's alive?" she asked, choking on her words.

"He's alive." The doctor gave a small smile. "But it's not all good news, I'm afraid. His pelvic and thigh bones were pretty badly shattered in the accident. He will need at least one more reconstructive surgery--his pelvis was stabilized in today's surgery — but it is too early to say whether he will be able to walk again."

'I don't care if he walks,' Layla's first thought was. 'I just want him alive.'

"His brain's alright? He hasn't suffered any memory loss or personality changes or anything? He'll still know us, be able to think like he did before — the accident?"

"Yes, his brain, miraculously, is fine."

Layla exhaled.

"Sometimes," the doctor continued, "traumas cause patients to forget moments around or during the accident, but it would be a matter of minutes, if anything. And it usually goes away with time. We'll know more once he's woken up."

"Thank you, Doctor," she said.

When he had walked away, she looked at her parents. Her father reflected the smile of relief that she gave him, but her mother's brow was furrowed. "What if he can't walk?" she said. "If he is stuck in a wheelchair, and you with the kids so young, oh Layla!"

Layla didn't understand at first. He'd be alive. Their kids would grow up with their father. She would have her husband. Then she realized that her mother was thinking about the day-to-day practicalities of her life. If she had to take care of the kids without Peter — actually, the kids AND Peter — that would become her life.

"It's ok, Mama," she said. "He's alive, that's the most important thing..." Layla pictured what getting everyone dressed, or fed, or actually, any moment of any day, would look like. "Of course it'll be hard. Very hard. But he's alive. That's the best that could have happened." Actually, the best that could have happened, she thought, was for this accident never to have happened.

"Did the driver even stop?" she asked her mother now. "I mean, does he know what he's caused?"

"I think so," her mother replied. "I thought I saw the car stop and a driver get out. Maybe I saw him talking to the police when they arrived? I'm not sure; I was so focused on keeping the kids calm, and on trying to see what the ambulance staff were doing with Peter."

"Let's not talk about that now," her father said. "It won't get Peter any better any faster."

"The doctor said it will be at least another hour before Peter wakes up," Yasmine added. "Let's go get something to eat or drink downstairs—I hear their cafeteria isn't at all bad. Then we'll take it from there."

As they walked down a hallway, Layla's eye caught a brassy glint from some touristy Pharaonic kitsch displayed on a cart along the side of the hallway. There were also some stuffed animals and other items for sale, presumably to cheer patients up, and Layla distractedly wondered if anyone ever bought that stuff, and what good, at all, they expected it to do.

38

Sydney
2009

After only a little discussion, it was decided Dalia would be given the plot of land her grandfather had set aside. At first, she didn't know what she would do with more money, other than invest it. Goodness knows she didn't have time to spend it; work kept her far too busy for that. She had returned from her hiatus in Egypt more appreciative of the work she did and more focused on why she had begun doing it in the first place. She had, however, with Liam's prompting, pledged to take more frequent vacations, even if they were just three or four days off every few months to go someplace else. And to leave work early enough at least one day each week to have dinner with her parents.

Liam would be coming with her, both to dinner and on vacations. He had proposed one night in Cairo, as they were walking home from a dinner out, the cool evening air warmed by the many motors of cars passing and by the smells of food emanating from the restaurants along the street. He had bought her a ring at an antiques jeweller in Old Cairo; the diamond's cut and setting were ones that had been very popular in 1920s Cairo, and Dalia had fallen in love with it. On either side were tiny turquoise stones, set in an intricate design on yellow gold.

It was only a day, or maybe two, after this that Dalia decided exactly what she would do with the money she had so suddenly found herself possessing. She would

give all of it, past and future earnings, to the girls'
boarding school to keep its doors open. The desire to
do good that had drawn her into the practice of law
was so very satiated by the idea of doing this that she
had not hesitated. The money wouldn't be enough
alone to keep the school running, but Dalia's gift had
inspired the school's board to start a fundraiser
program, allowing donors to "adopt" a girl at the
school and personalize their donations.

She and Liam would themselves adopt the cluster of
girls they had grown so close to over their weeks in
Cairo. These girls, and the "daughters" who would
come in the years after them, would stay in touch with
Dalia throughout their lives, many of whom fulfilled
the promise that someone had seen in them so early.
They called Dalia their second mother, and indeed, she
would field more than one midnight phone call over
the years as one of these girls would call her collect in
Sydney, oblivious to the time difference, seeking her
guidance in some life-changing decision. Dalia would
joke that she hadn't avoided being woken up in the
middle of the night by her children after all, despite not
having any toddlers of her own. And though she
would likely never say so out loud, those girls' calls
always brought her joy.

39

Sydney
2009

It was many months later, after Aida and I were
settled in our suburban Sydney home and had taken
up our old routines, that the cancer returned. For those
cautious months, we thought we had beaten the odds,
odds which were stacked against her, given how far
the cancer had advanced. Aida had, after all, decided to
return to Australia for her chemotherapy courses and
been treated by renowned physicians. And for a while,
everything had been fine. Aida and I would take a
walk every morning together, walking through our
neighbourhood, and often stopping for some tea or
coffee at the corner café, before starting the projects
and tasks with which we occupied ourselves now.
Dalia had kept her resolution to have dinner with us
once a week, almost always bringing Liam, and rarely
skipping a week.

But on the day of Aida's doctor's appointment, she
had been nervous. "It's just a routine screening," I had
tried to reassure, though I myself had begun to feel a
knot grow in my own stomach at Aida's worry. Aida
would tell me afterwards that she had known they
would find something; she had felt something wrong.
The prognosis, when we got it, was deafeningly final.
There were no further treatments. After we left the
doctor's office, I dropped Aida off at the house then left
again on foot, inventing an errand during which I had
tried, and failed, to clear my mind. When I entered the
house, I found Aida staring out the back window at her

garden, her cup of tea long since cooled in her grasp. I
looked at her hands and the engagement and wedding
bands she had worn every day for decades. The lines of
her fingers were still as graceful as when I'd first put
those rings on the excited young woman she had been.
The skin on her finger joints was wrinkled now, the
lines around her eyes and mouth more pronounced.
'How,' I thought to myself, 'have we aged so much
without noticing? Where can I look for all those years
passed by?'

"I think," she finally said, after I had pulled the cup
from her hands, drawing her out of her trance, "I think
it's time to go home."

"You are home, habibti," I said, worrying that the
shock of the news could have so disoriented her.

"No, I mean home to Egypt," Aida responded.

Because I wasn't ready to process this, my mind
immediately went to the practicalities. "Where would
we stay? Don't you want to be here in your own bed?"

Aida smiled at this. "I do love our bed, Tayib. I love
our room. I love our house. I love the shelves that you
installed for me in that cabinet so I could store all my
teas. I love all the pictures that hang on our walls."

I waited for her to continue.

"But all these things are for the living Aida, the Aida
who makes plans and has things to do today and
tomorrow and next week. It all seems a little pointless
now, don't you think?

"The apartment I grew up in Cairo, that's where I
learned to love the things I love, and make the perfect
cup of tea! It's where I became the woman you
married, and I want to return to being that person for
what time I have left. I want my last meals to be the
foods I grew up with and love, made by hands that

have known me as long as I've known myself, and love me."

I didn't respond. I knew Aida didn't mean anything hurtful in what she had said—I had never been much of a cook—but it was hard to realize that this place that I thought was ours, together, was not where she felt most loved. It had not, in fact, become the place she was most rooted, as it had become for me.

"Will you tell Dalia? Because I don't think I can do it. Tell her, remind her, afterwards, that I wish I could be around to see her live and grow older? I wish that more than anything. If I could spare her, and you, this pain, I would. I'm sorry, Tayib."

Dalia had tried to take the news, and her mother's decision, stoically. I found her, minutes after we had told her, sitting outside our front door, hugging her knees, pure anguish on her normally indomitable face. I sat down next to her. Finally, I said, "You and I have to put aside our own preferences and make Mama as comfortable as we can. She wants to be around people who love her."

Dalia nodded in agreement. Then she added, "but I love her," not bothering to hide her tears or the crack in her voice.

I thought about how to answer. "I know you do, habibti," I said quietly. "As do I." How could I explain to my daughter, who had only ever known one place as home, how it felt to be always pulled between the life one had been born into and the life one had built. I myself had embraced the present: while I loved my family and friends in my home country fiercely, it was the life I had built here that fit me most comfortably. Aida, on the other hand, had never forgotten, or stopped trying to recapture, the life into which she had been born, always trying to weave it into the life she and I had built together here, feeling the absence of each in the other, as if trying to weave the threads of her life across the thousands of miles, each place bound to the other, and finding the threads too different to make a cohesive whole.

I thought about how the greatest gift we may have given Dalia is a sense of home in one place, even as she had a deep appreciation for the treasures of her parents' home. And I thought, again, how it was only right that I should honour my wife's wishes, and for this last time, let her be home.

40

Cairo
2008

It had been 10 days since the accident. Peter had undergone an additional two surgeries to set his thigh bone and further stabilize his pelvis, but it was too early to know yet if he would be able to walk. To distract him, and herself, from dwelling on this question, Layla was keeping them occupied with news and books, a constant stream of which was being supplied by Tayib and Yasmine. Peter also looked forward to the daily visits from the kids, who were staying with Tunt Amira, and being thoroughly spoiled.

Amira, now retired from her practice, had insisted on taking the kids so that Tayib and Yasmine could focus their attention on Layla and Peter. Even though she had never had children of her own, Amira had shelves of her living room dedicated to books and toys for Layla's kids. Some of them had been for Layla when she had been a child. Maggie and Tado loved going to Amira's house. They considered her their third grandmother, and the one who was most lenient about bedtimes and most willing to sit down on the floor with them and play for hours without rushing off, like the other adults they knew, to make dinner or use the telephone. It comforted Layla to know that the kids were with Tunt Amira; she had predicted, rightly so, that as long as they were with her aunt, days would pass before they would express any interest in returning to their parents.

Motherhood cares relieved temporarily, Layla was reading the daily newspaper, Al Ahram, out loud to Peter. This was a morning ritual they had developed since he had been in hospital. That morning, she had looked up at the sound of a tentative knock on the door. A man she did not recognize was standing at the door, some flowers wrapped in newspaper in his hand. "Ostaz Tafe-stook?" he asked tentatively.

"Aywah," confirmed Layla, wondering how this man knew her husband. "Meen hadretak?"

"I just came by to check on his health," replied the stranger, addressing Layla but not answering her question about who he was. "My car is the one that hit him."

Layla froze. The police had told them the day after the accident that no charges would be pressed, since the pedestrian, Peter, was in the street, and there was no indication that the car had been speeding. She and Peter had accepted this on its face, choosing instead to focus on Peter's recovery. Yasmine and Tayib, however, had fumed about a ridiculous system in which, in front of a park where streams of pedestrians crossed all day, the police could say that a car driving too fast to stop in time could not be faulted.

"Believe me," the man said now, addressing Layla even though both Peter and Layla were looking at him. "The professor has not left my thoughts since the day of the accident. Is he badly hurt? Is he going to heal, ensha-allah?"

"What gives you the right to ask that question?" The voice was not Layla's or Peter's. They both looked behind the visitor, in the doorway where Yasmine had just appeared, her eyes burning with anger at the visitor.

"I was there," Yasmine continued. "I saw how quickly you made that turn, barrelling down the street as if you don't know that people are crossing there all the time. Or rather, as if you don't care. So why do you care now all of a sudden?"

"Madame," the man responded, "the police said I was not at fault — "

"I don't care what they said. They weren't there. I was."

"Madame, I did not have to come here today. But I really did want to be reassured that he will be ok."

"Be reassured?" Yasmine retorted. "How considerate of you. The man may not walk again, but at least you can go home reassured."

"I didn't come here to — " the man began.

"No!" Yasmine began, but then a new voice spoke up.

"We thank you for coming," said Peter, "you did not have to trouble yourself." The man, stunned to hear Peter speak Arabic, just looked from Yasmine to Peter.

"Kattar khayrak," Peter continued. "But I've been told to get as much rest as possible, you understand, so I think the doctors would think it's better — "

"Of course, of course," the man responded now, finding his voice. "I don't wish to disturb you. I just wanted to leave this for you," he said, indicating the flowers and laying them down on a side table. "May God grant you a complete recovery, sir." Giving a less than civil glance to Yasmine, he walked out of the door, shutting it behind him.

"The nerve of the man," Yasmine had sputtered. "Did he tell you his name? We can sue him, you know. I'm sure I can find a lawyer…"

"He didn't tell us his name, Mama," Layla had responded.

"Besides," Peter continued, looking at the wilting bouquet on the table, "what good will it do? It won't undo the accident. Whether I walk again or not won't depend on a law suit. No," he continued, "I'd rather spend my energy focusing on getting better. Besides, something tells me his guilt will be more than enough punishment."

Yasmine looked at her son-in-law for a moment, and then, with a small smile, gave a final nod. "You're right, Peter. May God grant you a full recovery indeed." Her smile grew a little wider, and Layla felt a tension ease between them. Yasmine continued, "I'm going to go get us some sandwiches. What will it be, Peter, shawerma or ta'maya?"

41

Cairo
2009

Four weeks after they first entered, Layla was wheeling Peter out of the hospital. "You know," he was saying, "this is a motorized wheelchair. I don't know why you insist on pushing it yourself."

"Because I can, and because it makes me feel like I am taking care of you," she said. "Besides," she said with a smirk, "after all those spinach and cheese fillos from the hospital cafeteria, I could use the exercise."

Peter's surgeries had all gone very well. He would be in physical therapy for the indefinite future, but the doctors and therapists felt confident that Peter would walk again, though likely with a limp. "We'll get you a fancy cane," Layla had joked when they had first been told. "One with a marble replica of your favourite Pasha or Emir or something." Peter had given her a feigned look of annoyance: the fact that she couldn't keep these details of her own national history straight, she knew, never ceased to astound him, given how fascinating he obviously found it—he'd gotten his doctorate in it, after all.

Layla and her father had, in the weeks after the accident, eventually gone back to the subject of the discovered account. Her father thought she should start drawing from it now. She could use it especially now, he'd explained, to get some extra help with the household.

"But what about the condition that I have to work?" Layla had asked.

Her father looked at her for a moment. "Layla," he responded, "I remember our conversations after you quit your job and were trying to explain to me why. Think of it: this is your chance to do with your life exactly what you want to do. As far as I'm concerned, the stipulation about working doesn't say you have to be paid for your work. You do work! You don't stop moving from morning til night. But this money is supposed to free you from earning a salary out of necessity. Just do what you want. Do you know what that is?"

"Not yet, Baba, but I'm starting to get some ideas."

Peter's colleagues, meanwhile, had been nothing but supportive. When the time came, the family returned to London for him to finish out his grant project. He continued his physical therapy there, his work schedule accommodating his recovery.

Layla hired a university student to spend several hours a week with the kids while she drove Peter to his physical therapy sessions, and, when necessary, accompanied him to the library or meetings. In the car or waiting rooms, the two found themselves with the time to speak about everything, most importantly about what had occupied each before the accident. Layla talked about her mixed feelings about not going back to her old job, about how to live at peace with her decision—particularly considering the ramifications the decision might continue to have on her relationships with her parents. Peter talked about seeing her restlessness, but being at a loss as to how to alleviate it. They talked, finally, about what the coming years might hold for them, and what each would wish for.

As the grant project neared its completion, Layla and Peter sat down for the obligatory conversation about whether to stay in London, where Peter could likely have found a faculty position, or return to the AUC. It was not a long discussion; they both missed Cairo.

The evening they returned permanently was the end of a hot day, a day in late October when the Cairene weather should have had some hint of autumn in it, but was nothing but smog and heat. Tayib and Yasmine had picked them up and taken them to their own home first. While the grandparents put the kids to bed, Layla and Peter had stood outside on the balcony, a sweating glass of ice water in each of their hands, and looked at the passing cars and pedestrians below, and the shops still lit and busy, and smiled. They were home.

Now, in the mornings, Layla and Peter and the kids would leave the house together. After dropping the kids off at school, the pair would stop at a coffee shop outside the AUC and have a few minutes together to talk quietly about the kids, about each other's work, about what was on their minds. Then Layla would walk with Peter to his office, carrying his briefcase for him (his limp was severe enough that it made carrying anything longer than a few meters very uncomfortable). Then she would head back home to her office, where she had decided to begin a design and organization business, taking on projects as small as reorganizing a small office or family apartment, to cataloguing estates and arranging for their distribution.

She and Peter would pick up the kids at the end of their day, and she and Peter would spend a few hours with them before dinner, which the cook they had hired would prepare. In this way, their days passed. The money from her grandfather, who she had never known but now was tremendously impacted by, allowed her and Peter to live the life she did not know she could want. They did not travel often to exotic places; there would perhaps be time and money for that when they no longer had school bills to pay, and that was alright.

Her parents and Tunt Amira, as they often would, had come over one evening for dinner, and seeing that it was a rare Cairene evening that was neither too hot nor cold, and not too humid, they decided to eat outside. The balcony of Layla and Peter's apartment overlooked a quiet courtyard belonging to an old building behind them. They were celebrating the end of the school year for the children and for Peter. Peter had finished a busy year that had been made more intense because it was the university's first year on its new, sprawling campus just outside the city. It had moved there from its historic site at Medan el Tahrir, where she and Peter had met so many years ago. Seated around the table were her parents, Tunt Amira, Peter, and the kids. Listening to her parents tease her children, and to the mixture of their eager voices and the more somber ones of her aunt Amira and Peter conversing, her mind's eye lifted above the table where they were all sitting, and she saw their laughing faces as they would look many years from now, when they'd all grown older and this moment held nostalgia. She was, for a moment, transported to a place where time had frozen them just as they were, without the layers of age and circumstance. There was enough time after all, for her work, for her kids, and for Peter. And she knew then that they were, above all else, fortunate.

42

Cairo
2008

At my age, I do not have the luxury of leaving unfinished business to the future. After breakfast one morning, I took the phone number Layla had given me for my old friend Hany Abdelmallek in Portugal. Our first phone conversation had been warm, if somewhat stilted, as I might have expected from years of distance. Hany said on multiple occasions how happy he was to be hearing from me, and asked me again for my forgiveness for not giving me the letter sooner. I had responded that God arranged it to come at the perfect time for our family and told him to think nothing of it. Eventually, Hany mentioned that he would be coming to Cairo for a visit the following month. His son was a neurosurgeon there, and he was too busy to visit his parents, so they returned every several months to Cairo to visit him and the rest of their family. "It is a blessing," Hany said, "to live the life of an emigrant but still get to return home so often." We had talked then about how much Egypt had changed in the intervening years, about our children and grandchildren, and finally, agreeing to meet in person when Hany visited Cairo, we hung up.

Yasmine had been shocked to hear we were meeting again. "Aren't you worried about stirring up old memories? Or souring the relationship you have?"

"What relationship?" I answered. "Look, if I am being honest, it was my own pride that caused our fall out in the first place. Hany has never been anything but kind and good. It was I who assumed less than good intentions about him, because…because I think I was jealous of him. Life had always seemed to go so easily for him. No father dying prematurely, all the girls adoring him starting from when we were 13, him sailing through medical school. But I'm an old man now. I know it wasn't the way I remember it; nobody's life is without its pains. And I don't want to leave our relationship dead. He was my good friend, Yasmine, a brother when I lost my father. I want reconciliation."

Yasmine had looked at me then, and after a pause, said, "You are always so true to your convictions, aren't you? Even to the point of entering an awkward conversation or even risking some personal humiliation."

"Perhaps," I responded, "what you see as humiliation, I choose to see as humility."

"Yes, I've learned that about you, my beloved Tayib. And I respect it."

There was a moment of comfortable silence before she continued, "you know, I don't remember, I truly don't, what your rift with him had been about in the first place. I remember that he'd been kind enough to recommend me for a project. I think it was a patient of his, and he was looking for an architect to build him a summer home. That project launched my career: it was the first project to give me the reputation as a modern—but also classical— architect, wasn't it? I think we probably owe a lot to Hany. Not that you are contacting him out of a sense of obligation; I know that. Or if it is, it is only an obligation to yourself and your own integrity."

I agreed, but didn't say anything. Yasmine reached over and patted my hand, but said no more.

When we met some weeks later, Hany and I greeted each other with big smiles and a bigger hug, with much patting on the back. We complimented each other on how we looked just the same as always, then teased each other about the grey hairs that seemed to have grown and multiplied over the years. After more catching up about where life had taken us in the intervening years, we returned again to the subject of our last parting.

"But let us speak frankly now, as brothers," I began. Hany nodded agreement.

"Layla said you'd told her there was a rift between us: why would you have thought, after all these years, Hany, that I was still upset with you?"

"Tayib, have you forgotten how hard you took it when I recommended Yasmine for that project over you?" Hany was looking at me with incredulity. "I don't think you realized how intimidating you can be."

"Intimidating! Are you serious? What did I say to intimidate you? I rarely said a word!"

"Precisely. I could just picture all the judgements you were passing about me inside that head of yours. Everyone thought the world of you and your family. I was what, 25 or 26 years old? If you disapproved of what I was doing, I could only conclude that it was I who was in the wrong. Don't tell me you weren't upset with me."

"I was, Hany, but I was also 25 or 26 and a young fool. We are old men now, so I can tell you this. I didn't know if I was any good as an architect yet, not back then. I thought maybe Yasmine was a better architect than I was—that would have been hard to take! Or maybe even that she would end up, I don't know, spending time with other men I didn't know, who

274

would flatter her with compliments. She was like a sparkling diamond back then—strong and smart and so beautiful—and she still is. But in those days, despite the fact that we were married, I didn't know her well enough to know that I could trust her to keep her head with that kind of attention. And I directed all that on you."

"How could you think I would ever violate my friend's trust that way? Yes, absolutely, Yasmine was an utter beauty—I am sure she still is—but you were my brother!"

"I know, I know. I'm sorry, Hany. But I never told you that I was upset, so I didn't think you knew. I certainly didn't think I had caused any rift between us. When you stopped coming around or calling, I assumed it was because you were busy with your doctor friends and your life. And at first, I was happy with that, but then I eventually forgot about it. Had I only known you've been carrying this around all these years—I never would have let it happen."

"Maybe, brother, we are still fools, then," Hany said with a smile. "It is true that you never said anything to cause the rift, and I presumed your thoughts. Or maybe I felt a little guilty; I should have approached you first rather than cutting you out and going directly to Yasmine."

I gave a soft snort at that. "If Yasmine heard you say that, she'd tell you that's ridiculous, and it isn't for me to give permission for her work. No, I think if anything, you were just ahead of the times. Or maybe you'd already adopted the western way of addressing women."

We were silent for a moment, each remembering, as old friends do.

"Tayib, did Amira ever say anything to you about…"

I looked at my friend then, and the realization dawned on me that my anger may have taken something more than just the friendship between the two of us. Amira had never said anything to me about it, all these years.

"We never talked about it. Maybe she knew how I would have responded had she said anything. Is it possible I could have been so thoughtless?"

"Who knows what might have happened," Hany said with a small smile. "I trust she's had a successful life…"

I gave a subtle nod, which he acknowledged before adding, "I think I too have…"

We were silent for a moment, wondering. Then Hany said, a note of reconciliation in his voice — or hopefulness, I couldn't tell which. "Sometimes pride robs us of the best we could have had. I am sorry that we have lost all these years of friendship."

I knew what it was to lose a loved one against his choosing, and found to my surprise that I was tearing up. "And I too am sorry. I should have tried to call you back then."

We sat in silence for a few minutes, sipping our drinks. Then, as if to mark a new chapter, I said, "So your son is a neurosurgeon? Which hospital does he practice at?"

"Dar El Fouad," replied Hany.

"Really! My son-in-law — Layla's husband — was there recently. He will be fine, thank God. What a small world."

The talk turned then to the accident, to our children's lives and wellbeing, and before long, we realized that we had been sitting there for over four hours.

Promising to meet again before Hany returned to Portugal, we said our goodbyes. We were with each other as we had been many decades ago.

As I stepped into the street, quieter now without the rush hour, but still full of people and the smells of food, I thought of our conversation. I thought, as I walked, of the life I had lived in this city I loved, and the life my dear friend had lived, a stranger in the world beyond. It occurred to me that we don't change who we are in the end, but what changes is our understanding, and because of that, our choices. Hany is as kind as he ever was, our feelings of brotherhood as strong as they ever were. Whether he had stayed in Egypt, whether I had gone abroad, this conversation would still be possible. And yet. And yet sometimes I look around me at what my city has become, at the choices my friends have made, even at the way the young people of our country choose to live their lives now, and I feel myself a stranger here. Sometimes I feel the world moving away from who I am—or perhaps it is I who is withdrawing from it into who I truly am. In the end, I am not yet home.